Praise for Anne Louise Bannon
and Fascinating Rhythm

Fascinating Rhythm is reminiscent of Agatha Christie or Dorothy Sayers' novels of the time period. A very nice story to cozy up to a fire with and imbibe. Legally, of course.

Literary R&R

Those who love a great (who-done-it) mystery will enjoy Fascinating Rhythm.

Sheri Wilkinson

JuniperGrove.net

Praise for Tyger, Tyger

I like Bannon's main character, Brenda, enough to follow her anywhere. Her boyfriend (no! wait! they're "just friends") trains animals for the movies, and between Brenda, the BF and his tiger, "Sweetness," they are a fun, crime-solving trio. I enjoyed this book.

Petrea Burchard

Author of Camelot and Vine

Stopleak

Anne Louise Bannon

An Operation Quickline Story

Healcroft House, Publishers

Healcroft House, Publishers, a subsidiary of Robin Goodfellow Enterprises, Altadena, California, United States of America

Acknowledgement

There are a lot of people who make a writer's life possible. In my case, my number one supporter is my husband, Michael Holland.

Sweetie, I can never thank you enough.

Dedication

To Dad.

May 14, 1983

The sky was overcast, a little unusual for that time of year in Southern California. I zipped up my ski jacket against the bite of the cool mountain air and headed away from the cabin in search of a quiet place to think, which is the point of going on a retreat. We were somewhere near Big Bear Lake. The area was a crowded one for the mountains, but certainly not as crowded as L.A. It had that special stillness, with the constant whisper of the wind in the pines.

"Hi. Going for a walk?" asked a voice behind me.

I jumped and turned to face Father John Reynolds. He was a tall man with salt and pepper hair and solemn brown eyes.

"Yeah," I replied quietly.

"Mind if I join you?"

"Mind if I be honest?"

He smiled. "Go ahead."

"Well, I did want to get away from the group for a while," I replied, shrugging helplessly. "I need to get some perspective on a couple of things."

"Maybe I can help."

"I appreciate the offer, but I don't think so."

Father John gently took my elbow and steered me down the road.

"I'd like to talk to you, Lisa," he said. "I think it's important."

"Alright," I sighed.

We walked in silence for a moment, as Father John mentally put his words together.

"Your small group asked me to talk to you," he

said finally. "They think you're holding out on them."

I thought back to that morning. They had been trying to draw me out, Frank Lonnergan in particular.

"Maybe I am," I said slowly. "But sometimes you just can't say things to people."

"Something about your boss?"

"Not that," I said. My boss, Sid Hackbirn, is an eccentric freelance writer. I'm his secretary. I also happen to live in his house. Of course, everyone who knows about it jumps to the obvious, however erroneous, conclusion.

"Well, if you're not living in sin, some other kind?"

"Father, I know you're just trying to be helpful, but please don't ask. For once, I'm not guilty. I'm not in trouble or anything like that."

"You're carrying something around, Lisa. It looks pretty heavy to me."

"Even if it is, it's just something I've got to carry."

"Confession isn't just for sin."

I looked at him and thought about that a moment. All of a sudden, my secret felt just too big and burdensome.

"Father," I began slowly, not at all sure I should be saying anything. "If I were to tell you, it'd have to be you only and you'd have to guard it as if this were a confession."

"Alright, I will."

"This is going to sound crazy." I thought back to how it had been explained to me. "But within the structures of the FBI and CIA are several smaller organizations so secret people don't even know they exist. They are involved in espionage and counter-espionage. My boss is a member of one called Operation Quickline and so am I."

"Ah hah."

"You don't believe me." My heart sank.

"No, no. I believe you. I was just trying to imagine you as Mata Hari."

"I've heard she was a lousy spy."

"And you are a very good one. I never suspected."

"Well, now you know why I'm holding back. I have to." I looked down at my feet. "I can't even tell my family."

"It's better you don't. Your kind of knowledge is dangerous." Father John smiled quietly.

"Tell me about it. I've been afraid so much." I could feel the tears forming but held them back. "When we were talking about fear of death today, all I could think of was being shot at in Washington, D.C. and watching a man die, and I couldn't say a word about it."

He nodded. "That's a heck of a thing to carry around by yourself."

"Sid tries to help me. We're really very close. But he doesn't quite understand where I'm coming from a lot of the time. His background's so different from mine and our value systems are diametrically opposed anyway."

"You must have some common ground."

"Some. In some ways, quite a lot. But where it counts..."

"I know. It's very difficult for you." John put his arm around me and gave me a gentle squeeze.

I heard a car go by. Looking up, I thought I saw a familiar dark slate blue fender disappear around the bend. I started.

"Something wrong?" John asked.

"I thought I saw Sid's car." I let out a nervous chuckle. "I've been so afraid he's going to pop up here with some problem. I must be letting my imagination run away with me, seeing his car everywhere."

"Lisa, if it's that big a strain for you..."

"But it isn't." I shook him off. "Most of it's desperately dull. I just need to get some perspective on those times that aren't so dull, like when someone dies as a result of my actions. The time I'm thinking of, he was the enemy and he was going to kill us. Sid says it's a lot like war. I suppose he ought to know."

"I'm afraid I don't have an answer for that. There's

the concept of the lesser of two sins, but I don't think that makes it any easier."

"It doesn't. I don't know. I keep hoping there's an answer."

Father John thought about it, then shrugged. " 'Now we see as through a glass, then we shall see face to face.' First Corinthians thirteen. I suspect that's all the answer you're going to get."

"I was afraid of that."

Father John stopped walking and put his hands on my shoulders. "Lisa, yours is an important job. I truly believe you were chosen for it and not by Sid Hackbirn. God is very good at putting us where we're most effective and He doesn't throw things at us we can't handle. You are in your admittedly unusual position because someone else would not be able to handle it."

I looked down the road.

"You know," I said, slowly. "I really like my job, all of it, not just Quickline."

"Do you like Sid?" He stepped to my side and we began walking again.

"Of course, I do. I like him a lot. We're very good friends."

"And yet, you're so different where, as you say, it counts."

"I know. But we've learned to respect each other's beliefs. I don't agree with Sid's fooling around any more than he does with my celibacy, but we respect that it's our choice and leave it at that."

"Maybe you shouldn't." Father John looked up at the pine trees surrounding us.

"What do you mean?"

He stopped walking. "As closely as you two work together, maybe you should try to understand each other and where you're coming from."

That was a new idea. I thought about it for a moment.

"You're going to end up challenging each other," John continued. "You, most of all, might have to think about some things you've always just accepted."

"Sounds dangerous." I let out a wary chuckle.

"Yes, but more dangerous for Sid perhaps, than you."

"Why?"

"You have the power and protection of Almighty God on your side. Who does Sid have to call on?"

I laughed. Sid's a confirmed atheist.

"Come on," John said, turning around. "It's time we got back."

I almost missed it as we approached the cabin. But parked next to Carl and Erin MacArthur's dark blue Nissan four by four pickup was the slate blue Mercedes 450SL that belonged to my boss.

"Oh, no," I groaned. "I was afraid it was him."

John just smiled.

"It can't be that bad," he said.

"Oh, yeah? I told him he'd better not come up here for anything less than World War Three starting."

"Let's hear it for Armageddon. Come on."

I hesitated. "I've got too much to sort out yet. I'd rather not talk to him. It's probably just a moved-up deadline anyway."

A small, dark figure appeared in the cabin's doorway, Esther Nguyen.

"Oh, there you are, Lisa," she called, and then inside. "She's back."

"Too late," John chuckled.

Esther stepped back to allow Sid to get through the door. He was immaculate, as usual, in a dark pinstriped three-piece suit. He's not a tall man, barely three inches taller than me and I'm about average height. His dark wavy hair is always precision trimmed and never out of place. His face is handsome, in fact quite striking with bright piercing blue eyes and a cleft chin. He's slender with a well-proportioned figure. In short, he's a very attractive man with a sensual air about him, very handy for him since his hobby is sleeping around. I'll admit I've been tempted, but I happen to believe sex is for marriage and that's that.

That day, his manner was urgent, even grim.

"Will you excuse us, please?" he asked Father John without waiting to be introduced.

I swallowed.

"When are the missiles coming?" I asked wearily as John left.

"What missiles?" asked Sid. "Oh. Your World War Three condition."

"The sole circumstance under which you were to come up here."

He sighed. "Alright, it's not W W III. But it could be something equally bad for us. We've got to get out of here."

"Why?"

"I'll explain in the car. Let's go." He started towards the Mercedes.

"No."

He turned and glared at me. "Lisa, I don't want to argue about it."

"Well, I don't want to leave without a darned good reason. This weekend is important to me."

"How about your life?"

"My life? Sid, what's happened? Come on, we can talk on the road."

Sid looked around quickly then went with me in the direction I'd just come from.

"There's been a leak," he said quietly. "The news came this morning. We've been ordered to pull out fast and report to Washington D.C. by Tuesday morning."

"Do they know where it is?"

"No. That's why we're reporting to D.C. We've been elected to find it."

"How? We don't know anybody else in the business."

"We'll find out Tuesday morning. But I've got a bad feeling we're going to end up bait for a trap."

I swallowed. "Wonderful."

"In the meantime, we've got to get out of L.A.

We're flying to Washington tonight. We'll be staying with Hattie Mitchell."

"Correction. You'll be flying out tonight. I'm staying here 'til this retreat is over. I'll meet you at Hattie's"

"Are you out of your mind?" Sid glared at me, his piercing blue eyes sparking with worry.

"No. I am for all practical purposes out of L.A. The only people that know I'm here are Mae, Henry James and you. Heck, I didn't even tell Mae where the place was to prevent you from badgering her into giving her the address."

"I know," Sid grumbled.

"Look, Sid, I really need this time."

"Alright, you can stay. I don't like it. Henry told me they found a female operative dead in San Francisco yesterday. She'd been raped and strangled, but it was a little too clean to be just your standard thug."

"I'll be careful. I promise."

"I'm sure you will." He sighed. "Just in case, have you told anyone about the business? Even Mae and Neil?"

Mae is my sister, Neil is her husband. They live in Fullerton with their five kids. I'm really close to them. So is Sid, strangely enough. They kind of attached themselves shortly after I started working for them.

"I haven't said a word to Mae or Neil. I wish I could."

"It's better for them if you don't. Anybody else?"

"Not anybody that could be the source of a leak."

"What?" Sid looked shocked.

"I just told him this afternoon, just as you drove up, so it's impossible."

"You told somebody?"

"I told Father John Reynolds, a priest and he promised me the secrecy of the confessional."

"The what?"

"The secrecy of the confessional. It's a vow priests take never to divulge what a person tells them in the course of a confession, currently known as the Sacrament of Reconciliation. It'll sound insane to you, but most priests, John among them, would literally rather die than tell somebody some ten-year-old lied to his mother three times last week."

"Lisa, why?"

"Because I can't take it anymore." Turning away, I wiped my eyes dry. "Sid, I really do like the business and I don't want to quit, even if I could. But even you admit there's a lot of pressure, and things happen that I have trouble justifying. I just need somebody to talk to whose beliefs are more in tune with my own."

"I see." He didn't.

"And don't worry about him being the leak. I only just told him. Heck, I saw your car go past us."

"I thought that was you. You mean that guy with his arm around you was a priest?" Sid was really shocked. "Why wasn't he in black?"

"He's wearing his civvies this weekend."

"But the arm..."

"Sid, there is such a thing as affection without sex. He was just offering me a little comfort and support, a little paternalistic squeeze if you will."

We started back with Sid shaking his head.

"So, when are you done here?" he asked finally.

"Tomorrow afternoon. I'm not sure when."

"I'll find out exactly before I leave. I took the liberty of packing for you. I also included Janet Donaldson's I.D. and credit cards and ring. They're in a wallet at the bottom of the suitcase. Carry both your I.D.'s on the plane, and wear the ring. I told Hattie I wasn't sure who we were coming as and that I was going to check out the situation there before I decided."

"Alright. Why don't you leave my ticket also? I can change it at the airport."

"I haven't got it. They're both waiting at the reservations desk. I'll change it and call you from the airport to give you the time. You got any cash?"

"A little."

Sid pulled out his slim snakeskin wallet from his inside breast pocket and opened it.

"Just a loan," he said before I could protest and handed me a fifty and two twenties. "You'll need it for meals and taxis. Keep an eyeball out for tails. I don't know how you'll get your shoulder holster on around here but wear it. It's in the carry-on, plus the shield for the metal detectors at the airport. Put some steel in your hair, and you might want to wear jeans and your running shoes. I packed those also. I don't want you running around unarmed, is that clear?"

"Alright," I grumbled. Sid knew I didn't like carrying weapons. He didn't like carrying them, either. But the way he automatically held his suit jacket closed as he put away his wallet told me he was wearing his shoulder holster. He probably had hidden about his person a variety of spring steel lockpicks, transmitters, and other potential weapons. [To the teeth, my dear. You can always hide something SEH]

As we came up on the cabin, Kathy Deiner, a tall slender black woman with her hair cut close to her head, broke away from a small group at the door.

"Hey, Lisa," she said pulling me away from Sid. "The rest of the group and I want to talk to you before you leave."

"I'm not leaving," I said.

"You're not? But what about the boss's interview?"

I headed over to the Mercedes where Sid was taking my suitcase out of the trunk.

"It's not 'til Tuesday," I said. "He just thinks he can't handle the background work himself. I'll be flying out Sunday as it is."

As I reached down to pick up the suitcase, Sid slipped the luggage tag he'd taken off into my hand.

"Be careful," he whispered. "It's not yours."

I slipped the tag belonging to my alter ego into my coat pocket.

Frank Lonnergan, a tall pleasant looking man with dark hair, appeared in the doorway.

"Kathy, Lisa, hurry up," he yelled. "They're calling ten minutes."

"She's not leaving," Kathy called back. "She talked the boss out of taking her."

"We've still got to talk. Come on, Miss Wycherly."

I looked at Sid, shrugged my shoulders and followed Kathy into the cabin carrying my suitcase.

It was rather odd that the six of us had ended up in the same small group at the retreat. Kathy, Esther, Frank, Jesse White, George Hernandez and I were already close friends. I had even been dating Frank and George, and usually on retreats, they're trying to get you to meet other people. We met upstairs in the "girls' dorm."

"Lisa," Frank began. "John talked to us and, well, we kind of owe you an apology."

"What did John tell you?" I asked, puzzled and a little scared.

"Just that there's sometimes things you can't share with us," Kathy said. "He said that he talked to you about it and agreed that you had a good reason and we have to respect that."

"We just want you to know we care about you." George put his arm around me and squeezed. He's average height, with features that remind you of Montezuma and still seems like a cuddly teddy bear.

"I know and I appreciate it. I love you guys."

"We love you too," said Jesse, who's about average size with dark black skin. It was good to get a hug from him. I'd kind of embarrassed him a couple months before by asking him out. Jesse's liberated. He just wasn't used to white girls asking him for dates. I think he has a crush on Kathy, too.

We were tangled in a group hug, when Susie Talbot came up, giggling.

"Oh, Lisa," she said. "You should see your boss."

"What's he doing?" I asked, afraid that he was trying to pick someone up. [Why would I have wasted my time?   SEH]

"Father John's trying to talk him into staying through mass and dinner."

"I don't think Sid's interested," I said nervously. "He's not exactly religious."

"That's not stopping John," Susie giggled. "Sid told John he's a confirmed atheist and John just said at least he was committed. Of course, everyone else wants him to stay, too."

"Shavings!" I was downstairs in seconds to rescue Sid.

Frankly, I would love it if Sid would convert. But at the same time, there is nothing worse than a bible thumping zealot trying to win your soul. I hate it when it happens to me, and I'm already converted. My friends at church aren't all that bad, but I did want Sid to like them, and I didn't think the odds of them hitting it off were too good if they found the sorry state of Sid's soul too tempting.

Sure enough, Sid was surrounded when I got downstairs.

"Come on, you guys. Lay off," I said.

"Lay off what?" asked Carl MacArthur. "We're just trying to be friendly."

"Right." I looked at Sid. He was starting to get angry. Suddenly, very much I wanted him to understand. "You don't have to stay if you don't want to. I don't want you to feel pressured. But, please, try to understand, they only want to share something with you that means a lot to them, and to me, too."

Sid's eyes pierced me, then slowly, they softened.

"Would you like me to stay?" he asked with surprising tenderness.

"I don't want you to feel obligated. It would be nice if you did. It might help you to understand where I'm coming from."

"I can only stay through dinner," he said softly. "I don't want to miss my plane. Hattie's expecting me."

"Dinner's enough." I was very touched. I knew how hard it was for him to stay. He's very comfortable with his atheism but feels out of place in religious settings, and he doesn't like it.

Mae's oldest daughter, Janey, had conned Sid into going to mass with us on Christmas and Easter, so he wasn't totally new to it. But mass on a retreat is certainly a more casual affair than the high masses of Christmas and Easter. We had a couple of tense moments that night.

The first was during the "sermon." Actually, it was a discussion. Sid had to make the comment that he thought Jesus's actions in the gospel reading were rather snotty. The room was stunned. I buried my burning face in my hands, thinking decidedly un-Christian thoughts. Father John came to the rescue, however, saying that Sid did have a good point and then proceeded to put the situation in a completely different light so that even Sid had to agree there was justification for the acts.

During the prayer of the faithful, we just made spontaneous requests instead of the usual pre-written prayers. Kathy prayed that Sid and I would have a safe trip, little realizing how unsafe it was likely to be.

The second tense moment was during the sign of peace. In a regular church situation, we just shake hands and say "peace be with you" to the people around us. On Christmas and Easter Sid had merely stood and smiled politely. He was pretty startled that night when we suddenly all got up and started hugging each other. He backed off into a corner pretty quickly.

I went ahead and went over to him, even though I was very nervous about it. I guess I didn't want him to reject me, but I couldn't see not doing it.

"Thanks for staying," was all I could say.

He smiled and then I put my arms around him and he put his arms around me and just held me like a friend.

"Thanks for being here," he said softly into my ear.

After communion, we had a spontaneous round of thanksgivings. I was almost as surprised as Sid when I thanked God for him being there.

"And thank you, Lord, for the friendship Sid and I have built," I continued, still blushing. "And, dear Jesus, take care of him and watch over him."

Sid did a minimum of teasing through dinner. For a minute, I actually thought he was behaving for my sake, but then I noticed he seemed very thoughtful.

"Do you spend a lot of time doing that?" he asked later as I was seeing him off.

"Doing what?" I asked.

"Praying for me."

I blushed.

"All the time," I whispered, and braced myself.

With Sid, the rejoinder could have been as caustic as the one I got was tender.

"Thanks." He smiled warmly. "I'd better get going. See you in Washington."

He got into the car, inserted the key in the ignition and buckled his seat belt.

"I'll see you there," I replied. "You take care now."

"You too."

He drove off and I went back to sort things out.

May 15 - 17, 1983

When I got dressed Sunday morning, I dressed for a very long day. The retreat was supposed to end around three. We would get back to the church sometime after five. Then I had a few hours to kill before my plane left at 11:53 p.m. Sid had said when he called that there weren't any earlier flights, and suggested I get a nap before I left and sleep on the plane because I would be arriving in Washington at 8:07 a.m. and he thought it would be better if I were ready to go.

Dressing without anyone around was impossible. There was even a communal bathroom. I put on my jeans, a pink oxford shirt, and a gray herringbone twill sport coat. I was able to put on my black armored running shoes without anyone questioning it. Then again, to look at them, you'd never suspect I had a knife, two screwdrivers, lockpicks, wires, a transmitter and batteries hidden in the soles.

I ditched the final talk so I could get my shoulder holster on but then realized we still had a lot of hugging to get through and I'd never get it past anyone. Frustrated, I dug out Janet Donaldson's wallet and put it in my purse, hid her luggage tag in my jacket pocket, and slid a two inch by one quarter inch piece of spring steel behind the barrette I had in my hair.

Unfortunately, Frank, Kathy, Esther, George, and Jesse all insisted on taking me to dinner after the retreat and then to the airport. I managed to talk them into parking the car while I picked up the ticket and got checked in.

"It'll be a lot easier if I just do it by myself," I

explained as I got out of George's Range Rover. "They don't need a crowd to confuse things. I'll meet you by the metal detectors."

"But you've got two suitcases and a carry-on," said George.

"I'll have to carry them when I get off the plane," I replied. Esther handed the cases over the back seat.

"Park the car, George," said Kathy.

I was glad I had gotten there two hours early. There wasn't a line at the desk. Just in case, I waited to put the luggage tags on my suitcases until the last second. Kathy came into the terminal just as the clerk handed me my boarding pass. I jammed it into my purse.

I was a little nervous getting through the metal detectors, but the shields worked. I purposely led the gang to the bar, which made Frank happy. After about an hour, I heard them announce a flight to Atlanta. I checked my watch.

"That's mine," I said, standing up. "Listen, why don't we say goodbye here and get it over with?"

"We don' mind walking to your gate," said Esther.

"I'd just as soon stay here," teased Frank. He talks more than he drinks, and he'd only had one beer.

Kathy shoved him.

Jesse yawned. "Far be it from me to actually agree with Frank, but I'm bushed. I'd just as soon say goodbye here, too."

"Then this it." I held out my arms.

"God go with you, Lisa," said George when his turn came to be hugged.

"I hope so," I replied.

Then unexpectedly, he kissed my mouth. As we pulled away, I looked into his sensitive brown eyes.

"Hey, I want my turn," Frank said loudly.

Laughing, he grabbed me and planted a loud smacking one on my lips.

"Frank, you rowdy." I laughed and turned. "You want a shot at me, Jesse?"

"Sure." And he came over and kissed me quickly.

"You guys take care," I said to them.

"You take care, now, Lisa," said Kathy. "We'll be praying for you,"

"Please do," I replied emphatically. "You don't know how much I'll need it."

"Oh, we met Sid," put in Esther grinning. "We know."

They announced the last call for Atlanta.

"I've gotta go. God bless." I headed for the gate, waving to them.

They waved, then George pulled Frank out of the bar and they headed for the escalators. I waited until they were out of sight, then went to the restroom and put on my shoulder holster in the stall. Before leaving, I got out Janet's wallet again and got the wedding ring set that was in it.

Sid and I had traveled together as a married couple before. It attracted less attention. I took a moment and gazed at the rings. It was a nice set, though I wouldn't have chosen it for myself. Sid had picked it out. It was tasteful and quiet, the diamond being big enough to belong to a reasonably prosperous couple, yet small enough to be discreet. Taking a deep breath, I slid the set onto my left ring finger.

I tried snoozing while waiting for the flight I was really taking. It was a red-eye, which would land early the next morning. Fortunately, I conked out the minute the plane was airborne and felt quite awake and alert when it landed, about ten minutes earlier than scheduled.

I was surprised to see Sid waiting for me when I got off the plane. Hattie Mitchell was there with him. She's a tall attractive woman in her middle fifties. She owns, among other businesses, a couple defense plants and is up to her hips in espionage-related issues. Sid ostensibly knows her because she owns and edits a magazine that he does a regular column for. In truth, she was involved in a case Sid and I were working.

She greeted me with a quick hug and a kiss on the cheek and she called me by my own name. Anxiously I looked at Sid.

"We're ourselves," he said, smiling. "You can ditch the ring in the car."

The car was Hattie's limo, a sleek black Cadillac complete with chauffeur.

"Have you found anything out?" I asked Sid.

He shook his head. "We could be leaving tomorrow. We could be stuck here a month."

"You're to make yourself completely at home," said Hattie to me. "Mi casa es su casa. I'm afraid, however, I do have other commitments, so I won't be able to entertain you."

"That's okay," I said. "I can usually keep myself busy."

"Well, Sid told me you enjoy sewing, so I took the liberty of getting a sewing machine and all the other tools you'll need. My dressmaker set it all up, just in case you find yourself with time on your hands."

"Gee, thanks. It's very nice of you." But a little short sighted, all the same, though I would have died sooner than say so. Sewing can be pretty time consuming and I didn't want to start anything I couldn't finish.

A lot of good that did me. Like most people who like to sew, I have an incredible fabric habit. I know when Sid had us dropped off near the Air and Space Museum so we could do some sight-seeing, that was where he was planning to go. But he got sidetracked by a men's wear store nearby, and I started looking at dresses, and we ended up window shopping until I stopped at this absolutely huge fabric store. There were three floors of the most wonderful fabrics. I was as close to heaven as I'd ever been. [But then, you hadn't slept with me yet   SEH]

I dragged Sid in and we didn't leave until eleven thirty. I had a terrific time. Sid was bored stiff, but followed me docilely, until I came across this one bolt of broadcloth in a very striking shade of blue.

"That'd make a nice blouse," I said aloud, feeling the fabric. "It's got a nice hand to it. I love that color. What do you think, Sid?"

"Whatever." He'd been saying that a lot.

But as I looked at him, a new thought occurred to me.

"You know that blue really sets off your eyes," I said, and then looked at the end of the bolt.

"It's an okay shade."

"Hm, one hundred percent cotton. The more I look at this, the more I like it for you."

"For me?" He gaped.

"Yeah." I pulled the bolt off the shelf. "How'd you like me to make you a shirt?"

"No thank you, Lisa, I have a shirtmaker in L.A. who does a very nice job."

"So do I. You can't tell what I've bought and what I've made."

"Maybe so, but..."

"Don't you like the fabric? It really does nice things for your eyes." It did look good next to him, and I knew that if anything would sell Sid on it, appealing to his vanity would.

"You really think so, huh?" Sid is hopelessly vain.

"It'll leave them breathless."

He chuckled. "Not you, though."

"Don't worry. I'll be admiring the fine handiwork. Come on, let's find a pattern."

I, of course, found several things for myself, which slowed us down some. Sid remained apprehensive about the whole shirt issue. He fussed mildly when I went ahead and took all the measurements I needed in the store. I had to take chest, neck and arm length as it was so I knew what size pattern to buy and how much fabric I needed. Sid made certain I knew he was not necessarily going to wear the shirt. I managed to turn this to my favor when we had an argument over who was going to pay for it. I won and it was absorbed into the substantial addition to my Master Card balance

We had another argument over lunch at the Natural History Museum. Sid wanted to pay for it and I wanted to go Dutch treat.

"What is your problem with me buying things for you?" he groaned as we sat down at our table.

"It just doesn't feel right."

"Lisa, I would hope that by now you'd know me well enough to know I am not going to ask you for favors."

I blushed. "I know, but maybe I don't, Sid. I mean, we talk, but you're not always that open."

"Trust me. I don't operate that way, not with you, not with anyone. I deal with any trade issues up front and above board."

"It's not even that, really. It's just... You're my boss. I feel like I'm taking advantage."

"Why not? The way you sit on every penny, I'm surprised you're not leaping at the chance."

"I bought all that fabric today."

"All the while proclaiming how much more it would cost you ready made and you still winced when you signed the charge slip. Face it, Lisa, you're cheap. In fact, I strongly suspect that the reason you're passing up a free meal has very little to do with taking advantage. You just don't want to have to order something good for you."

Sid is a health food nut. He won't touch red meat, salt, sugar, believes in small portions. I like healthy food. I also like not healthy food. I like to eat, in large quantities, if possible.

The waitress chose that moment to take our order. I glared at Sid.

"I'll have the double chili burger with lots of onions and cheese, and don't forget the dill pickle."

"Would you like coleslaw or potato salad?"

"Potato salad and a large Coke." I smiled in triumph.

Sid's face became a cool blank. "I'd like the grilled chicken salad, please, vinegar and oil on the side. Do you have non-fat milk?"

"No, sir."

"Perrier, then."

"Thank you." She took our menus and left.

Sid waited until she was gone and then moved in to renew the attack.

"That stuff is going to kill you."

"Not half as quickly as most the other things you've got me doing."

"What the salt alone in that dill pickle is doing to your blood pressure "

"Sid, the last time I went to the doctor's "

"I know, he had to give you an EKG to make sure your heart was still beating."

"No. He said if it was any lower I'd be dead. One occasional dill pickle is not going to hurt me."

"What about all that junk in your chili? That stuff is loaded with salt, MSG, preservatives, artificial colors, and my god, there's the hamburger underneath it all. Do you realize how lethal those things are?"

"Yes, if the hormones don't get me, the fats will. I seem to remember having this argument before and I'm getting tired of it."

"Not tired enough to change your ways. Which reminds me, even your precious scriptures tell you to take care of your body."

"They say a whole lot more about not doing what you do with yours."

"If you want to play that way, my sex habits are not doing near the harm to my body that your eating habits are doing to yours."

"What about social diseases, with which you are not unfamiliar? And while I'm on the subject of disease, Mr. Paragon of Health, must I remind you who had flu twice last winter? Not to mention that little bout with the stomach flu last month."

"Stomach flu is a misnomer. It was a bacterial infection."

"Misnomer or not, I wasn't the one who spent nine

hours straight puking out his guts.”

“Here we are,” said the waitress, cheerfully placing our plates before us.

We smiled politely and waited until she left. I started in again quickly. I was on a roll and I didn’t want to give Sid a chance to break it.

“I might also add I’m not the one who drinks his morning prune juice religiously and won’t leave his front door without a Metamucil fix.”

“Can you imagine the shape I’d be in if I didn’t eat properly?”

“Well, I don’t and I don’t have any problems like that. I might also remind you of that week you let me eat anything I wanted. I am fifty dollars richer because I didn’t gain an ounce and you gained three pounds on a diet.”

“You didn’t lose any either.”

“I’m skinny as a rail. I don’t need to.”

“Eat your lunch.”

I was already shoveling it in between sentences. I grinned. I had him and I knew it. I let him pay for lunch because I knew how much paying for that chiliburger would bug him. Actually, I got the feeling he thought I was patronizing him. [Nope. You were right the first time   SEH] Either way, smug, happy, and, for once full, I enjoyed the rest of the afternoon.

We got back to Hattie’s estate in Mount Vernon by six thirty. I ate dinner as quickly as I could get away with. The little sewing room next to where I was sleeping was indeed fully stocked, and with projects in hand from that morning, far too tempting for me to resist.

I cut out and put together Sid’s shirt that night. I was still on California time, but I was pretty tired when I finally sewed the last button on. I yawned and went to bed. The next morning, I overslept and Sid had to come after me to go running.

The morning run is one of the more dismal aspects of working for Sid. Every morning except Sundays, from six to seven, we run. I hate it. I'm not a morning person, to begin with, and until I went to work for Sid, I firmly believed in the complete avoidance of physical exercise. I have to admit it's gotten easier. I'm a lot stronger and I do have a lot more stamina. I still hate running.

Sid went to the meeting with whomever shortly after breakfast, leaving me alone. I knew Hattie was working elsewhere in the house and I didn't want to disturb her. I didn't want to go wandering around the estate because of the possibility of needing to leave quickly after the meeting, nor did I want to start another sewing project. I thought of putting the shirt I'd finished in with Sid's stuff but realized I didn't know where he was sleeping. Yawning, I elected to nap.

Sid came home shortly after lunch. He handed me a slip of paper with a phone number on it and told me to call the number at three fifteen sharp and take down the instructions. Then he went off to find Hattie.

At three thirty, I hung up the phone. I was moderately perturbed. The instructions were in a code I recognized but could not break because I did not have the keyword. Obviously, Sid did but at that moment he wasn't exactly approachable, and I was afraid the instructions were urgent.

I deliberated for another five minutes because I knew where Sid was, and I knew he wasn't alone. It doesn't happen very often. Sid is good about keeping his priorities straight. But one of my more unpleasant tasks is getting him out of bed long enough to get some work done.

Sid was in Hattie's bedroom. He'd been sleeping there since he arrived. Hattie hadn't moved out either.

I was pretty surprised when I found all this out. I'm not saying Hattie was an unattractive woman. She was just quite a bit older than any of the women I'd seen Sid date.

In any case, I decided business first and went to Hattie's room, hoping I wouldn't be too embarrassed.

I listened at the door before I knocked. There didn't seem to be any point in interrupting anything... Well, you know.

"I just hope you don't mind, Sid," said Hattie's warm voice.

"Why should I?" His voice had a purring, comfortable feel to it. "You're fun, and I'm very fond of you."

"Well, forgive my insecurity, but I find your being so nice to me rather odd. After all, I'm not a nubile, young beauty."

Sid chuckled. "Who needs them? Oh, alright. I admit it's not often that I make love to an older woman. But it's more an issue of availability than anything else."

"Oh dear. I was afraid you weren't being very picky."

"The older women aren't available. The only time I'll jump anything I can get my hands on is when it's been a while and I'm very horny. Fear not, Hattie. I'll take a woman with your experience over a nubile young beauty any day. Yours is a very special charm."

"Oh, it is?"

"Mmhm."

The noises I then heard were starting to get embarrassing. I felt a little guilty about listening so long and knocked.

"Uh, Sid? I know you're in there," I called.

"Caught again," Sid chuckled. "What's up?"

"A certain phone call you had me make."

"Ah. It can't be that late." Sid made this little gurgling sound and Hattie yelped and giggled. "Damn it, if it isn't. Meet you downstairs in fifteen minutes."

"Trouble?" I heard Hattie ask.

"Who knows?" Sid replied. "But I'm afraid I must end this pleasant interlude. By the way, Ben Franklin was right."

I walked away wondering what he meant by that. Then I remembered the old saw about taking an older mistress. I groaned in disgust.

Sid must have been more concerned about the phone call than he was letting on because he showed in ten minutes carrying his jacket, his vest open and tying his tie. Sid almost never starts anything without first making sure his appearance is perfect.

"So, what was the message?" he asked, laying the jacket over a chair.

"I don't know. You have the keyword."

We were in the drawing room. I put the message on the top of a burlwood grand piano. Sid came over and looked at it, all the while mechanically working on his tie. Still reading, he fished the tie pin from his pants pocket and slipped it through his shirt collar, under the tie and fastened it. He shook his head, picked up the paper and tore it into tiny pieces.

"So, what's going on?" I asked, sitting in a chair.

He looked at me, then absently slipped the shredded paper into his pocket.

"You know we're supposed to find the leak and plug it." He buttoned his vest as he talked.

"But how?"

"We'll be making a series of drops. One at each of the suspected stations. Each drop is a piece of information that will produce a specific reaction. What that information is, I don't know. I do know that it's part of an elaborate trap."

"Why do I get the feeling we're the bait?"

"Because we are." Sid walked over and slid on his jacket.

"Nice to know we're dispensable."

"We're not." He gently tugged me to the piano and sat me down facing the keys. "We were chosen because we stand the best chance of surviving. You and I have a very good track record."

"You in particular."

He shrugged. "G major."

"Oh, help." I glared at the keys. "There's G."

I tried sounding it out. Sid shook his head. He

plays the piano very well. His preference is classical music, but he can play anything. He also sight reads and transposes. A few months before I had made the mistake of confessing that I wished I could play like he did. He'd been casually trying to teach me ever since. He wasn't getting very far.

"Lisa, G major is the one with just the F sharp."

I slid off the seat. "Then you do it."

"You could try practicing." He took my place, played the scale and the chord, then moodily gazed at the keys. "But back to the matter at hand. That message was our itinerary. Friday, we go to New York City, after that Orlando, Florida, New Orleans, Chicago, Yellowstone, the Grand Canyon, Seattle, San Francisco, then San Diego. We'll go into town tomorrow and pick up the drops."

After a pause, Sid played a series of slow heavy chords. I recognized the progression, and absently hummed the Barry Manilow tune that went with it.

"No, no," said Sid, shaking his head and still playing. "I'm playing the original."

"The what?"

"The piece that song is based on. Chopin, number twenty, in C minor, of the Twenty-Four Preludes, Opus 28."

"Oh."

I lapsed into silence. I didn't really listen as Sid started on another prelude. Instead, I thought about the proposed itinerary. All of the stops were either major urban centers or tourist traps. That made sense. In our business people were always moving around and all the stops were places transience wouldn't be noticed.

"I take it we'll be traveling as the Donaldsons," I said, as a new thought occurred to me.

"Yes, we will. We're less conspicuous that way."

"Then maybe we'd better not go first class."

Sid stopped playing and turned to me. "Why on earth not?"

"Well, tourist class is more inconspicuous and I assume that's the objective."

"Yes." He paused for a moment, then looked at me. "You do realize, don't you, that you can't get a suite in tourist. We'll have to share a room and it'll look pretty funny if we ask for a double."

I was pretty uncomfortable with that, but I shrugged my shoulders.

"So, I have to sleep on the floor."

Sid has a very special little smile he pulls on me occasionally that, well to be blunt, gets me hot and bothered. He had that little smile on his face and I could see him mulling over the possibilities.

"You could be a gentleman and offer to take turns," I snapped more fiercely than I'd intended.

"I will." He grinned, turned back to the keys and bounced out a tango. "This could be interesting."

I felt like slamming the cover onto his hands.

"You'd better not get any ideas," I growled.

"Me?" He stopped playing and looked at me innocently. "Heaven forbid, my little ice cube."

"Is there anything else I need to know?" I asked, very coolly.

"No."

"Then I'll see you at dinner."

I left as Sid launched into a piece that I think was Tchaikovsky. I was frosted at Sid for deliberately pushing my button like he did and at myself for letting him get to me.

May 18 - 19, 1983

I poked my head into the drawing room where Sid sat staring at a blank notepad in a padded leather cover. Surrounding him were pages of statistics. He twiddled his favorite Mont Blanc fountain pen in his hand.

"Um, what time are we making that pickup?" I asked.

"We'll leave right after lunch." He looked up at me. "Why?"

"Well, I was just wondering if I'd have time to give this to Hattie." I went in the rest of the way and sat down on the piano bench.

"You're finished with that sidebar already?" Sid did not look happy.

"It was only two hundred and fifty words, and I didn't have to do any research."

Sid was writing the main article on the different choices women were making for their lives, namely to stay at home or work. We'd had a lively debate over the issue with Hattie the night before, and she decided she wanted an article on it. Disgusted, Sid capped his pen and put it away in his suit coat.

"I can't even get an outline down," he grumbled. "How am I supposed to do interviews if I don't know what to ask?"

"Maybe you ought to start with how they feel."

"Maybe Lisa ought to be doing the main article," said Hattie, coming into the room.

"I'm happy with the sidebar," I said. I was thrilled. This was the closest I'd ever come to being really published, and to get paid for it? "I just finished it."

Hattie took the sheet and put on her reading glasses, which she had on a cord around her neck.

"Hm." She looked over at Sid. "Sid, have you got your angle on this?"

"I'm getting there," said Sid gloomily.

Hattie looked down at the blank notepad. "You're not very far. Perhaps you don't have the right feel for it. Sid, I want you to reduce the stats to the sidebar. Lisa, you do the main article."

"What?" yelped Sid.

"The piece needs a woman's voice."

"I couldn't," I gasped. "Hattie, I've never really done anything like this."

Sid glared at me. "Lisa, you are being offered an opportunity on a silver platter. Grab it, woman."

"Lisa, your writing is excellent," said Hattie. "I'm sure Sid will be glad to help you develop the reporting, then it's just a matter of getting the words on the paper."

"Okay."

"I'll see you two at lunch." Hattie left.

Sid glared at his notepad.

"You're mad, aren't you?" I said.

"I can't say I'm happy about it." He looked at me. "Actually, you're right. I'm pretty teed off. But it's not your fault, Lisa. Hattie's right. It needs to be written by a woman."

"But you'd rather she wasn't me."

Sid looked me over. "I don't get it."

"It's the younger sibling syndrome," I grumbled. "Mae would do something, like drama or choir, and I'd have to get involved too, and sometimes I was better than she was, like skeet. It really bugged her to work so hard on something only to be pre-empted by her baby sister."

Sid laughed. "Yeah, that about describes how I'm feeling. At the same time, I want to be noble about this. After all, Lisa, if you want to write yourself, I really do want to support you."

"It would be nice," I said with a small smile. "But I don't want to get into competition with you."

"I doubt that will happen. Even on the same subject, I think you and I would write two very different articles." Sid got up and stretched. "At least we're not on deadline with this." He paused. "I don't want you to feel like you have to ask me to help you just to make me feel better. But if you do want it, I'll be there for you."

"Thanks. I'll probably need it."

He smiled at me. "Why don't we get this mess cleaned up and go to lunch?"

We drove into Washington in a rented car. Sid was still acting a little funny. He was not happy about having to hand the article over to me, but he kept bringing it up, asking me about the outline, what interviews I planned, and generally discussing various plans of attack.

"Sid, are you still trying to write this article?" I finally asked.

He winced. "I hope not. I'm making a very genuine effort to be supportive and share a little of my journalistic experience. I've got the background academically and I did sell stuff before you came along."

"How often?" I asked out of curiosity.

"Well, only about two or three articles a year, but I did have to do everything myself, and there was an awful lot of Quickline business that I had to take care of."

I laughed. "Sid, the only reason you didn't get published more often was that editors didn't want to take the time to fix your lousy sentence structure and spelling. Since we got that cleared up, you've been going gangbusters. I'd be a fool not to listen to you, especially since my writing experience is all academic."

"Still, it's your article. I have no right to be butting into it." He looked at me and grinned. "I'll find some other way to get even."

I stiffened. "You'd better be careful."

"Very careful," he snickered.

I would have slugged him but he was driving, and he pulled into a parking garage anyway.

The drop was at a music store filled with all sorts of pianos and a long wall of sheet music with more bins next to them. Sid and I browsed casually for a few minutes, he through the bins, and me through the racks on the wall. A title caught my eye and I pulled the music out.

"Doesn't that about say it all?" I told Sid, handing him the music. He handed me the book he was holding, then looked at the title of mine and laughed. The song was "You and Me Against the World."

"How are we doing today?" asked a young preppy salesman.

"Oh, fine," said Sid. He handed the song back to me and meandered over to a cherry wood upright piano.

"That's a nice little starter instrument," said the salesman. "Do you play?"

Sid winked at me. "Sometimes."

I grinned back. Sid was setting the poor guy up. We both love doing that to salespeople who try to sell us stuff we don't want.

"Here, let me play a little for you," said the salesman. "So you can hear how good it sounds."

Of course, the last thing he wanted was for us to find out how hard it is to make music until we'd heard how easy it is first. Sid beat him onto the bench and tapped out a tentative "Chopsticks"

"I don't know, honey," he asked me. "What do you think?"

"We have an excellent lesson program," said the salesman as Sid continued playing "Chopsticks." "And lessons do come with the purchase of your piano."

"Lessons, huh?" Sid asked. "So I can play like this?"

Sid launched into the two-handed version, then improvised, getting more and more complicated as he went.

The salesman laughed. "I thought you said you

played sometimes."

"I didn't say how well," said Sid. He looked over at me. "Sweetheart, would you give me that book I handed you a moment ago?"

I gave it to him. He thumbed through it to the page he wanted, flattened it on the music holder, counted and burst into "The Flight of the Bumble Bee." The salesman gaped, then nervously looked at us.

"You're them. I- I'll ring this up for you." He grabbed the song I was holding and fled.

"Our drop?" I asked Sid softly.

Sid nodded, still concentrating on his music. A minute later, a tall, matronly woman wandered over with my sheet music in hand.

"Good timing," she said softly. She handed me the song.

There was a thick manilla envelope inside. I slid it into my purse. The woman looked at us sadly.

"I'm the Dragon, 53-Q, code level 12-A," she said. The code meant she darned near ran the organization. "This is going to be a dirty one."

"So we've been given to understand," said Sid. He stopped playing and turned to face her.

"I must warn you that the tree you're working has been flaky for a long time. We've already tried sending marked drops through. Whoever the leak is, they're very clever, and they're quick, and as the girl we sent to San Francisco found out, they're deadly."

"Well, we're going in with our eyes open," said Sid.

"You'll be calling me for check-ins and to arrange the drops and me only. I'm code Strawberry 5150. If the Strawberries have wilted, bail out and go to standard identity change format. You'll be cleared to leave the country. If you can't make a pickup, you can buy passports through the Company, or any other supplier. For check-ins, I'm only giving you fifteen minutes on either side of your assigned hour. If you can't get me, call the next day, regular time. If I don't answer a second time, bail out and leave the country immediately, however you can, and get passports through the first Company station you can find."

Sid nodded, his face unreadable. I tried to keep mine blank, but it wasn't easy. A standard identity change meant completely changing your identity, often for the rest of your life, and starting over someplace else. As for leaving the country, we normally had to clear even day trips to Tijuana a week in advance. We were headed for some real trouble if we were cleared ahead of time without a specific plan and set up to buy fake passports from the C.I.A.

The Dragon looked us over. "The biggest danger for you will be carelessness. It's reasonably safe to assume that your first few stops or so will produce no response at all. But when things do break, they'll happen quickly. I'll try to warn you where I can."

"Thanks," said Sid softly.

The Dragon smiled at us, then left. Sid took the sheet music from my hand.

"Do you know this song?" he asked.

"A little. I've heard it before."

"Hm." Sid looked over the music as he turned back to the piano keys.

I sang softly. As we finished, Sid looked up at me.

"It says it all," he said with a wistful smile.

We were quiet in the car back to Hattie's. About halfway there, I sighed.

"We're really looking into the gun barrel on this one, aren't we?" I asked nervously.

Sid shifted. "It's not a suicide mission. They've given us too many escape routes."

"Yeah, but."

"That's it precisely." He glanced over at me. "You know, I think our best chance at coming out of this alive is to be aware of the danger, but not to let it get to us. Caution is in order, paranoia will kill us."

"You're probably right. But could it be you're not owning up to your own fear?"

"Who me?" Sid tried to chuckle and failed. "Maybe."

Pause. "Probably." He sighed. "Lisa, right now there's a job to be done, and I can't deal with that kind of paralysis. Let's get the job taken care of, and then we'll deal with the emotions."

"Assuming we get that far."

"We've got to stay positive and believe that we're going to stay alive. Period."

"Okay. That makes sense." I was still pretty scared and I could tell Sid was too. But there wasn't anything we could do about it.

Well, I did something. I called my parents after dinner from the phone in the drawing room. My parents own a resort in South Lake Tahoe, and that's where I grew up. They also own a place in Homestead, Florida, which is where they're from. Daddy bought it just after I left for college. Grandma Caulfield was raising Cain about not seeing Mama enough, and my parents were getting a little tired of eight feet of snow seven months out of every year. So they live in Homestead from the end of October to around Easter. The night I called, they'd been back in Tahoe for a month.

"Well, how are you, Lisle," said Mama in her soft southern drawl. "I was just thinking about calling you."

"Oh, well, I'm not at home. Sid and I are doing research. I just happened to be waiting around, so I thought I'd call and say hi."

"From a pay phone?"

"No. A friend of ours. Don't worry. I've got the money thing all worked out."

"Oh, really. Well, that's awful nice of your friend."

"Is Daddy there?"

"I'm 'fraid not, honey. He had to go into town. You remember Bill and Dottie Shakespeare?"

"Oh yeah." Actually, I remembered their really awful sons better. Bill was a commercial real estate agent.

"You know Bill was behind that time share company that bought the Bowers' motel."

"I didn't know the Bowers had sold it."

"Oh, Lisle, they had to. Martin got so sick, and Ernestine just was not up to all that work by herself, and with the kids grown and moved off, there was no way they could keep it. And the time share people were real anxious to get it. You know how that place had all those huge suites and all. Bill fixed them one sweet deal."

"That's good, but what does that have to do with Daddy?"

"Well, that time share company is going in everywhere, and they were so happy with Bill that they invited him to get into it, putting money behind it, I mean, and Bill thought your Daddy might be interested in investing also. In fact, we're supposed to go out to Yellowstone to look over the operation sometime next month."

"Is Daddy interested?"

"Oh, yes, and I'm looking forward to the trip. It'll be fun to get someplace besides Florida and here for a change."

"How are things down south?"

"Oh, the relatives are just being as tiresome as usual."

She launched into some tale about my Aunt Marie, who is pretty tiresome as a rule. I didn't hear much of it because Sid wandered in and made it clear that he was not happy that I was on the phone. Fearing the worst, I broke in on Mama.

"Oops, there's Sid now, Mama. I've got to take off. I'll talk to you soon." I hung up fast.

"What the hell were you doing?" Sid demanded.

I opted for the best defense. "I was calling my mother. I have a right to do that."

"Not when it could get her and you killed."

"Hattie swears her phones are clean, and nobody knows about our business, so nobody is going to tap my mother's phone."

"It's still taking chances. Why on earth would you do that?"

I blinked back tears. "Why do you think?"

Sid paced for a moment longer, then sat down at the piano and began the first of the Twenty-Four Preludes.

The next morning at breakfast, Sid got called to the phone. He didn't seem too ruffled up by it until we left the dining room. Hattie took off to take care of whatever business she had. Sid motioned for me to follow him upstairs.

"What's up?" I asked as I followed him to Hattie's room.

"That phone call. It was from the Dragon."

"She called you here? How did she know?"

"She told me to come here in the first place. Anyway, one of the Washington operatives who has been watching this tree got called to meet with one of the suspects at three o'clock this afternoon. We're to watch the meeting, and tail the suspect."

"That doesn't sound too bad." I waited in the doorway while Sid went in and got our transmitters and receivers out of his suitcase. "We might even break this thing right up front."

Sid smiled and shook his head. "We can but hope. Unfortunately, our shopping trip is going to make it hard to wear jackets."

He meant our shoulder holsters. We couldn't wear suit jackets to cover the holsters because a three piece or even a two-piece suit is a real nuisance to get in and out of when you're trying on clothes. Also, Sid's suits and shirts are all custom made, which is why we were shopping in the first place. We were supposed to be your average middle-class couple, and Sid always says it's the details that trip you up faster than anything when you're undercover. It would have looked pretty funny if he were dressed in one of his super expensive suits and shopping at the Gap.

He was wearing khaki slacks and a light orange Polo shirt, which was the least conspicuous outfit he had with him. Since he was wearing that, it would have looked funny if I were wearing a suit, so I wore the lavender shirtwaist dress that I'd finished the night before. Except for Wednesday morning when I was writing, I'd been sewing pretty steadily and had another sundress and short sleeved shirt in progress. I learned a long time ago that I can get a lot more done if I work on batches of outfits instead of just one item at a time.

I had stuff to buy as well. While my vacation clothes were compatible with our cover, Sid hadn't packed any of them, just my business wear. All I had were the three t-shirts and pair of jeans I'd worn on the retreat. We knew we'd be gone at least three weeks, so what I had wasn't going to get me very far.

Shopping with Sid is, in a word, interesting. He's the only man I've ever met who doesn't mind browsing, although when he's buying for himself, he does have the male habit of getting what he wants and getting out. Things were a little difficult that day because off the rack clothes don't fit him too well. He is a little on the short side, so all the pants were too long. He isn't stocky or square-shaped at all, but his chest and arms are pretty muscular because he works out on weights, so most of the shirts and sport coats that were big enough for him were also way too long. Anything that fit, he bought on the spot.

"That's going to be an awful lot to carry," I pointed out as he stacked up six pairs of Jordache jeans. They came in specific lengths, so we didn't have to worry about shortening them. We already had two pairs of casual slacks and another pair of dress slacks that I was going to hem for him. We'd taken a chance and paid for emergency alterations on the navy blazer and tan sport coat. And then there were all the different sport shirts and sweaters we'd bought. Sid is a clothes horse.

He shrugged. "I need the clothes, and as you can see, I can't just walk into a store and buy them."

"Well, what about packing lightly? It's a little

more realistic."

"No, it isn't."

I lowered my voice. "Maybe not for a rich kid like you, but for the rest of us, it is."

His voice dropped also. "Believe it or not, there was a time in my life when I didn't have any money and I still managed to keep a decent wardrobe."

"But we have to carry all this stuff."

"I'll carry it, and gladly, too. My days of packing lightly are over."

I snorted. "What? Managing with only one suitcase was a little rough?"

"Try hitchhiking cross country with one pair of jeans, two t-shirts and three pairs of jockey shorts. I swore never again and I meant it."

"Well, five suitcases is just a bit too far in the other direction."

"I suppose," he sighed. "We'll just get four of these."

He put back two pairs of jeans as I shook my head. He nearly went nuts watching me. I was the exact opposite. Everything fit, but I didn't want to spend the money. And if that wasn't bad enough, Sid kept pushing me to buy long, full-skirted sundresses instead of the shorts and jeans I prefer.

"But I like shorts," I protested as he put yet another pair back. "I'm comfortable in them."

"You can't hide a gun in them," he said through gritted teeth.

"Oh."

"You can hide all sorts of stuff under this." He handed me a blue chambray skirt with a white eyelet petticoat.

I took it. "I have a pattern like this." I examined the side seams. "And the pattern has pockets."

"Just buy it, will you?"

The only other problem was getting a swim suit. Sid had left mine. It was pretty ratty. He'd brought his.

"You don't mean your birthday suit, do you?" I said, teasing.

"No. It's a genuine, bona fide swim suit." He looked me up and down. "You've got the figure for a bikini."

I blushed. "Would you mind terribly if I did this by myself?"

"Why?" he asked innocently. Yet as he did, one eyebrow lifted and he smiled that really hot little smile.

I swallowed and forced myself to smile back. "I think you know."

Sid chuckled. "I'll meet you back here in twenty minutes."

I got a black one piece and told Sid when he met me that he'd see it soon enough.

We left the stores from there and went to a restaurant near the Watergate Hotel. In the restrooms, we each hid a small micro transmitter and receiver on ourselves. I slid my transmitter onto my bra strap, and parked the receiver behind my ear, brushing my hair over it. Almost immediately, I heard a toilet flush and the raucous laughter of two men. I switched my transmitter on.

"Coming in," I said softly.

"Loud and clear on this end," said Sid's voice in my ear.

I left the ladies room. Sid went to wait in the car, which was parked on the street out front. The restaurant was a nice, if trendy, place, with lots of hanging plants, and booths topped by more planters. I wandered around the dining room, looking for a young man with a purple tie reading Plutarch's Parallel Lives. He had sandy hair and tortoiseshell glasses and wore a gray pinstriped suit with a purple tie and matching color in his breast pocket. I took a table across the room from his booth to the consternation of the hostess.

"Excuse me, miss," she said, smiling through gritted teeth. "It would be better if we could get you a table in the other section."

"I'm waiting for someone," I told her. "I want to be where I can see the door."

"We can arrange that," she said.

"I'll stay here, thank you."

A minute later, I heard her behind me. I couldn't see her through all the plants topping my booth.

"We've got another one that won't budge. Table twelve."

"Aw hell, and that jackass on fifty-three. Why do they always have to spread out on the days we're short-handed?"

Just then, the Washington operative jerked. The book tumbled out of his hands as he fell forward, the back of his head a red mess. My stomach tied itself into knots. A waitress approached the table and screamed bloody murder, literally.

I looked everywhere but at that table.

"It doesn't sound good in there?"

"It's not," I whispered. Terror settled into my limbs and kept me pinned. "Um, has anyone left the place in the last thirty seconds?"

"Yeah, about five people. You'd better get out of there. Go the back way."

Trembling, I got up and slipped back and around towards the bar. There was a closed section next to where the operative had been sitting, and in it, a booth that backed up to the booth where the operative was. On the table was a glass of water, half empty, and a crumpled napkin.

I got to the car just as the police pulled up. Sid took his time getting going.

"What the hell happened?" he asked.

"He just went over," I said. "I didn't hear anything, but he must have been shot. Someone was in the booth behind him."

"Did you see who?"

I shook my head. "The planters blocked the view."

"And a silencer, too." Sid shook his head. "That's a professional job if ever I've seen one."

"I wonder who set it up there. Not one of the booths backs up against a wall, and everything is screened by planters."

"But who'd try a hit like that in broad daylight? Whoever's behind this has guts."

Apparently, the Dragon concurred when Sid checked in with her from Hattie's. I just wanted to put it all out of my mind, so I concentrated on finishing my projects. It worked. I not only finished them but got Sid's pants hemmed and pressed. I just didn't get to bed until three a.m., not that I would have been better off going to bed earlier. Something told me I wouldn't have slept much.

[I didn't sleep much either. You were right about the fears I didn't want to acknowledge, and the worst fear was that you or I would die before we had a chance to know each other's love, the physical kind, of course. I had no idea there was any other. That night, I made love to Hattie and felt terrible because in my mind I had made love to you. I vowed then and there that sometime on that trip I would make it right for you and we would make love. I eventually banished you from my mind and made love to Hattie, only to have it happen all over again - SEH]

May 20 - 23, 1983

The flight from Washington was short. Sid seemed tense but stayed awake for a change. I, on the other hand, dozed. Sid woke me as we circled over Manhattan.

"We forgot something," he grumbled.

"Huh?"

"We forgot something," he repeated. "Something critical."

"Oh, help." I dove under my seat for my carry on and the huge tan leather purse Sid had talked me into buying the day before.

"It's something we forgot to get yesterday," said Sid.

I yawned. "I can't imagine what."

"A camera. We're tourists."

"I've got mine." I got out my purse and pulled out the black case containing my Canon SLR. "I even remembered the flash."

Sid all but gaped. "When did you get that?"

"I've had it since last November. Jesse helped me get it wholesale."

"Figures. But how did it get here?"

"I had it on the retreat with me."

"Oh, great. Don't tell me you have film with your friends on it."

"Nope. I'm not that stupid. I shot off that roll in Washington and left it. Hattie said she'd send it back with the rest of my fabric and stuff. Oh my, those skyscrapers are so close. What a great shot."

I pulled the case off my camera and squeezed off

a few.

We landed about ten minutes later at La Guardia. We were on one of those early commuter flights, and so it was only nine o'clock when we got on the bus to Manhattan. We settled into our seats, and I checked my copy of Frommer's New York City.

"Good lord, look at these prices!" I gasped.

"Welcome to New York," said Sid.

"Hey, get this, the Algonquin is moderately priced. That's moderate? Good Lord. Here's one on 42nd and 8th."

Sid grimaced. "That's right off of Times Square. It's not a nice neighborhood."

"This says it's right in the middle of the theater district. Can't be that bad."

"True. Alright."

"It's the cheapest one there is." I shook my head. "My daddy would be a millionaire at these prices."

Sid just chuckled.

At the hotel, we had to store our suitcases and carry-ons. Our room wasn't ready, but the desk said he'd send our stuff up as soon as it was. In the meantime, Sid and I hit the phones. I didn't know what he was up to, but I had a drop to arrange.

"So what do we do now?" I asked him when we met again in the lobby.

"Go sight-seeing," he said. "We'll come back and change for dinner."

"Okay."

As far as I was concerned, he was dressed for dinner in one of the casual slacks I'd hemmed the night before. They were a tweed-like synthetic linen, with a pleated front. The yarns were mixed white and light blue with navy blue slubs here and there. They just happened to match the shirt I had made for him, which he just happened to be wearing, along with the light blue sweater he'd bought the day before, which also just happened to match.

The shirt, itself, was short sleeved with square

patch pockets and epaulets. Instead of just throwing his sweater over his shoulders and tying it in front, as usual, he'd buttoned the epaulets over the sweater's sleeves. The whole effect was stunning, far more so than I wanted to think about.

"You got your sweater?" he asked. "It's a little chilly out there."

"Yeah, but maybe I should put it with our stuff." I looked at the beige shetland wool in my hands. "It's going to warm up, and this purse is bad enough. I don't want to be dragging a sweater all over, too."

I had put on my lavender shirtwaist again, with tan sandals that tied around my ankles. The heels were a modest wedge, and in them were pieces of assorted hardware.

"Wear it around your shoulders," said Sid.

"They always fall off when I do that."

"Maybe you're not wearing it right. Put it on."

Rolling my eyes skyward, I flipped the sweater around my shoulders. Sid just smiled and shook his head.

"No wonder it falls," he said, plucking it off. He deftly folded the neckline over. "Here, see how I fold this?" I took my purse in my hands and he swung the sweater over my shoulders. "Then you just lay it on, so that all of the sleeves are over your shoulders, then tie it like so." He did. "And you're ready to go."

There was a strange, but not awkward, pause, as we stood and looked at each other. His lips parted. I felt my heart stutter.

"Uh, yeah, well." Sid turned from me to one of the mirrors decorating the lobby and ran a reassuring hand over his perfectly arranged hair. "You got plenty of film?"

"Yeah," I replied softly and gathered my things together.

There is an energy to Manhattan that when you're in the middle of it, fills you with an exhilaration that goes beyond words. Times Square was ugly, without a doubt, trash all over the place, tacky stores, and crowds like I had never seen before, but I loved it. The only other time I had been in New York City, I was in a cab going through Queens from La Guardia to Kennedy. No matter what the danger was, I couldn't help filling up with the incredible life of the city around me.

"New York, New York, it's a wonderful town," I sang. "The Bronx is up and the Battery's down."

"The people ride in a hole in the ground," said Sid. He doesn't sing. [Under certain circumstances I do, just not in public. They arrest people for that - SEH] "Come on."

He gently took my elbow and steered me into the hole in the ground. It was dark, dirty, graffiti everywhere, and it stank.

"This is great," I giggled as we stood on the platform.

Sid laughed.

"Cut that out," I said. "I can't help it. I mean this is the New York subway. I've heard about it all my life and I'm really here."

"You get excited by the strangest things, woman."

We got off at the Battery. At the edge of the park was a wagon vendor. I got out my wallet.

"A hot pretzel, please," I asked the vendor. Sid cleared his throat. I turned on him. "Don't start. Don't even think of starting. I experience the world with all five of my senses, and I'm not about to stop now." I turned back to the vendor. "I'd like a bag of peanuts, too, and... a strawberry soda."

Sid winced as I squirted mustard over the pretzel. That was only the start. I basically ate my way through lower Manhattan. From the Battery, we walked up to Wall Street, then over to the World Trade Center, where Sid decided the line was too long for the ride to the top. I got a bagel and cream cheese downstairs.

Then we went up Broadway, past City Hall Park, and walked around the shops in Chinatown where I got take out - marvelous mu shu pork, exquisite egg foo young and a yummy spare rib, then on up through Little Italy where I ate two slices of pizza from two different places, a half pint of tortellini that I'm certain God Himself made, and a quarter pound of an incredibly delicious salami.

"Fats and salt," said Sid, morosely shaking his head.

"And lots of garlic to thin out my blood." I stuffed in another slice.

"I know. I can smell it."

"You can? Maybe I'd better get a breath mint."

"Oh no. Not one of those revolting peppermints. Please. The only thing worse than garlic on your breath is peppermint and garlic on your breath."

From Little Italy, we walked through SoHo and up into Greenwich Village where I stopped eating long enough to take some pictures of Washington Square Park.

"So this is the infamous Village," I said.

"Mm-hm." Sid nodded. "It's gotten a lot nicer since I was a kid. I was born not too far from here, you know."

"That's right. But you were pretty young when you left. Do you remember a lot?"

"I was only three when we moved." He frowned, digging up the memory. "We lived over this little Italian grocery. My earliest memory is of the grocer. He was an old guy, with ice blue eyes. I don't remember much else from when I lived here. Stella and I came back a lot, though. It was a pretty interesting place."

"I'll bet." Then something I'd been looking for caught my eye and I headed for it. "Alright."

"Where are you going?"

"That hot dog wagon. I've been looking for one of those since I got here."

"You can get one later." Sid caught my arm and pulled me away. "You may not believe this, but I am actually hungry and would like to eat a responsible, healthy lunch."

Read boring, but actually, it wasn't bad. The

little restaurant served a variety of organic salads and something called tofu. I had an avocado sandwich with tomato and lettuce on whole grain bread. The salad they put in front of Sid had all sorts of weird things growing out of it. I managed to cop a taste from him, and it was pretty good.

"There, you see," he said. "Healthy living does not have to be deprivation. This food is as delicious as anything I've watched you put in your face today."

"I never said it wasn't. I just like the other stuff, too."

Sid sighed in surrender. We spent the rest of the afternoon ambling up Broadway. I got cookies, more pizza, falafel, gyros, Lindy's cheesecake and the most heavenly pastrami sandwich it has ever been my pleasure to sink my teeth into.

"This is the pastrami I have been waiting all my life to eat," I announced, licking the mustard from my thumb.

"Are you finally getting full?"

"You're just jealous."

"Not a bit. In fact, I'm rather enjoying the thought of the incredible indigestion that's headed your way."

"Not my way." I patted my tummy. "It's cast iron. Can handle anything."

As we neared Times Square again, I spotted another hot dog wagon.

"No," said Sid. "Don't you want to save some room for dinner?"

"It depends on whether or not I get to pick out where we're eating."

"I've already selected a place and made reservations."

"I'm not eating dinner at any restaurant that serves alfalfa sprouts. I've done that once today and that's enough, so if you'll excuse me, I'll get my kraut dog now."

He caught my elbow. "In deference to your gluttony, we're going to a very nice little French restaurant that

I know of."

"It's not that nouvelle cuisine that's supposed to be good for you, is it?"

"No. It's traditional French cooking in all its glory."

"Really?" That sounded a lot better. "Maybe I will wait on that kraut dog."

It was almost three o'clock then, and time for me to check in, which I did at the first pay phone I could find that worked.

"Well?" asked Sid as I hung up.

"The drop's set up for tomorrow."

"Good."

When we got back to the hotel, Sid grabbed his clothes and the bathroom.

"Put on that black backless dress you got yesterday," he called.

"Okay." I also got out my makeup and redid my face. If the place was that fancy, I wanted to look good.

It took me a few more minutes to find my black nylons. I got undressed, put on the black nylons, and had just slipped the black dress up over my hips when the bathroom door opened.

"Sid!" I yelped, pulling the top up over my bare chest.

His face was damp, his five o'clock shadow was gone, and he was equally bare-chested, with a light tan that highlighted his muscles, just enough to suggest power without all that exaggerated bulkiness.

"Oh, sorry," he said, going over to his carry on. "I thought you'd be dressed by now."

"But, Sid-"

"Watch that name stuff. You never know."

"You did that on purpose!" My face was purple with rage and embarrassment.

Sid, who was on his way back to the bathroom, turned back to me with his very bored look.

"Why? I'll confess to some curiosity, but in the first place, there just aren't that many variations on the theme, and we both know it would go nowhere, so in the final analysis, looking is utterly pointless. And in the second place, nude bodies in all circumstances aside from immediate sexual pleasure just don't get me that excited."

"Huh?"

"I don't give a damn whether your breasts have clothes on them or not. Your bare breasts are not going to get me all fired up. As far as I'm concerned, they're just mammary glands, unless I happen to have my hands or my mouth on them, which is a very pleasant thought, indeed, but not too damned likely to happen. I just came out to get my brush, and I'm sorry I caught you." [Okay, I wasn't being entirely honest. I found your topless body quite pleasant to look at and was very happy to have had the chance. But it was an accident that I got it - SEH]

I didn't believe him. He went back into the bathroom and I finished getting dressed. When he came out, we were both dressed.

"Did you shave again?" I asked.

"Mm-hmm. I always shave twice a day. My beard is unfortunately too dark and grows too fast for me not to."

The topless incident remained unmentioned.

Dinner was excellent. Sid almost ate like a normal person. He stuck with chicken and oil and vinegar on the side for his salad and requested no salt when he ordered. He also refused dessert. I didn't. While I was happily consuming my pastry, he told me what those other phone calls were.

"Tickets to the theater and the ballet?" I actually stopped eating. "You're kidding."

"Not in the least. We've got American Ballet Theatre tomorrow, and a nice little off-Broadway show tonight."

"On a weekend? How'd you do it?"

"I have my ways."

I leaned over and spoke softly. "You didn't blow our cover did you?"

He also spoke softly, mocking my tone. "Not even close. I just know who to call."

I settled back in my seat.

"Wow," I giggled. "That's terrific."

Between dinner and the play, I got down a Hagen Daz ice cream cone. During the play, which was very good, I ate a chocolate bar. After the play, I finally got my kraut dog (perfection).

"I've never seen any one person eat so much in one day in my entire life," Sid said when we finally got back to our room.

"There's a lot of good food around." I came in from the bathroom, dressed for bed in nightgown and robe, stirring bicarbonate of soda into a glass of warm water. I handed it to him. "Maybe if you didn't baby your system so much, it wouldn't be so hard on you."

Sid winced at the taste of the mixture. He heaved himself out of the chair and headed for the bathroom to change for bed. I noticed his pajama bottoms and robe folded neatly on top of his suitcase.

"You forgot something," I called out. I picked them up and handed them through.

"Sorry."

That was one of the most awkward things about us rooming together. Sid doesn't normally wear anything to bed. He was very nice about volunteering the pajama bottoms but got a little testy about the robe until I reminded him he didn't have to sleep in the robe. It was just for between the changing room and bed, as the bottoms were rather sheer and the flies on those things were always popping open. Sid promptly retorted in that case, he could dispense with the bottoms once in bed. I said I didn't want to know about it.

"I'll sleep on the floor tonight," I called. "Since you're not feeling well."

"Thanks."

We had gotten an extra blanket from the hotel. I took the bedspread off the bed, laid it down on the floor, grabbed the second pillow, and taking it and the blanket, made myself comfortable. After taking off my robe, I laid down, trying to silently release the excess gas in my stomach.

The next morning, Sid let me sleep until seven thirty before he nudged me awake with his foot.

"Leave me alone," I mumbled, pulling the blanket over my head.

"We're going running." He was ready to go.

"We're supposed to be on vacation."

"In the first place, we are in fact not on vacation, and in the second place, people on vacation do go running in the morning. Don't you want to be able to say you went running in Central Park?"

"No."

"Get up."

I did, growling and grumbling and fumbling my way around. I wake up very slowly. As I became more alert, I made several pointed remarks about the possibilities of encountering the muggers, rapists, and other assorted violent types generally associated with Central Park. Sid pointedly ignored me. I also complained about running the twenty blocks up to the park through all the crowds of people trying to get to work when we could have taken the bus or subway. Sid ignored that too.

Two hours later, over breakfast, Sid briefed me on the small, coded dossier on our suspect that we'd found in the envelope with the drops.

"His name is Merle Wadkins, Jr.," said Sid. "He's caucasian, six one, brown hair, green eyes, no distinguishing marks. Cover is a freelance salesman in the greeting card and novelty business. He lives in a fourth floor walk-up in SoHo. He was adopted in 1969, has a good solid record, including several investigations, but nothing spectacular. He's considered the least likely source of our leak, but you know how that goes."

"I can imagine." I was nervous. Sid and I were wired, but that was small consolation.

We took a cab to the Metropolitan Museum of

Art. Sid ditched me just after we got in the entrance. Around eleven, I found myself in the European Artist's Gallery looking for someone looking at Rembrandt's "Aristotle Looking at a Bust of Homer." Wadkins arrived precisely on time at five after. He wore a dark tacky spring overcoat. I casually came over to inspect the Rembrandt. Standing close to him, I quickly glanced around. People milled about the room but paid no attention to us. I slipped an envelope out of my purse and into the pocket of the overcoat.

"Thanks," muttered Wadkins and then moved off.

I stayed looking at the painting a minute longer, then sauntered off to meet Sid in Arms and Armour.

"Mission accomplished," I said slipping up to him.

"Great. Let's make tracks out of here."

"Do we have to?"

Sid looked at me and shrugged. "I suppose we could stay if you want to. I was thinking of taking in the Statue of Liberty, myself. It may be our last chance before all you know what breaks loose."

"Oh. That's right." I sighed. "Alright, let's go."

We had a lovely day. The Statue was great but extremely crowded. Sid absolutely refused to stand in line to walk to the top. The Dragon had nothing for us when we checked in, so we goofed off and window shopped at the South Street Seaport and just barely got back to the hotel in time to change for dinner and the ballet. Then I almost made us late by insisting on checking the times for mass at St. Patrick's Cathedral.

The next morning, I told Sid he could stay at the hotel if he wanted to, while I was at church. He insisted on walking with me.

"It'll look better if I go with you," he said, as we started off.

"Well, you don't have to stay."

"So I'm bored for an hour."

"You're not bored, you're bugged. Why the sudden interest?"

"Strictly for appearances." His tone told me he'd

been bracing himself for this. Attending mass was the last thing he wanted to do. I took pity on him.

"If that's the only reason you're going, then don't. Mixed marriages aren't all that uncommon. Nobody would think twice about a man dropping his wife off at church."

"You sure?"

"Positive."

"How long will you be?"

"About an hour. Tell you what. Sak's is right there. I'll meet you there in two-and-a-half hours."

I was surprised when he didn't argue or insist that we go wired.

I was looking at a dress in Sak's Fifth Avenue when it happened. I didn't have to meet Sid for another half hour, and so I was more absorbed in whether or not I should try the dress on than I should have been. A pair of hands slipped from behind to cover my eyes. I didn't scream but rammed my knuckles into the tendons above the wrists. The hands gave way, and I whirled around with my elbow looking for a place to connect. One of the hands stopped me.

"Hold on," Sid said wincing and chuckling at the same time. "It's just me."

I turned on him, utterly furious.

"You," I gasped, then continued in a low angry voice. "You of all people ought to know better than to pull a stupid stunt like that."

"Did I scare you?"

"I only tried to jump right out of my skin."

"Well, you got yours back." Grinning, he held up his wrists, then rubbed the spot where my knuckles had hit home. There was something funny about the way he was acting.

"You seem to be in an awfully good mood," I said.

"I am. I just resolved a problem that I thought was going to make things difficult for us, especially if this fiasco turns out to be a long-running affair."

"I don't get it."

Sid grinned and brushed my nose with his forefinger.

"You're not thinking again, my dear. What's a supposedly happily married man supposed to do when he's horny and his wife won't co-operate and nobody can know why she won't?"

I blushed. "I think I know what you were doing while I was at church."

"Each of us to our own first loves."

"That is disgusting." I stopped and looked at him. He laughed. "But apt."

"So what are you looking at?"

"This dress. I was debating trying it on."

"Go ahead."

"I don't know. It's very expensive."

"Oh no." Sid groaned. "Must you..?' "

"That is why I wanted to meet you out front, to prevent this argument."

"How much is it? It's probably not that bad."

"Details..."

Sid looked at the price tag.

"It's not that bad," he said. "You could afford it."

"I suppose," I sighed. "But I don't know if it's my style."

I took it off the rack and walked over to the three-way mirror. Sid followed me over.

"I don't know," I said again putting it up to myself and looking into the mirror. "What do you think?"

"Looks nice." He nodded.

"Maybe." Without thinking, I put the dress up to him. "Here, hold this."

"What?" He took the hanger as I stepped back a few paces and looked at it.

"I can't tell."

"I should hope not, up against me." He handed the dress back. "Here, go try it on. Please?"

"Alright. Will you take my purse?"

Sid feebly took the strap, gazing skyward and asking, "Why me?"

Needless to say, we bought the dress. As the salesgirl was wrapping it, I sniffed at my wrists, trying to make up my mind about the two perfumes I'd tried on them. I noticed Sid raise an eyebrow at me, so I asked his opinion. I stiffened and tried to calm my racing heart as his soft, gentle hands took each wrist. He sniffed expertly at one, then the other and pronounced judgment. Our next stop was the perfume counter, where we bought the approved scent.

"We should get something for you," I said as we left the store.

"Maybe we will." Sid held the door open for me. "Why don't we make this our shopping day? I'd just as soon keep moving."

"Why?"

"We'll be harder to hit."

We spent the day walking up and down Fifth Avenue and Madison Avenue. We didn't buy much. We knew we'd have to carry it. Sid spent a lot of time smiling and shaking his head at what he called my "childlike delight" over anything I liked.

"It's utterly fitting for you, innocent one."

We were in front of Tiffany's and I had more or less glowed at finding myself peering into its windows. We'd already been to Cartier, which I know is a classier store. But there was something special about Tiffany's.

"Please," I replied, blushing. "I prefer to think of myself as a more sophisticated woman."

"But you are in your own way. That's part of your charm. You, my dear, are a fascinating woman of contrasts."

"Oh, I am?" I blushed even harder. "I suppose you're waiting for me to tell you what a dashingly clever, charming, and handsome fellow you are."

"I already know I am."

"Then I won't tell you."

Sid laughed. "Come on, let's go inside."

"Better not." I looked at the door longingly. "I'll fall in love with something and you'll get mad at me because I won't buy it."

Sid leaned back against the building, with his arms folded and looked out at the traffic.

"Maybe... I think I will." He nodded and looked at me. "This is a promise. I don't know how yet, but someday, I am going to find a way to put you in a position where you cannot protest and I am going to drag you in here and I am going to twist your arm until you tell me exactly what it is you want and I shall buy it for you."

He was smiling and his tone was light, but he was serious. I don't know why it made me feel so uncomfortable.

"Well," I said, desperately trying to break the moment. "The only position you'll be able to get me in is standing or sitting."

Sid's eyebrow lifted and his hot little smile sent my heart racing.

"I can do that." There was not the least trace of lechery in his voice, and yet those four words were the most sensual and steamy that I had ever heard.

My face went vermillion.

"I should know better than to say things like that to you," I said, walking off.

Sid chuckled. "And I should probably have let it pass, but a set up like that is just too tempting."

"I suppose." We walked in silence for a minute. "You know, I really am not saying anything."

"Believe me, I'm well aware of how innocent you really are. I guess I do it because A- It is funny. Even you laugh."

"Yeah, I do."

"And B-" He looked out at the cars and people. "There's a certain safety in keeping you mad at me."

I had to admit there was that.

Then there was the problem of all the stuff I saw for my five nieces and nephews back home.

"Anything we buy that we cannot personally use represents clues that an enemy might use against us," said Sid.

"We can't send it, I suppose."

"And give an enemy an address to latch onto?" Sid shook his head. "I'll admit the odds are pretty low that we're being watched right now, but we're not going to stay alive by being careless."

"I'm going to have to call Mae sometime. She's going to start wondering, and that could be dangerous, too."

Sid sighed. "You've got a point. Let me think about it and I'll figure something out. But we've got to stay on our toes every step of the way."

"You certainly know how to set a person at ease."

Sid softened. "Let's not worry about it too much. I don't want us to be miserable, just alert."

I tried cheering up, but it took more of Sid's teasing to jolt me out of it. It was my idea to stop at the t-shirt shop.

"This looks nice," said Sid, holding up a beige one with the city's skyline silk screened onto it.

"Yeah." I managed a half smile, then a thought hit me. "You know we could get matching shirts."

"No way in hell. I wouldn't be caught dead."

"Thanks." I sulked.

His hand softly landed on my shoulder. "Hey, matching you isn't the problem. It's matching." His face scrunched up in disgust. "It's so cutesy and juvenile."

"It might help our cover."

Sid rolled his eyes. "We're not a couple of junior high kids going steady."

"True. Why don't I get this other one, and you can have that."

"I don't particularly want it."

"You have no problem with me getting it."

"You have more up front to fill it out with."

I glared at him. "That was tacky."

He grinned. "You walked right into it."

By that point I knew he was pushing my button deliberately to get me out of my depression, so I decided to play along. I looked at the t-shirt again.

"Of course," I said slowly. "If you keep working out like you do, you could have more than me. I mean some of those guys at the gym could wear D-cups."

Sid laughed. "I, however, am not about to take the steroids to do it."

"Are you serious? They do that?"

"Hell, yes."

It was my turn to make a face. "Who would want to take drugs to get all distorted looking? Yuck." I looked at the t-shirt again. "You'd still look good in this. Or I could cut out the arms and neck for you and make it a tank top."

"Don't bother. There's a rack full of tanks right here. I guess I could use a couple new t-shirts to play racquetball in."

"You only change shirts three times a game."

Sid sweats like a horse when he plays.

"I didn't think you'd noticed." Sid looked up at me with one of his sly smiles.

We belong to the same gym because that's where Sid signed me up when I first started working for him. But when we're there together, we don't really cross paths much. Most people would be surprised we even know each other.

I'm only a beginner at racquetball and Sid's a thousand times better, and I'm on a different weight program again because Sid's been there a lot longer and is more advanced and because I'm a woman. Strangely enough, Sid doesn't go to the gym to pick up women, although he doesn't turn down offers. He says it's his time to be with the guys.

"Well, Karen and Mindy have spotted you," I said referring to the gals I hang out with. "They talked me into watching that tournament last month."

"Really." Sid's eyebrow lifted.

"Don't waste your time. Karen is happily married and Mindy is too busy with law school to bother. We just like ogling the meat, that's all."

"Meat. Hmmm. Alright. As the current representative of the male sex, I accept your point and concede that it is well put."

Laughing, I licked the end of my finger and chalked up my point on the air.

At check in time, the Dragon told me to make a pick up near the U.N. and drop it with our suspect the next morning. I got the pickup, then Sid and I took advantage of where we were and toured the facility. We were not happy about the drop. Sid called us cheese for the mousetrap. But that was why we were there.

Later, I talked Sid into tickets for that night for one of the big musicals. We got back late, completely exhausted. It was my night for the floor, and I was so tired, I didn't care. It was the only reason I slept.

We were both tense the next morning. We went to the drop wired. Sid scoped out the set up first. Of course, I didn't think anybody would be crazy enough try a hit in the toy department at Macy's, but after that restaurant in Washington, we weren't taking any chances. We'd made it a code one, which meant no contact at all, to make it even harder for someone to get in close enough for a knife, or even a small pistol.

I'd been told about a doll in a doll bed, and sure enough, it was there.

"You're clear," said Sid's voice in my ear. He was within reach, but not where he could be seen. "Anyone hiding would have to be a leprechaun."

"I don't want to chance them, either," I grumbled, going over to the doll bed.

I put the drop under the doll and retreated quickly.

Nothing happened. I browsed through the games. No one went near the bed. I waited for five minutes.

Sid came out from behind the luggage department.

"Keep an eye out," his voice said in my ear. "But I'll watch here."

He looked over the stuffed animals. A woman in a business suit wandered through. She picked up a toy gun and eyed Sid. I moved in quickly, but she went back to the register. Sid moved out of range. The toy clerk came out from the stockroom. The woman bought the gun and left. The toy clerk went over to Sid.

"Help you today?" asked the clerk.

"Not today." Sid backed off quickly and slid around the corner.

We waited another five minutes, then I went over to the doll bed, got the drop and we got out of there fast.

"Something's wrong," I gasped as we hit the street.

"Keep moving," said Sid. His eyes were everywhere. Suddenly, he darted onto a bus, pulling me with him. The bus pulled away downtown. I watched out the door as Sid paid our fares.

"Well?" he asked as we made our way to the back.

"Nobody noticed or cared," I said. "Typical New York."

"Lucky for us," said Sid. The bus took us down Broadway and we got off in SoHo. We found the brownstone where Merle Wadkins lived without problem. The front door was locked and had a buzzer on it. We lucked out and someone left the building and all we had to was slip in after.

"Gloves," said Sid softly. I dug the two pairs of black kid leather gloves out of my purse, and we put them on as we went upstairs. Sid had drilled it into me that anytime I was someplace I wasn't supposed to be, I wore gloves.

We knocked on the door to Wadkins' apartment. There was no answer.

"I don't like this," said Sid. "I hate daytime jobs."

But he scratched his hair and pulled out of it a small piece of spring steel.

"Keep your eyes open," he said working on the door. "And get your hand on your gun."

I already had my hand on the S and W model thirteen revolver in my purse. The bolts slid back with a clunk and the door creaked open. Sid stepped back. We checked the landing for people. I drew my gun and, with my back to the door, eased myself into the apartment. Behind me, Sid bent down and retrieved the twenty-two automatic he keeps strapped to his left shin.

Utter quiet blanketed the destruction in the tiny room. Papers and greeting cards were everywhere. Cushions and pillows had been torn apart, chairs had lost their seats and drawers were upended.

"Damn," muttered Sid.

"What now?" I whispered.

"Better see if somebody found something." Sid moved past me towards the back.

I went over to the turned over couch and righted it and gasped loudly.

"What?" Sid was at my side in a second.

He doesn't swear often, but when he does, it can peel paint off walls. In rare form, he pulled papers away from the corpse and checked it. I turned away, feeling nauseous.

"Damn it. What's the matter with you?"

"Is he dead?"

"As stiff as they come. Jesus, will you pull yourself together?"

"Don't use that name in vain."

Sid groaned. "Go check the kitchen."

I stumbled into that room, but couldn't get through the door. Every cupboard had been emptied as had the refrigerator, and the floor was completely covered with pots, pans, broken glassware, limp vegetables and thawing tv dinners and meat. I hesitated but pushed my way in. Even the safe at the back of the cupboard had been broken into and cleaned out.

"Well, well," said Sid. He came to the kitchen door and showed me a used syringe.

"Was Wadkins a junkie?" I asked.

"No, but that's who we're supposed to think did this. Come on. Let's go."

"What about...?"

"It's just a dead body. It can't hurt you."

I took a deep breath and scrambled through the

front room.

"You are going to have to do something about that," Sid said as we hit the street.

"About what?" I grumbled.

"You and corpses." He headed uptown.

"I'm sorry. But you've got to admit my experience with them hasn't exactly been the best."

He sighed. "No. It hasn't, damn it. But past trauma or no, you've got to find a way to stop panicking every time you see a stiff or you're going to end up one."

I shuddered. "Are you sure it wasn't a junkie who tore up that place?"

"Positive. There were no forced entry marks on the door, and that place was too clean. No junkie would have found that safe, or taken the time to crack it. That was a professional job."

"Terrific. What killed Wadkins?"

"Probably the ever-popular blunt instrument. There was a nasty soft spot at the back of his skull."

"Do you think the police will be fooled?"

"Not likely, but it won't do them any good. Even if Wadkins didn't keep his tracks covered, a job like that is going to be mighty hard to crack, and it just might throw someone off."

Sid hailed a cab and told him to take us back to our hotel.

"We're leaving," he told me in the elevator. "Don't waste time trying to figure whose stuff is whose. Just jam it in the first open spot and let's get out."

"But what about check in?"

"We'll stay in town long enough for that, but not here. A moving target's harder to hit."

Sid took the bathroom while I removed bags from purchases and started cramming. We were out in ten minutes with nothing left behind. It took us longer to pay up at the desk.

We stored our bags at Grand Central Station, then went to find lunch.

That afternoon we had the first of a series

of remarkable talks that popped up periodically throughout the trip. After lunch, we went to Central Park. We ambled along the path, heading for the zoo, each of us lost in our own thoughts. It was a pleasant, comfortable silence, and much needed given all the tension we were working under.

"Do you ever think about dying?" I asked suddenly, without even thinking about what I was asking.

"I try not to," Sid replied, casually. "Generally, I'm successful."

"And when you're not?"

"I try to think of something else."

I stopped walking, turned and looked at him.

He shrugged. "It's not one of my favorite topics to dwell on." There was a pause as we continued our walk. "How about you?"

"I never used to, at least not much. I've been thinking about it a lot more recently."

"That's one thing that's always puzzled me about you."

"What?"

"You say you believe in God and all his promises about going to Heaven when you die, and you're afraid of dying. I would think you'd have thrown yourself under the wheels of some car long ago."

"Well, I believe life is a gift from God, like a sacred trust and you don't go around throwing gifts back in people's faces."

"No."

"Besides, I believe there's a purpose for my life and when I've fulfilled it, God'll take me."

"Then why are you so scared?"

That was a hard one to answer. I knew Sid just wanted to know. I don't think I wanted to convert him. I knew that was almost impossible. But I was anxious that he not get a bad impression. I stopped walking and looked at his face. There was something about the look in his eyes that made me decide to just be myself and not worry about bad impressions.

"Sometimes, it's the process itself that scares me, the actual act of my soul leaving my body." I paused. "Most of the time though I'm scared I won't measure up somehow."

"It'd have to be a pretty cruel God, not to let you in. I'm surprised you still believe."

"I believe because intellectually I know it's not God, nor my perception of him that's the problem. It's my perception of myself. Most of the time, I'm aware of my goodness, if you will, but there are times when I'm not terribly convinced emotionally. I guess it's the sin in my life."

"Sin?" Sid smiled. "I don't see how your occasional petty misdeeds could be classified as sin."

"I suspect my so-called petty misdeeds are worse than your so-called grand scale sinning. I know better."

"You shouldn't be so hard on yourself."

"Maybe not. I may be a Christian, but like the bumper sticker says, I'm not perfect."

"Just forgiven." Sid chuckled. "That's always sounded like a cop-out to me."

"For a lot of people, it is. That's why I don't like it. It's too easy to just sit back and forget about growing. I don't want to live that way. If I'm not growing, I'm dying." I paused and blushed. "Oh, geez, listen to me. I sound so holy."

"I wish more people were holy like you."

I swallowed and blinked back the tears that had come rushing to my eyes.

"Thanks. That was the nicest thing you've ever said to me."

"You're welcome," Sid said, softly.

We stood there silently for a moment, looking at each other, stymied by the one barrier left between us. A breeze wafted by, carrying on it a light friendly scent that delighted my nose and gave me the graceful escape I was looking for.

"Popcorn," I said, sniffing and turning. "Where is it? I can smell it popping. Where is it? I'm hungry."

Sid burst out laughing. "You're hopeless, woman. Utterly hopeless."

I spotted the bright red wagon some ways away. I grabbed Sid's hand and pulled him after me.

"Come on. I want to get it while it's fresh out of the popper."

"I shouldn't be supporting this, you know." Sid pulled his hand away to save himself the indignity of being dragged more than anything else. I smiled as he hung his thumbs in his belt loops and sauntered after me.

Sid checked in that afternoon. The Dragon said she'd find what she could on Wadkins' murder and told Sid we were not to go to Orlando until the next day. Sid told her in no uncertain terms that we were not staying in New York that night.

So we went to Kennedy airport and to Atlanta, Georgia. We stayed at a small motel near the airport. I decided to take a shower and shave, so I let Sid have the bathroom first. While he was changing, I made up the "bed" on the floor and then gathered together the toiletries I was going to need that I could find.

"It's all yours," said Sid, coming out of the bathroom.

"Thanks," I mumbled, and then to myself, "Where is that blasted thing?"

"What are you looking for?"

"Oh, you'd know. You packed the stuff in the bathroom. I can't find my shaver."

"That little cheap white supermarket job?"

"Yeah, where is it?"

"I left it."

"How am I going to shave my legs?"

"Go ahead and use mine. Just make sure you change the blades when you're done."

"Thanks, where is it?"

"It's in my kit. I left it on the toilet tank."

"Um, there's nothing embarrassing in it, is there?"

"Shouldn't be."

I retreated to the bathroom. Sid's black leather shaving bag was where he said it was. I rummaged through it.

"I can't find it," I called. "Oh, never mind."

I saw the top of the razor and opened the section. All sorts of necessities were strapped onto the wall of the kit.

"Oh, my god," I groaned.

"Honest," I heard Sid call. "Whatever it is, I promise I did not know it was there."

"Oh, you knew about this." I opened the bathroom door and leaned in the doorway. "Honestly, Sid, a gold-plated tortoise shell razor?"

It was his night for the floor and he was already under the covers. He rolled over onto his stomach and squinted at me, grinning. Sid's very near-sighted and had already taken his contacts out.

"I have expensive tastes," he said, propping himself up on his elbows. "Besides, it's weighted very nicely, has a good comfortable feel to it."

"I'll bet. How ostentatious can you get?"

"Plenty. Don't forget to change the blades."

"I won't."

I didn't forget. I just couldn't figure out how to do it. I left the refill right on top of the razor where he could see it and went to bed.

May 24 - 28, 1983

We were up early and ran, as always. I got the bathroom first, dressed, then repacked the bags. Our flight to Orlando wasn't leaving until two, so I figured I might as well.

"Damn it! Lisa!" Sid suddenly bellowed.

"I thought we weren't supposed to be using names," I said as he came to the bathroom door.

He was wearing his jeans, but no shirt, and his face was half covered with foam. His left forefinger was pressed against the dimple in his chin. He spoke quietly, but he wasn't happy. "Did you remember to change the blades on my razor?"

"Well, I remembered, but..."

"Then why didn't you?"

"I couldn't figure out how to do it. I left the new one right beside it so you'd see it. I was going to tell you, but you were asleep and I kinda forgot."

Sid sighed and looked at the blood on his fingertip.

"You just slide the blade assembly off the base." He replaced his finger. "It's very simple. You can't even misalign it."

"Oh."

"Please remember that. I don't like cutting myself."

"I'm sorry."

"Apology accepted." Sid sighed and withdrew to finish shaving.

When he came out, I had to look for the cut to find it.

"Do you cut yourself often?" I asked as we left the motel. "I mean with that dimple and all..."

"Almost never. Of course, it took a certain amount of practice. My aunt was fond of saying she was surprised I had a chin left."

"Why didn't you grow a beard?"

"I don't like beards, or any facial hair, for that matter. I did have a mustache in high school, though, one of those thick Sergeant Pepper things. I graduated with it. I was one of the few guys my age who could grow one." Sid chuckled in reminiscence. "I shaved it off at boot camp and haven't grown one since."

I sat back in the rental car and tried to imagine him with a Sergeant Pepper mustache and then with a beard. I decided I liked the cleft chin more, though I didn't tell him. He was vain enough as it was.

We still got to the airport by ten fifteen that morning. We went ahead and checked our luggage, then Sid phoned our contact.

"I was afraid of that," he grumbled, as he left the booth.

"What's the matter?" I asked, worried.

"The drop's set for Disney World."

"How fun. I'm excited."

"You would be. I suppose you'll be dragging me on all those silly rides."

"Oh come on. Loosen up a little. Do me a favor and dump the dignity for a while. You might even have some fun."

"Are you implying that I don't know how to have fun?"

"Not at all. You're just limited."

He sighed.

We still had an hour or so to kill. I talked Sid into the cafeteria. He opted for an early lunch. I pored over some brochures I'd found.

"Let's see..," I mumbled between bites of polish sausage and french fries. "They say here Epcot costs extra, but they have combined passports..."

I dug a pen out of my purse and did some figuring on the paper placemat. Sid shook his head. He was eating a chef's salad, but had picked out the ham slices and set them aside.

"How long do you think we'll be there?" I asked. "May I have your ham?"

"At least through Friday and no you may not. It's not good for you."

"That's just a myth." I reached over and took it anyway. "There is no trichinosis in that meat." I continued with my figures.

"Maybe not, but there is an enormous amount of fat, and even if there's isn't, it's probably salt cured. That's not even count—"

"Shut up. I'm trying to divide." I worked at the math a few moments longer and then smiled at the results. "Okay. The four-day passport is the best buy, but it hardly seems worth it if we're probably leaving Friday. So we should probably get the three-day passport."

"I'd like to keep our time at the parks to a minimum."

"Oh, come on. Disneyland is about as safe as you can get."

"I wouldn't know," Sid said, bored. "I've never been there."

"You've never been..?" I was aghast.

"Nope."

"But you've lived in California all your life. Heck, my parents weren't rich and we still managed to make it down from Tahoe at least once a year."

"I couldn't afford it."

"Oh, come on."

"I'm serious. I was dirt poor as a kid. I didn't come into my money until my second year at Stanford. Being a communist made my aunt rather hard to employ."

"I suppose but... well, how'd you learn to play the piano so well? That takes years of lessons and that's not cheap."

A faraway look came over Sid's face, he quietly laid his fork by his plate and wiped his mouth with his napkin. Slowly he placed the napkin by the fork.

"Stella taught me," he said finally. Stella was the aunt who had raised him, and as far as he knew, his only living relative. They hadn't spoken since Sid was nineteen because he allowed himself to be drafted instead of going to Canada. Sid had never been close to Stella. According to him, she'd never wanted him in the first place. So this sudden emotion over her surprised me a little. "She was a student at Julliard when she broke with her family and changed her name. I don't know if she continued there after that, or not. I'm not even sure if she graduated."

"Why don't you know? Didn't she tell you?"

"Stella never told me anything about her background or mine. What little I know, I pieced together from various stories I heard from people who knew her at the time."

"Could you tell me what you know?" I leaned forward and smiled warmly.

Sid looked at me for a moment and returned the smile. He leaned back in his seat and took a deep breath.

"As far as I know, Stella had been a communist and was broken off from her family for some time, when my mother got pregnant. She got disowned and sought out Stella. Stella took her in, very unwillingly, and managed to convince my mother that an abortion would just be asking for trouble."

"That's right, they were illegal, then."

"Mm-hm."

"Do you know what your mother was like?"

"I don't remember her at all. I have heard that she wasn't exactly an innocent victim. Stella was rather fond of hinting that my mother didn't tend towards chastity, even after she was pregnant."

"Like mother, like son."

Sid laughed. "That's exactly what Stella said when she found out I was into fooling around. But that's another story. Anyway, Stella took pretty good care of my mother, but when she went into labor, Stella panicked. She took my mother to the hospital, but couldn't get her admitted. I've heard all sorts of reasons, such as my mother had never been married and wouldn't name the father, or more likely, Stella just didn't have the money and got unpleasant about it."

"Oh no. You were born on the sidewalk."

"Almost. Apparently, it was quite a scene. My mother sitting on the curb in labor and Stella standing over her screaming Communist propaganda. Finally, they were rescued, by of all people, a priest and Stella was furious about that."

"How wild."

"It's not necessarily true. The man that told me all this was prone to big lies, especially when he was stoned, which he generally was." Sid smiled. "Donovan Smith. Sheesh, I haven't thought about him in years. He was the closest to a father figure I ever had. Used to pop in and out of our lives periodically. I hitchhiked cross-country with him several times. Sometimes Stella came with us, too. He was the only man I ever suspected of being her lover. She was strange that way, not gay, just completely indifferent, like it was a nuisance."

"What happened to Donovan?"

"He died, in '67, I think. I heard he took a bad trip on LSD and jumped off a building."

"How sad."

"I suppose. It was no surprise. Stella always said he was headed for it."

"But what got you started on the piano?"

"Oh that. That was Stella's idea. I remember that day. It was my sixth birthday. I was also excited because kindergarten was almost over. I hated it. I was always in trouble and the teacher was always making me do stupid things, like building houses out of blocks, and they had to be just so and when I asked her why, which I did often, she had fits."

"My teacher did that too. She always made us put roofs on our houses and I got mad because we couldn't play with them that way."

"I wonder if it was the same lady." Sid laughed, while I shrugged. "Back to the piano. I came home from school and Stella told me that the time had come for me to receive my legacy. Neither she nor my mother had anything to give me in material goods, they belonged to the people, anyways, and the Revolution was not Stella's to give. But Stella said she could give me music and that would be my legacy." Sid paused. "I didn't even know what the word meant. For years I thought it was playing the piano. Anyway, she sat me down at this old battered upright and started me playing scales. That's how it all began and every day after that for years I worked on my music for hours. When there wasn't a piano available, I was drilled on theory. It was the only thing we shared." Sid fell silent for a minute, then looked at me. "So tell me about your childhood."

"I was basically happy. Very comfortable. I was sick a lot as a little kid, though. I got pneumonia every year without fail until I was seven, then I got double pneumonia. After that I was healthy. I always said I got it out of my system early. But when I was well, I had a good time. I was Daddy's girl. Don't get me wrong. He never played favorites. He loved Mae very much. But I was special because they almost lost me so many times."

"Really?"

"Yeah, Mama said her obstetrician was surprised I lived at all."

"I don't understand."

"Well, Mama never had any trouble getting pregnant, she just couldn't keep them. She miscarried twice before Mae, carried Mae to term, then had five miscarriages in four years before she got pregnant with me and I showed up two months early. I barely weighed four-and-a-half pounds at birth."

"Is that bad?"

"Average is seven to eight."

Sid whistled low under his breath.

"Anyway, Mama miscarried three more times after I was born. Then I kept getting sick, which was to be expected, I guess."

"You must have been one tough little girl."

"Yep. Of course, part of that was Daddy's fault. You see, I doubled as his son. He was disappointed when he found out I was a girl. But he told me when I was eleven that when he saw me in the nursery struggling just to breathe, he knew I was going to be a very special baby and he loved me very much because of that."

"Is that why he's so protective of you?"

I laughed. "Yes, that's part of it. Of course, he's very protective of Mae, too. Neil used to work for Daddy, put himself through dental school that way. Daddy almost fired Neil several times because he thought Neil was making moves on Mae and that was before they fell in love with each other."

"He seems to like Neil well enough now." Sid's tone was a little rueful.

Daddy has never liked any man that Mae or I have dated. He really can't stand Sid. He considers Sid's urban polish effeminate, which bugs him. He's convinced Sid has designs on my body and is going to lead me straight into living in sin. [The man had a point there - SEH] Worst of all, Daddy is insanely jealous of Sid, more than he's ever been of anybody I've dated, which I can't figure out for the life of me.

"Well, Neil is his son-in-law," I said.

"How is the old cuss, anyway?" Sid asked. He's not terribly fond of Daddy, either.

"Just fine. I didn't get to talk to him when I called in Washington. But that reminds me, if we go any further south, we'll have to drop the Donaldson's. There are parts of Dade County where I can't spit without hitting a relative."

"Dade County?" Sid grinned. "As in Anita Bryant?"

"Yes," I groaned. I hated those jokes. "My parents

are from Dade County."

Sid chuckled. "It figures."

"Will you please? He is my father."

"Alright. But what are the odds of us running into them?"

"Almost nil. They're already back in Tahoe. Summer season starts this weekend. It's Memorial Day, you know."

"Ah, that's right." Sid looked up as they announced the flight to Orlando. "That's us. Let's go."

We had a pleasant afternoon. We got checked in at the motel outside Disney World without a hitch, then went to change into our swimming gear.

At first, I was a little nervous. The time had come when I had to face Sid in my swim suit and him in his. I was afraid he would have one of those little knit bathing suits that leave nothing to the imagination, but he came out of the bathroom wearing, brief, but sufficiently modest, trunks out of a blue Hawaiian print and an open short-sleeved shirt out of the same fabric. He, in turn, was surprised when he saw me. My new bathing suit was discreet, but just barely, a halter with a front that plunged and closed just before you could see anything and a back that dipped becomingly low.

"I thought you'd be wearing something that covered a lot more," Sid said.

So I told him what I thought he'd be wearing.

"I'm not an exhibitionist," was his reply.

Sid brought a magazine with him to the pool, but when he discovered there was no shade, he decided to swim with me.

"Didn't you want to work on a tan?" I asked. "Not that it's much work."

Sid chuckled. "I can't out here. We don't want people to complain to the motel management."

"At the risk of further inflating your ego, I can't see anything to complain about."

"I can't either. But you see, I don't believe in tan

lines, and some people find that objectionable."

"Oh." I could feel my face growing hot. "I thought you said you weren't an exhibitionist."

"I'm not. Just because I don't exhibit my body for show doesn't mean I am uncomfortable in my natural state."

I confess I did briefly try to imagine him that way, but it was just too embarrassing. Sid noticed and laughed.

Disney World and Epcot were a blast. Okay, the Magic Kingdom was almost just like Disneyland, but that didn't bother me because I love Disneyland. Sid made the drop without trouble. He even went on the rides without complaining.

By Thursday, however, Sid was getting a little touchy, and made a few pointed comments about the number of frozen bananas, orange juice bars, hamburgers and boxes of popcorn I consumed. It didn't help that we were given a second drop to make the next day. By then, Sid was positively distant.

"I just don't feel like communicating right now," he told me after breakfast.

"Okay. But the last time that happened, we ended up in that really awful fight and it just made it harder when things blew up."

He sighed. "Alright. Point taken." He turned to me and gently touched my cheek. "But the only resolution for what I'm feeling at the moment is something you don't want to get into. Can you bear with me until Sunday?"

"Oh. Yeah." I felt guilty, but Sid was right. I didn't want to get into that.

He was still sulking at lunch.

"We'll have to take time out from your food and ride fest to make that second drop," he grumbled. "The layout is pretty good from our standpoint. I'll be at the hotel bar, and she'll talk to the bartender. It'll be pretty hard to pop me with someone right there. I want you to be extra careful on the perimeter sweeps."

I was, but there was nothing to be seen. Nobody was in the bar in the middle of the afternoon. The bartender was very friendly and I could hear Sid chatting pleasantly with him. I moved around behind the bar. Static crackled in my ear, and instead of Sid, I got the radio from the monorail. I stepped into the ladies room and took off my transmitter. Fat lot of good that did. I whacked it a couple times.

"Approaching station," said the professional voice. "All clear."

I went back to the bar. Sid met me out front.

"Let's go," he said.

"Everything go okay?" I asked. "My transmitter cut out and picked up the monorail."

"So did mine." He paused. "Listen, is your heart still set on another run through Space Mountain?"

"Yeah."

"Then why don't you spare me? I'll meet you over there after check in."

I wondered what was up, but decided to take advantage of it. While in line to Space Mountain I ate a bacon cheeseburger. [So that was what I smelled on your breath - SEH] As it happened, I did feel for him, but there just wasn't much I could do about it, besides the obvious, and no matter how I tried to justify it, I couldn't.

Sid just got grumpier and grumpier. We flew to New Orleans the next day. As usual, Sid slept the whole way, so I didn't say anything about the problem.

In New Orleans, we found a nice little motel in the French Quarter. At the desk, the clerk said all they had was a double (a room with two queen sized beds).

"That's it?" Sid asked.

"Oh, darling, let's take it," I butted in quickly. "I know it's more expensive, but it's Memorial Day weekend. I don't want to take a chance on not finding a place to stay."

"Alright," replied Sid, quietly.

He paid for the room and gloomily followed behind

the bellhop and me. It was a very nice little room with a private bath and a balcony overlooking a courtyard and, of course, the two beds. I waited until the bellhop had gone before I bounced onto the bed closest to the balcony.

"No sleeping on the floor," I crowed, flopping backward and gazing at the ceiling. "How wonderful."

I thought I heard a faint sigh. I looked at Sid, who was sitting down with his back to me on the far edge of the other bed.

"Isn't this just perfect?" I asked.

"Yeah, " grumbled Sid. "Too bad I can't have company."

"Well, I could make myself scarce."

"I'm not bringing anyone here, anyway. It's too dangerous."

I rolled over onto my stomach and looked at him.

"Are you sure there's not something else bothering besides you know what?"

"I'm fine. Just leave me alone will you?"

"Come on, what's eating you?"

Sid let out a short high-pitched sarcastic laugh, and I thought I heard him mutter the Lord's name, but I chose to let it pass.

"I'm sorry. I just find it a little hard to believe you are this upset because you've missed a few nights."

He turned around and glared at me.

"I am not upset, but I am that horny. I'm also trying very hard to remain civil and pleasant, but it's not easy."

"Well, hang on, Sunday's coming. Better yet, I'll go do something by myself today."

"No, I don't want you wandering around on those streets by yourself. I'll make it til tomorrow."

"You could always try running twenty laps around the French Quarter and then a cold shower."

"Very funny."

"I thought so. Maybe you ought to pretend you've got V.D., something drastic, like Herpes."

"Mention not that dread name, even in jest." Sid was deadly serious.

"Sorry." I rolled over onto my back again.

"Will you cut that out," Sid snapped turning away from me.

"What?" I folded my hands underneath my head.

"What you're doing."

"I'm not doing anything. I'm just laying here, looking at the ceiling."

"I only have so much control."

"What do you mean?"

"You laying on your back. Don't you have any idea how inviting that is?"

"Oh, Sid," I gasped as the light dawned. "I'm sorry. I didn't mean to. Look, I'm not even laying down anymore. I'm really sorry. I didn't even think..."

"I know." Sid turned to me. "That's the problem."

"I can't help it. I just don't think that way."

"Maybe it's better that you don't."

There was a pause.

"That bad, huh?" I asked.

Sid nodded. "Your presence isn't helping any, either."

"Well, that settles it." I stood up and grabbed my purse. "I'm taking off, and by myself, too. You do what you want."

"No, I'll go with you. I don't want you out there by yourself."

"Enough with the chauvinism. It's broad daylight, I can take care of myself and I'm not going to take any stupid chances. I'll be fine."

"So will I. Let's go."

"No. Sid, I don't want to make it any harder on you than it already is. I'll go. You can do whatever and I'll be back by four. Okay? See you."

"Alright."

I had to pass him to get to the door. As I did, he goosed me. I turned on him angrily.

"Do you want me to sock you in the jaw?"

"Might help." He shrugged, helplessly.

"Don't tempt me." I shut the door. The poor thing.

There was another reason I didn't want Sid around that day. While on the plane, I had remembered his birthday was the following Wednesday. Now, obviously, Sid isn't exactly the type to appreciate being reminded that he is getting older. But I felt I had to do something. He had been very generous to me on my birthday earlier that spring.

So, happily rid of him for several hours, I explored the French Quarter stores, searching for just the right gift. It wasn't easy. If Sid wants something he just buys it. Back home, in Los Angeles, I had a sweater half-way knitted for him, but Sid hadn't thought to bring my knitting. I don't knit fast enough to have started from scratch again. There was also the problem of carrying it.

Most of the stores carried tourist-oriented goods. The stores on Bourbon Street carried a lot of items that were along the lines of Sid's extracurricular activities, but I decided I didn't know enough about what I was doing. I was too embarrassed anyway.

Towards mid-afternoon, I went into a little antique shop off of Andrew Jackson Square. They had a lovely collection of antique jewelry. I found Sid's gift sitting in a case with some china. It was a gold pocket watch with a chain and fob attached. It was open, and I could see the time was the same as on my watch.

"How much is this watch?" I asked the shopkeeper.

"Hundred and fifty dollars, ma'am."

I bit my lip. On one hand, it was a lot of money for me to be spending on Sid and we were supposedly on a budget. On the other hand, Sid wouldn't like anything cheap and a hundred and fifty dollars wouldn't seem like a lot to him.

"Um, could I see it?"

"Certainly, ma'am. Nice little piece." The shopkeeper opened the case and pulled it out. He wound it up and gentle music came tinkling out of it.

"Has a music box."

"How enchanting. I know that piece."

I was entranced, but the money it cost made me hesitate.

"I'll have to think about it."

I knew as I left the store that I wouldn't find anything better. In fact, the more I thought about it, the more I was convinced that Sid should have it. I continued shopping but was utterly preoccupied with the watch, until a sharp female voice jolted me alert.

"How'd you like to see yourself as a blonde, honey?" she screeched.

I stopped. She leaned in the doorway of a wig shop, a heavy set blonde with a style like Dolly Parton's. I had a feeling she was wearing her stock.

"Excuse me?" I asked.

"How'd you like to see yourself as a blonde?" she repeated. "Got a piece of hair'd suit you right nicely."

"Oh," I giggled. "I suppose it wouldn't hurt to try it on."

"Course not."

The effect was incredible. I couldn't believe the stranger with the ash blonde shag cut I saw facing me in the mirror was me. So, impulsively, I bought the wig. After all, what's a spy without one good disguise? Still in that frame of mind, I also bought a pair of indoor/outdoor sunglasses with nice contemporary frames.

Then I went right back to the antique shop. As I entered, my heart stopped. I heard the gentle music of the watch and saw another couple looking at it and smiling. I didn't breathe again until they sadly shook their heads and started out.

"I want that watch," I told the shopkeeper before the couple had even left. I dug frantically through my purse for my wallet. "Chain and all. You have a box for it?"

"Yes, I do, ma'am."

"Great. What do you want? Master, Visa, American express?"

"Whatever you wish, ma'am."

I don't know which card I gave him. I was just glad I'd left my real I.D. in Washington. Knowing me, I'd have given him a card with the wrong name. While he wrote up the sale, I inspected the watch once more.

"Do you gift wrap?" I asked.

"Yes, ma'am."

"Could you wrap the watch for me? How much extra will it cost?"

"Not a cent, ma'am."

"I'm going to tell my friends about this place. Thanks."

Checking my watch, I saw that it was getting close to four. I hid the gift-wrapped box in my purse and hurried back to the motel.

"I'm back," I called, coming in the door. I shut it firmly.

The room was empty. The bathroom door was shut, and I heard the whine of the blow dryer coming from behind it. Underneath the blow dryer, I thought I heard singing. Puzzled, I slowly put down my bags. The blow dryer clicked off, but the singing continued. It was Sid's voice, alright. But I'd never heard him sing before. He was singing "All Day, All Night, Marianne." At least that was the melody. He'd rearranged the lyrics and they were filthy. It figured.

I noticed his suit jacket and vest laid out neatly on the bed. On the dresser was the matching tie, a pair of cuff links and tie pin.

"Sid?" I called again, more hesitantly. "I'm back."

"Great," he called back, over the sound of water running. There was a pause then, "Enjoy yourself?"

"Yeah."

"Terrific." Pause. "Why don't you get on your black dress? I've got reservations for us at..." pause "...one of the nicest restaurants in the French Quarter."

"Do you think that's wise?" I asked.

"Sure..." Pause. "...We can afford to splurge a little."

"Alright."

I got out the dress, wondering a little. He seemed to be in a lot better mood. The bathroom door opened and he came out humming "Marianne" and buttoning the top button on his dress shirt. Flipping up the collar, he crossed over to the dresser, picked up the tie and began tying it around his neck.

"I get the feeling you went out also today," I said leaning on the doors to the balcony.

Sid snickered. "This city's reputation is well deserved, I'm happy to say." The tie finished, he inserted the pin into the collar underneath the knot.

"I don't know. I can't tell if you're easier to deal with when you're horny or when you're satisfied."

"Satisfied? Me? Never." Sid grinned and faced me. "Like the song says, I can't get no... And how are you, my little ice cube?"

"Confused."

"About what?"

"You. I'm sorry, Sid, I'm really trying, but I just can't understand what the big deal is."

"What big deal?"

"Sex."

Sid couldn't have been more astonished.

"What do you mean you don't understand what the big deal is?" He sat down on the dresser. "It's...uh... my god, child, I know you're untouched, but haven't you ever been horny?"

"Of course, I have. I'm normal."

"I wasn't saying you weren't." Sid got up and started prowling about the room. "How can I explain it?"

"I know sort of what's supposed to happen. I guess part of the problem is that I've been hearing some conflicting reports."

"Such as..?"

"What my Grandma Caulfield told Mae right before she got married."

"And..?"

"She told Mae to close her eyes and lay still and it wouldn't take long."

"That's rubbish and you know it."

"I know, but what about all the horror stories I've heard from my aunts?"

"They're probably a bunch of gossipy frigid ladies with husbands who are only interested in slam, bam, thank you, ma'am. A decent sex life does take a certain amount of sensitivity."

"I'm sure it does, but..."

Sid settled on his bed. "How can I tell you? If I try to show you, I'll get my teeth knocked out. If I use graphic detail, you'll probably crawl under the bed and stay there."

"Sid, please. I guess what I don't understand is I've gone all my life without sex and you can't go a week without it."

Sid looked at me thinking.

"Well, I am hornier than most," he said, finally. "I guess it's largely because I never say no, except for the occasions when I pick up a little V.D., and that's rare, believe it or not. When I do and I see a likely woman I start reacting like I would normally. I start thinking about how it would feel. Under normal circumstances, I either move in, if the time's right or forget about her. But there's something about not being able to have her, for whatever reason, that locks her into my mind. I work at thinking about other things. But you know how it is when there's something you don't want to think about, inevitably that's what you find yourself thinking about. And when I think about it, I get horny. Having to say no only aggravates it. Worse still, I rarely run across just one woman. Anyway, that's why I get so grumpy. I like to think I've got better control over my thoughts than I do." Sid sighed, looked at me intently and then looked down at his feet. "Of course, you add a whole new dimension to the problem. Not only have I got you in my brain, I'm working with you, closely. Normally, I get hot, I transfer it to some other woman."

"You mean you think about me when..?"

"No. It's just when I look at you and the urge hits, I work it out with someone else. But now it's a lot harder to do that because there's supposedly no need for another woman, which makes her harder to come by. So I get horny. Do you realize you are the only woman I have really wanted that I have not made love to?"

"Oh, dear, I knew it." I bit my lip, trying not to cry. "I knew I was making it worse."

"It's not your fault."

"It's not? Come on. If I wasn't such a prude, you wouldn't need to be that way. When the urge hit, you could just have me."

"That part of it might be easier, but I think we're still better off as we are. One of the reasons you and I work so well together is because we're forced to take the time to talk with each other because we do believe so differently. If we were sleeping together, I don't know that we'd take that time."

"I still feel responsible, and guilty. I've always felt that teasing a guy was incredibly cruel. And here I am driving you nuts because I can't say yes."

"Be careful. You sound like you might be rationalizing yourself into a position I can tell you don't want to be in."

"And you're cheering me on."

"Oh no. If I was, I wouldn't have warned you. I'd have let you dig your hole and crawled in after you."

I looked at him, surprised, then smiled.

"Who'd have though my virtue would be safe with you?"

Sid chuckled. "I'd like to think it isn't entirely safe. I do have my pride, you know."

"Well, it does get shaky, sometimes, but I have a pretty firm grip on my resolve."

"Good." Sid's smile was tender and warm, then he looked at his watch. "Uh, oh, it's getting late. You'd better hurry, or we'll miss our reservation."

"Oh dear, yes. Let me see, here are my nylons. I'll

need my...where's my makeup bag?"

"In the bathroom, in your carry on. I hope you don't mind, but I borrowed your shampoo."

"You got dandruff?"

"No. I ran out of my own."

"That figures. You wouldn't allow dandruff."

"Very funny."

"I thought so. Where's my dress?"

Sid handed it to me and I retreated with it into the bathroom. I was a little mad at myself for not remembering that Sid already had a watch. Then I wasn't so mad because I remembered that he had several different watches that he coordinated with what he was wearing and not one of them was a pocket watch. Then I got depressed because that probably meant he didn't like pocket watches. Then again, it was possible it just hadn't occurred to him. I bit my lip. I really hoped he would like it.

"By the way," I heard Sid call as I slid into my dress. "By any chance, did you buy anything today?"

"You can be proud of me. I did."

"What did you buy?"

"Now, don't laugh. You promise?"

"No way."

"Sid."

"I'm not making any promise unless I know I can keep it."

"Well, it was very impulsive. The second most impulsive thing I've done in my life."

"What was the first?"

"Coming to work for you."

"Real cute. What is this thing?"

"It's in the tall round box."

"I was wondering about that."

Then I heard him laugh, very loudly and very hard.

"What on earth?" he gasped.

"The lady practically dragged me off the street to try it on. I was fascinated. I looked completely different.

I thought it might come in handy."

"Come on, disguises are for Inspector Clouseau and B-rate spy thrillers."

"Well, you never know."

"Are you ready yet?" He was still laughing.

"I'm not coming out of this bathroom until you stop laughing. I don't care if our reservations are at the White House."

"Alright, alright. I'm not laughing."

"I still hear a little snicker."

"No, you don't. I'm as straight and sober as can be."

I opened the door a crack. He wasn't even smiling. I came out. He didn't crack. I went to get my purse. He started breaking up.

"That does it." I fled towards the bathroom but Sid caught me before I got there and held me by the upper arms. "Will you please stop laughing? I admit it was a little silly, but for heaven's sake."

"Okay, I'll try." Sid's eyes sparkled merrily. "It's just so unlike you and at the same time very much like you. I love it, I really do."

He reached over and kissed my forehead.

"Come on," he said, sympathetically. He turned me around, put his arm around my shoulders and started walking me out of the room. "We shall now go and be terribly sophisticated and dine in elegance at our leisure. Then you can show me how to be utterly frivolous and childlike."

"Oh, Sid."

Dinner was marvelous, and oh, we laughed together. Then when we went walking and window shopped. A dress in a children's boutique stopped me.

"That dress." I pointed it out to Sid. "I made one almost like it for Janey when she was a baby." We moved on. "I was so excited when she was born."

"Why?"

"I was there. It was Friday and Mama and I drove

down because Mae was due that Sunday. I was still working at Daddy's store in Tahoe, but I came down with Mama to bring some of my stuff because I was moving in that fall to go to college. Mama and I pulled up at the house at three o'clock that afternoon, but there was no one there. Darby was at the neighbor's. Mae had been in labor all night and Neil had forgotten to call us. We went right over to the hospital. Mae's doctor was real progressive, and he had us put on scrubs and go right in. Half an hour later, Janey was born." My eyes filled. "Mae held her, then Neil, then they plopped her in my arms. I asked what her name was and Mae said Lisa Jane."

"They named her after you."

"Yeah. But we call her Janey to prevent confusion since I was living there. Actually, we're both named after Grandma Wycherly. I was supposed to be Lisle Frobischer, cause Grandma was German, but Mama didn't want me to have a funny name. She hated growing up as Althea."

"I can sympathize."

"So she and Daddy compromised on anglicizing the first name and hadn't decided about Grandma's maiden name when I was born. So when I had to be baptized right away cause they were afraid of losing me, Mama couldn't think of what to do and the nun suggested Jane after St. Joan, who was a strong fighting woman, and Mama said that sounded good, so that's my name. There wasn't time to ask Daddy."

"What did they do, whisk you off to the church right away?"

"Oh no. I was baptized right in the delivery room. In fact, I think Sister did it. They didn't want to waste time digging up a priest."

"But I thought only priests did that sort of thing."

"Under normal circumstances, sure. But in my case, it was a life and death emergency. Heck, in an emergency, any Catholic can baptize somebody."

"I don't understand."

"Well, if there's an accident or something and somebody's dying and wants to be baptized, but there's a good chance he's going to peg out before a priest can get there, I, or any other Catholic, could baptize him."

"What if he doesn't die?"

"He's still baptized. Baptism's baptism. Even in the old days, the church didn't re-baptize someone who was joining up if he'd been baptized in another faith."

"I don't understand. Isn't that how you guys initiate somebody?"

"In one sense yes. But baptism is a sacrament and that means it goes a lot deeper than the ritual you see. When a person is baptized, he's washed clean from original sin, which in the case of babies, is their sinful nature and in the case of adults also includes all their other sins."

"In other words, you have to be baptized to get into heaven."

"Basically."

"What if you don't get around to it?"

"There are provisions for those who believe but haven't had a chance to be baptized for whatever reason. One of them is martyrdom."

"Oh."

"The key is faith. You have to believe in it, first. So I wouldn't count on having me around when you cash in. Without faith, it won't do you any good. And besides, I'll probably get bumped off a lot sooner than you will, anyway. The idea is not to wait to the last minute, because you may not have a chance."

"Ah, yes. You realize that's the argument you religious types have in your favor. Death and what comes after."

"That undiscovered bourn from which no traveler returns."

"Precisely." Sid paused, then we walked on. "Back talking about death again, aren't we?"

"It must be the circumstances surrounding why we're here."

Sid smirked. "Maybe I ought to get myself baptized."

"What?" I asked laughing. "You?"

"Well, that point you made about not waiting to the last minute because you may not have a chance is well taken. You might even want to consider it, as a matter of fact."

"What do you mean?"

"Earlier this evening you expressed an intense curiosity regarding sexual intercourse."

My heart racing, I stepped up my pace. The problem was, I was curious and horny, and I realized all of a sudden just how hard he was to resist.

He caught my shoulder. "Hey, don't worry. I'm not asking. You're obviously not ready, any more than I am to believe in God. And I refuse to make love to you until you are."

I looked into his beautiful blue eyes. "It might surprise you, but sometimes I really think I am ready."

"I'm not in the least surprised." His fingers touched my cheek. "But until we can overcome the fear within you, it's not going to happen."

We went back to the motel from there. I almost took the cold shower. Sid didn't shower at all, but he sure spent an awfully long time in the bathroom. [You're kidding. Didn't you smell it? I was going nuts. I was going to die. That's what I thought. Either I was going to get myself between your legs, or I was going to die – SHE]

May 29 - 31, 1983

We got up rather late on Sunday. Well, later than usual. We went to brunch at nine. It was Sid's idea. He must not have been thinking straight because it was a buffet. I made at least five trips and scarfed down beignet, crepes, gumbo, bacon, sausage, grits, eggs, fruit and waffles.

"Is there any hope of you being finished within this lifetime?" he asked tiredly.

"Probably not," I replied. "But I am getting ready to change restaurants."

Sid shook his head. "Let's go over your drop. According to the dossier, the suspect is Blaine Winters, caucasian, five eleven, dark blonde hair, blue eyes, fairly heavy. His cover is independent electronics sales. He has a place out in the bayou, with a P.O. box here in the city. Same good record everyone else has, except he's a little weak in the area of investigations." He paused. "You're going to noon mass, aren't you?"

"Yeah."

"I, uh, will probably drop you off a little early and meet you at one thirty. Is that okay with you?"

"Take your time. My drop isn't til two and you don't have to be there."

Sid thought it over. "Wear your transmitter. I'll make sure I'm in the neighborhood in time. I don't like the alley set up, but there's no reason to believe they're expecting you."

Sid left me at St. Louis's Cathedral about fifteen minutes before noon mass. After mass, I killed about twenty minutes looking around the cathedral, then another half hour in the gift shop. The drop point wasn't far away. It was a small alley off of the square. About two doors down, sitting in the doorway was a man fitting Winters' description in a black beat up fedora and old dark raincoat.

"Excuse me," I said approaching him. "I've got a small package to deliver on Bourbon Street. Can you help me find it?"

"I'll draw you a map," he replied. "You got something to write on?"

I dug into my purse and pulled out a pen and pad. Under the pad was the sealed envelope. These I handed to the man. He wrote the directions down and handed back the pen and pad.

"Thank you," I replied and continued down the alley.

Ignoring the directions I'd been given, I left the alley at the first real street I came to. I had gone about half a block when I looked into a window and saw two men standing at the end of the alley I'd just left. One of them was short and fairly heavy, wearing a poorly fitting dark suit. The other was tall and had a dark green overcoat on. Neither was Winters.

After turning down a couple of streets, I discovered they were still close behind and getting closer. I walked a little faster. They picked up speed and started gaining on me. Wondering where the heck Sid was, I slid my hand up the sleeve of my dress and tapped out an urgent message on the transmitter. I turned a corner and broke into a trot. Checking behind me, I saw that they had not caught up with me yet so I ducked into a souvenir shop.

Apparently, they saw me go into it because a few minutes later they came in. I ducked behind the shelves, keeping one eye on the tall one, edging towards the door. The tall one was heading for the back. Just as I was almost to the door, I looked down the long aisle just in time to see the two of them spot me and come after.

That was enough. I dropped any pretense of discretion and ran full out, crashing through the doors, and headed in the direction I'd just came from. I looked back and saw the two of them running after me. But I'd gained almost a block's lead. I frantically tapped out another message to Sid. At the second cross street I came to, I crossed the street I was running along, then nearly got myself hit by a car, running across the cross street. I hit the sidewalk and turned onto the street I'd just crossed. I looked back to check the progress of my pursuers and ran straight into someone.

"Excuse me," I gasped without looking and tried to run on. Sid's hands held me firmly but gently.

"Oh, thank God," I gasped. "I'm being tailed."

Sid looked quickly around and pulled me after him through two saloon doors. Just before I went through, I saw my tails come around the corner and spot me.

Firmly holding my hand, Sid led me through the dark, smoky room, weaving between the crowded tables. It was terribly noisy in there with loud music and people trying to talk over it. I heard the catcalls but somehow didn't notice the ramp down the middle of the room.

"They saw me come in," I said in a low voice in Sid's ear. "They'd just come around the corner."

"Do you think they saw me?"

"I don't think so."

"Okay. We'll take a chance on assuming they didn't."

Sid found us a table in a dark corner, about midway through the room. A cocktail waitress came up and slapped two huge menus on the table. Smiling, Sid picked up one and opened it.

"Perfect," he said quietly. "Don't hold it so high it's obvious you're hiding, but this is excellent cover."

I opened my menu and looked at it. The bill of fare was pretty typical. I guess the lewd drawings were too, but I had never seen anything like them. I began to realize what sort of place I was in. I swallowed.

"Carefully now," said Sid. "Look up and check out the two gentlemen who just came in."

My eyes were adjusted to the dark by then, so I could take just a quick peek.

"That's them." I dove behind my menu.

"Are either of them Winters?" Sid asked.

"No. But I picked them up as I left the alley."

The waitress came to take our order.

"Just a few more minutes," said Sid and off she went.

Out of the corner of my eye, I could see my tails heading for the back. Sid suddenly got up and left for a minute.

"Okay, they're gone," he said, returning.

I lowered my menu. For the first time, I saw the woman dancing on the ramp. I froze.

"Oh my god, she's stark staring naked."

"She's not a very good dancer, either. Come on, let's get out of here."

Once outside, Sid put his arm around my shoulders and held me tight against him. I started to pull away, but his grip was too strong.

"Hang on to me," he ordered, as we walked quickly down the street. "It'll be harder for them to spot you."

I stopped pulling.

"Not that I think they'll get out of there any too quickly," he continued.

"Why not?"

"There's a cat house in the back there."

"How'd you know?" I looked at him suspiciously.

"Observation, my dear. I saw several men go back there, all escorted by obvious professionals. You got any cash?"

"Some."

"Oh." There was a pause. "I just spent my last hundred bucks to keep those goons of yours occupied."

"How?"

"I sent a couple of girls after them. Told them to say Jerry sent them."

"Who's Jerry?"

"Beats me."

"Are you sure that's going to stop them?"

Sid looked behind us. "Well, they're not following us. Besides, I was able to get a better look at them than you were probably able to. They looked like your standard thugs to me. I get the feeling somebody hired them to do some dirty work. That's just the type to take advantage of a freebie, even if it means being lax on the job."

"I hope so."

We got back to the motel without any sign of a tail. Still, we didn't leave again that night. The next morning, Sid left fairly early to look around. He returned just before noon, saying he hadn't seen hide nor hair of Mutt and Jeff, as we'd come to call my pursuers, but that I'd better not go out that afternoon. We could go out that night, under the cover of darkness. We ate lunch in the motel coffee shop and spent the afternoon playing cards. That night Sid told me he had a surprise for me the next day.

It was an all day riverboat trip on the Mississippi. We had a wonderful time even though I lost ten dollars to Sid when I dared him to spell Mississippi. He couldn't do it. But he challenged me to, and I didn't get it right until the third try. That hurt my pride more than it hurt my pocketbook.

We got off the boat just in time to check in with the Dragon. Sid was not happy when he hung up the phone.

"Guess who set up a phony meeting with Winters and asked me to tail him when he splits after no one shows," he said.

"Why would she do that?"

"Your friends, Mutt and Jeff." He looked around. "It's not 'til six thirty. Why don't we get some dinner and window shop for a while, then you can go back to the motel while I'm on Winters' tail."

"Sounds good, but don't you want to stay wired?"

"Uh, yes and no. The Dragon said I shouldn't hold onto him too tight, and I thought I might take advantage of the separation, if you don't mind."

"I guess not. When do I start worrying?"

"Tap in a message around ten. I'll make sure I keep my receiver on and give me, say, twenty minutes to respond."

We took our time and pretty much stayed near the waterfront, as the meeting was in that neighborhood. At six twenty-five, Sid spotted Winters at the restaurant.

"There he is. Now, remember, straight to the room."

"I'll see you later."

He watched me until I got half a block away, then got into position on the other side of the restaurant, where I couldn't see him. I did see Mutt and Jeff watching Winters, which I thought was rather odd. I didn't think they'd seen me, so I turned into a nice old fashioned drug store on the corner. Ordinarily, I would've done exactly what Sid had told me, but the next day was Sid's birthday and I wanted to get him a card. I had plans and I couldn't wait to surprise him.

Finding the right card for him was no easy task. Getting back to the hotel proved to be much harder. I had just paid for the card and stashed it in my purse when I saw Mutt heading my way down the aisle adjacent to me. I didn't wait. I pulled a wire rack of greeting cards into his path and took off.

After bursting through the doors of the store, I turned right into a dark green overcoat. Gasping, I pulled away and tried to run over a small foreign car parked at the curb. But Jeff pulled me down by the back of my sundress.

By that time, Mutt was there. He grabbed my upper arm hard and held me so tightly it hurt. Jeff took hold of my other arm just as tightly. They escorted me down the street, to a large, dark, four-door sedan. Mutt shoved me into the back seat and climbed in next to me, while Jeff seated himself behind the wheel. Mutt pulled a gun. I decided not to try anything.

I wasn't blindfolded and I do have a pretty good sense of direction, so I was able to pretty much keep track of where we were, even though I was terrified. I was too scared to play cool. It was all I could do to keep my head clear enough to think and not panic.

We parked in front of a line of seedy apartment buildings on the edge of the French Quarter. When Mutt pulled me out of the car I stumbled and fell, scraping my elbow. I was roughly dragged to my feet and escorted into the building we'd parked in front of.

The stairs weren't lighted or carpeted. The place reeked of urine and burnt food. Somewhere I heard an infant screaming. I was pushed up three flights and then down the hall.

The apartment I was pushed into wasn't any nicer. There were newspapers all over the floor, an old yellowed lamp in one corner, a couch with the stuffing coming out in several places and a kitchenette with a sink piled high with dirty dishes. At the end of the room was a door.

Mutt patted me down, missing the twenty-two automatic strapped to the top of my thigh. Sid had told me to wear it as close to my crotch as possible just because people usually avoid searching genitalia unless they have to. I was shoved through the door into a small bedroom with a foul smelling brass bed and a white ceramic stand alone sink up against one wall. In the other wall, was a window.

"Don't think of trying anything," said Jeff, as he shut the door.

I tried the window. Even if I could have opened it, there was no place to go but straight down three stories. I wasn't that desperate yet. I debated blasting my way out with the twenty-two. But while the gun was better than no gun at all, it was little more than a pea shooter, and with two of them, I figured the odds were pretty good I'd get hit before I could get them stopped without killing them.

I decided to listen at the door, to see if I could learn something useful. All I heard was that someone wasn't answering and snatches of debate about what to do in the meantime. I looked at my watch. It was eight forty-five.

Time crawled along. To calm myself, I recited the Rosary under my breath, counting the Hail Marys on my fingers. Shortly after nine, I heard the phone clatter onto its cradle. It seems whoever wanted me raped, strangled and dumped near the waterfront. Then they started talking about doing it together and arguing about who took the top and who took the bottom first. I had only a vague idea what they were talking about, and a bad feeling that I didn't want to know. It took them 'til ten-fifteen to settle it and they came after me.

I yanked up the skirt of my dress to get the gun. The fabric got in my way, then the door slammed into my hands.

Seeing me so close to the door really irritated Mutt and he backhanded me across the face, first one way and then the other. I stumbled, crying softly, as I felt the blood from my nose drip onto my upper lip. I saw him double up his fist and ducked just enough to catch it in my left eye. Then the room went spinning as another fist connected underneath my jaw. I fell backward onto my seat, my tongue throbbing on one side where my teeth had sunk in.

Looking up, I saw the both of them advancing on me. Jeff had come in without his overcoat and was playing with the fly on his pants.

"Holy God have mercy on me," I prayed in a low voice.

Mutt turned to Jeff. "Quit playin' with yourself and help me get her onto the bed. You can drop your drawers when we get her tied down."

That wasn't how I'd envisioned losing my virginity. I crawled backward as Mutt advanced on me. I tried to get my hand under my skirt again. Before I could get the gun, Mutt made a grab for me. I rolled away and scrambled to my feet. I think Mr. Fukaro, my martial arts instructor, would have frowned on my style, but I landed a good solid kick into Jeff's groin. I swung around and landed a rabbit punch in Mutt's ear and knee jerked him in the groin.

I found my purse in the other room and quickly checked inside to make sure everything was there. I guess they figured since they were killing me, they could always empty it later. With the transmitters on Sid and me, there really wasn't anything of obvious interest in there, except my gun, which was on the same table as the purse. Jeff groaned and stumbled out of the bedroom. I grabbed the model thirteen and put a slug in his shoulder. Then I ran.

I got out of the building okay, but as I started running down the street, a bullet ricocheted off the building next to me. As another passed through my skirt dangerously close to my legs, I ducked for cover in a doorway.

I peeked around the stone to see Mutt, still doubled over, but hanging out the window with a gun. A car came towards us. I was about a hundred feet away from the cross street. As the car passed, I darted out from the doorway, running behind the car, to the corner and headed down the cross street.

I got turned around a couple of times and was making a lot of turns anyway, to avoid being followed, so I didn't get back to the motel until eleven thirty. I couldn't take a cab because Mutt and Jeff did get the cash out of my wallet. Gasping and sweating from the run, I got the key from the desk and hurried onto the elevator. My hands shook as I inserted the key and opened the door. The room was dark. I breathed a sigh of relief. Sid hadn't gotten back yet. I had time to clean myself up and hopefully, he wouldn't ask any questions. I could always say that the transmitter hadn't worked.

I sank onto the edge of my bed closest to the balcony and blankly looked at the curtains. The key in the lock scraped and the door opened behind me.

"Where the hell have you been?" Sid was furious. "I've been worried sick about you."

"Just out." I kept my back to him. "I had to get something."

I wanted to get to the bathroom before he saw my face.

"Just out," snapped Sid. "I got back here at nine and you were gone. I found out from the desk clerk you never came in. I told you to come straight here."

"I had to get something."

"What, pray tell, did you have to get that took you four and a half hours to buy? Will you look at me?" Sid strode over. I winced as he grabbed my arm and turned me around. "Jesus. What the hell happened to you?"

"Will you please?" I groaned, trying not to cry. "I hate it when you use His name that way."

"I'm sorry. What happened?"

"Mutt and Jeff were watching Winters. I figured you'd seen them, but they found me. They knocked me around a little, but I got away. I kept an eye out. They didn't follow me."

Sid looked me over tenderly. A glance in the mirror told me I was a mess. My hair had gone wild from the run. My left eye was beginning to swell and redden. There was dried blood on my upper lip and out the corner of my mouth. My tongue had swollen and I was speaking with a slur. My upper arms were beginning to bruise. My elbow stung. My dress was filthy, with dark greasy spots all over it. My skirt had been torn away from the bodice in one section in the back and had a bullet hole in one side. My nylons were a mass of runs.

Sid bent and gently took off my sandals, which, amazingly, had held up. Then he turned down the covers on my bed and propped the pillows up against the headboard.

"I want you to stay put exactly where you are," he said, pulling my nightgown out of my suitcase. "I'm going to get some ice. While I'm gone, I want you to slip out of your clothes and into your nightgown. I don't want you to try and get up. I'll clean you up when I get back. Okay?"

"Okay."

"Will you follow directions this time?"

I nodded.

"Alright. I'll be right back. I'm taking my key, so don't answer if anyone knocks."

He left.

I did change into my nightgown. But he came back to catch me staggering out of the bathroom.

He set the ice bucket on the dresser.

"I thought I told you to..."

"I had to go."

He softened and gently picked me up. I was too tired and shaky to protest. He set me down on my bed with my back against the propped up pillows. Then he quickly gathered together the towels, ice, washcloth, bucket and first aid kit, and neatly laid everything out on the bed beside me. He sat down next to me and without saying anything washed off my face and arms. I closed my eyes and allowed myself to enjoy his gentle touch. His hands were soft as they very carefully, gently probed my nose and around my eye, searching for things out of place, and then inspected the bruises on my arms and the scrape on my elbow.

"Doesn't look too bad," he said, smiling. "Just a nice selection of bruises and scrapes. You're going to have quite a shiner, there."

"Terrific. Can I have a piece of ice to suck on? I bit my tongue, too. It hurts."

"Sure open wide."

I did so and he popped the ice in.

He improvised an ice bag out of a plastic bag and a towel and had me hold it to my eye. Then he bandaged my elbow.

"Feeling any nausea or dizziness?" he asked, picking up the stuff.

I shook my head.

"Good. But let me know if you start feeling sick."

He put everything away and then sat down next to me again.

"Now, I need to know exactly what happened."

So I told him, starting from when I first saw Mutt. He listened without comment, although I saw him getting mad when he heard about the attempted rape.

"So you got them where it hurts," he said and then to himself, "I wish I had." He looked at me. "I'm proud of you. You handled yourself well."

"Thanks."

"But why were you at the drugstore in the first place?"

"I had to get something."

"I know, but what?"

I bit my lip. Besides wanting to keep Sid's birthday a surprise, I knew he'd be furious if he knew I'd gone there just for a birthday card. Fortunately, Sid took my hesitation for something else.

"Is it time for your monthly?"

I blushed but seized on the excuse. "Well, not quite. I just don't like not being covered."

I figured that was close enough to the truth. I hadn't checked my calendar, but I knew I wasn't due for at least another week and a half, more like two.

"You could have asked me to buy whatever you needed. I don't mind doing that sort of thing."

"I'm sure you don't. But you know me."

"Afraid so. That was a damned stupid thing to do. Next time, ask me, will you?"

"I will." I watched him get up and go over to his bed. A question kept nagging at me. It was unpleasant, but I had to know. "Sid, I told you what they said before they came to me. Do you know what they were going to do?"

Sid looked at me sadly, then slowly nodded.

"What were they going to do?"

"You don't want to know."

"I do. It's bugging me."

Sid turned down his covers with a vicious snap

before he spoke. He looked at me.

"They were going to take you both at the same time, probably more than once."

"How?"

"One normally, one orally."

I put my hand to my mouth as my stomach heaved.

"That's sick," I said through my fingers.

Sid shrugged. "It's not really that bad. It's the rape element that's sick." Sadly, he pulled his pajama bottoms and robe out of his suitcase. "Why don't you go on to sleep?"

He helped me readjust my pillows, then disappeared into the bathroom.

June 1, 1983

Wednesday morning I woke up stiff. Sid made me do stretching exercises to relieve it.

"So what now?" I asked after we both were dressed.

"Nothing." Sid picked up the phone and dialed. "This is room two-eighteen. I'd like to order breakfast... Yes, the fresh fruit with whole wheat toast for two, a glass of prune juice." He glared at me as I giggled. "And a glass of orange juice. Oh, and I want the toast dry with butter on the side... Thank you." He hung up. "You need to recover so you are staying put today."

"Then you are, too. It's not fair that I have to stay cooped up, while you're out having a good time."

"I suppose."

Room service showed up pretty quickly.

"We'll leave the dishes in the hall," Sid told the waiter, tipping him.

After breakfast, Sid pulled out the deck of cards.

"Gin today?" he asked, shuffling them.

We were almost evenly matched. He never really slaughtered me, but he did usually win.

"Let's not keep score," I said, setting up the little night table between us. We sat on the edge of our beds, facing each other.

"Why not?" Sid shuffled and began dealing.

"I'm tired of seeing how badly I'm losing."

"You're not that bad."

I wasn't. But Sid is very good at gin rummy because he has a good memory for details, which helps him remember which cards have been played. A plan formed in my head. If I could break his concentration...

"Maybe not," I continued. "But what difference does it make if we keep score or not? I thought you communists were supposed to be noncompetitive."

"I'm not a communist anymore. But alright. You can start anytime."

I rearranged my cards and discarded the two of clubs. Sid picked it up. No big deal. He did that a lot of times, just to bug me.

"What was it like?" I asked.

"What was what like?" He dropped the ace of spades. I grabbed it and discarded the four of diamonds.

"Your education. You keep saying it wasn't terribly structured. I know you went to a lot of private schools, and if you were so poor, I don't know how you could have afforded it."

"Stella taught at almost all of them. That's how she supported us."

"They were all communistic, too, weren't they"

"Not all. Just radical. Of course, I didn't know that at the time. I thought I was normal."

"Was it really different? I mean you read all this stuff about the sixties and everyone's doing all sorts of strange things and taking their clothes off and all."

Sid chuckled and absently drew from the pile.

"Some of that's exaggerated," he said, looking at his cards. "But I did spend a certain amount of time in the buff. Sex was no big thing either. If you felt like it, you did it. If not, you didn't."

"I bet you were at it all the time."

"Not at first. Actually, I started relatively late."

"How late?"

"Thirteen."

"That's late?"

"Well, you've got to bear in mind, I knew lots of kids who started as early as eleven. I think my initial indifference had a lot to do with Stella's attitude. That, and well, with most people, puberty just sneaks up on you. With me, it was an explosion. One day, I couldn't have cared less and the next day I couldn't get enough."

Sid smiled as he lapsed into the memory. "Paula Frost. She came up to me one day and asked me why I was still a virgin. I said it just didn't seem worth bothering with. Then she asked me if I wanted to know what all the excitement was about. I was a little curious at that point, so I said okay. After that..." He sighed.

"Gin," I said, presenting my hand.

"Huh? Oh. Alright. It's your deal."

I dealt the cards. "So how'd you learn to read and all that stuff?"

"I don't know. Depending on the school, we studied various things. Usually, they just let us learn what we wanted. I was rather fond of math and science. I guess I was desperate for structure. I've always been the well-ordered type. I didn't get too much of it, though. That is one area radicals are notoriously weak in. That last school I went to had a good math teacher. He was gay. Tried coming on to me once, but I was having too much fun with the girls. He had a pretty steady lover, anyway."

"How come you went to so many different schools?"

"They kept folding. Usually, there weren't enough rich kids enrolled to support the ones that couldn't afford it. Fortunately, Stella had enough idealistic friends to keep me steadily enrolled somewhere. Of course, the last school I went to before high school was closed by the Health, Education and Welfare Department. I don't remember exactly why, but I think it had something to do with the fact that most of the kids couldn't read."

Sid discarded.

"Was that the ten of hearts you just dropped?" he asked, suddenly.

"I'll never tell." I reached over and lightly slapped his hand as he tried to remove the card he'd just discarded to see the card underneath. "No peeking, that's cheating. So that's why you ended up in a public high school."

"That and the fact that Stella couldn't get another

job and had to go on welfare. Was she mad about that. Then the social worker butted in and said I had to go to a properly accredited school or they'd put me in a foster home. So I ended up at San Francisco High School. Talk about a culture shock. When I saw all the rules and regulations that came with the enrollment papers, I about died. Fortunately, the dress codes were still pretty strict, so I didn't look that different when I arrived, which probably saved my neck. Before that, I had long hair and was generally pretty sloppy. Before school even started, I had to get my hair cut, get shoes, all that stuff. I remember reading the student handbook about a week before school started and thinking I was never going to make it."

{This is from a creative writing class that Kathy dragged me to, but it's all based on the original journal entry - ljw}

San Francisco High School. He'd passed by it many, many times before without giving it much thought. But now, the building seemed very imposing. Shaking his head, a very scared fourteen-year-old Sidney Hackbirn pushed his black horn-rimmed glasses up on his nose and swallowed. Being a freshman on the first day of school was bad enough. Being a freshman that was short, nearsighted, and (he thought) a little on the chubby side with a background totally different from the whirl of students around him, a background that had had no rules, that had been totally unstructured, was sheer misery.

Sid wasn't entirely alone. Three other kids from his old school were in the same predicament. But what good were three people in a freshman class of over four hundred? That wasn't even counting the students from the other three years.

Sid let the crowd of students carry him along and shuffle him through to the right spot to pick up his schedule. He already knew some jerk in an office somewhere had taken one look at where he was from and had dumped him in a remedial program, assuming he couldn't read, write, or do math. It wasn't an unfair assumption. Sid knew his three friends couldn't. But Sid could, even if he didn't know how well. Of course, they hadn't bothered to test him.

Sid looked at the schedule with disgust. For the first time in his life, he had not chosen what he was going to learn. He'd had two electives, but Stella had chosen them for him: orchestra and French. He didn't get to take French. He was a remedial student and had been given wood shop instead. First period was homeroom/social studies; second, math; third, English; fourth, orchestra; fifth, P.E.; and sixth, the despised wood shop.

He got through homeroom okay. A couple of girls giggled at his first name, but that had happened before. Mrs. Gridley was okay, even if she did get a little perturbed when Sid spoke out in class without raising his hand first. It wasn't that he didn't raise his hand that bothered her. It was that he asked her why he had to. He backed down when she threatened something called detention. He wasn't trying to be rude, he just wanted to know.

Mr. Carson, the math teacher, promptly announced the homework for the next day. When the books were passed out, Sid opened his and started right in.

"Mr. Hackbirn," growled Mr. Carson. "You do not write in your book."

"Oh. Sorry. I'll erase it." Sid erased the pencil marks and then rewrote the problems on a sheet of binder paper.

"Mr. Hackbirn, in class you listen to the lecture and you do your homework at home."

"But I know how to do the problems."

"We'll talk about it after class."

After class, Sid got a lecture on not talking back to the teacher and on doing things at the right time.

English was a bore, but at least Sid didn't get into

trouble. In orchestra, Sid was told they already had a piano player, he would have to learn violin. Sid did not want to learn violin. For once, he did not say so. Mr. McCready did decide to find out how well Sid could play in the event they needed a backup. Upon assuring Mr. McCready he could sight read, Sid was presented with a piece of unfamiliar, but easy music. Sid played it through halfway as it was written, then began to improvise in a jazz style, something he did when his aunt wasn't around. If it wasn't classical, Stella frowned on it. Mr. McCready asked Sid to transpose it. It took a couple of seconds, but he did. Feeling like he was getting somewhere, Sid started showing off and launched into Flight of the Bumble Bee. Mr. McCready asked Sheila Warner, the piano player, if she'd mind working on the violin. Sid ran an appraising eye over Sheila. After class, he made a pass at her.

"Sidney Hackbirn, what to you think you're doing?" she replied to him in shocked anger. "I'm a nice girl."

"Yeah, I thought so too." Sid was totally baffled by her reaction. "That's why I..."

Sheila was on her way. He sighed and went to lunch. In the cafeteria, he met Doris Ames, the only girl he knew from his old school.

"Where's Frank and Hector?" he asked, as they carried their trays to a table.

"I think they chickened out," said Doris, in utter disgust. "I don't blame them. What a bunch of clods they've got around here. All the guys are looking at me, drooling practically, and not one of them's made a pass at me."

"I believe it. I made a pass at a girl just now and she was furious. These people are weird."

"Not one lousy pass."

"I'll make a pass at you after school."

Doris smiled. "We'll go to my house."

"Okay." Sid smiled. The day wasn't going to be a total loss.

Sid got even more disgusted, as he sat listening

to the other boys talk in the locker room before Mr. Quickly called the class to order. They were rank amateurs, most of them probably virgins. Even in the relatively short time he'd been fooling around, Sid had done more than the boys had ever dreamed of. Sid sighed and shook his head. There was no point in even bothering.

Mr. Quickly was a former Marine who hadn't gotten it into his head that he had left the service. After a lecture on the importance of keeping fit, Mr. Quickly gave a pep talk on the armed forces, the Marine Corps in particular, and how great serving your time could be, especially in Viet Nam, where our boys, etc. He had all the boys except Sid, cheering.

"You're not cheering," Mr. Quickly growled at Sid.

"I'm a pacifist."

"Oh, you are, are you?"

"Yes."

"Yes, what?"

Sid was completely baffled. "Yes, I am?"

"Are you trying to be smart?"

"No."

"No what?" Mr. Quickly bellowed.

"No, I'm not trying to be smart. I don't know."

Mr. Quickly was scribbled furiously on a piece of paper which he shoved at Sid.

"Get to Mr. Frye's office. Right now. Hop to it."

Sid all but ran. He was completely frustrated and confused. Somehow he'd managed to get himself into trouble again and he didn't even know what he'd done.

Mr. Frye was the principal, a kind, gentle man. He knew about the four radical kids who'd been recently enrolled. He wasn't surprised to find one of them in his office.

"What happened?" he asked, after reading the note.

Sid told him. Mr. Frye nodded.

"Do you prefer Sid or Sidney?"

"Sid."

"Alright, Sid. I think you know you've got a problem."

"I just wish I knew what it was."

"Nobody ever taught you how to behave in a classroom situation. It's not your fault. But you're going to have to learn and learn fast. It's yes, sir or yes, ma'am; or no, sir or no, ma'am. That's what Mr. Quickly wanted to hear."

"Sir?"

"Yes."

"But why?"

"That's another thing you're going to have to watch. Asking why. In many ways, it shows you're alert and trying to find out. But a lot of people don't like it when you ask that."

"That doesn't make sense."

"A lot of things don't and you're going to have to accept that, I'm afraid. Sid, you can waste a lot of time knocking the system, or you can work within it to change it. It's up to you.

"Alright."

At least the rules in wood shop made sense. The tools were dangerous if used improperly. Sid still couldn't see any reason for being there in the first place. He was less than enthused about making a wooden trivet and correctly guessed that his aunt would be even less thrilled about having one.

After class let out, Sid headed for Doris's apartment. About two blocks from the school, several boys from his P.E. class caught him and roughed him up. Later that night, as he mended his glasses with tape, Sid decided pacifism would be the first thing to go.

In the days that followed, Sid found himself tagged as gay. He also spent several afternoons sitting at his desk in various classrooms after school, enduring detention for a variety of misdemeanors, most of them involving the question "why", and others involving comments that were either implied or directly sexual.

When this first happened, Sid couldn't figure it out. Nobody had ever told him there was anything wrong with sex. Mrs. Gridley explained, with much blushing, that one just didn't talk about such things and that sex was for marriage. Sid decided not to mention that he'd always heard that marriage was a crock.

Life was getting more and more miserable for Sid. Being called a fag wouldn't have bothered him, except that he knew he was considered the scum of the earth because of it, not to mention being beaten up all the time. The worst part, though, was that none of the girls would come near him and he was horny. Doris helped, but she wasn't terribly interested in being associated with a fag, not when she was happily getting a reputation herself.

Then there was Stephanie. She was a junior. The Friday of the first week of school, she stopped a group of boys from picking on Sid. She innocently took him to her apartment, so he could clean up and have a snack. After she very innocently mentioned her parents were gone for the weekend, Sid had her. She had no idea what was happening until it was over. Then she cried and insisted Sid tell no-one. She was a nice girl and didn't want a reputation. Sid finally found out what being a nice girl and having a reputation meant. He thought it was pretty stupid, but went along with it. He also got into the habit of stopping by her apartment every now and then.

By the third week of school, Doris was struggling with her work and about to go under. In desperation, she asked Sid for help.

"I'm sick of this," she groaned after they'd been studying for a couple of hours. "Come on Sid, make love to me."

"You've got to learn this stuff first. You want to stay with those clods forever?"

"No. I'm going to drop out anyway. I'm going to get pregnant."

"Not by me, you're not."

Doris showed him her diaphragm. "See, I'm covered. Don't worry. I'm going to really cause a ruckus when I do."

"What do you mean?"

"I think I'm going to let one of the senior football players be the father. Can you imagine the scandal?"

"He'll get off scot-free and you'll get all the blame."

"Not if I play my card right and I will. Come on, Sid, let's forget about these books. You don't study afternoons."

"That's because I'm ahead of everybody."

"You poor thing. And they think you're gay. What a joke."

"It's not funny. Being called gay really kills a guy's love life. I just wish there was something I could do. Can't you do some talking?"

"They won't believe me. But I know who they will believe and she's very good about talking. I've also heard she's very good."

"Who?"

"Liz Warner. She's in your home room."

"I've heard about her. Easy Lizzie. Aw, she wouldn't look at me."

"Screw her and your troubles are over, Sid. She's probably dying for somebody decent, anyway. And you're better than decent."

"I am, huh?" Sid grinned and reached for Doris.

But how to get to Liz. That was the problem. Liz avoided Sid like the plague, as did everybody, terrified of guilt by association. Finally, Sid came up with a plan. A little research provided promising results. All he had to do was wait.

He didn't have to wait long. One morning, near the end of September, Liz got herself put on detention by Mrs. Gridley. All Sid had to do was get on detention also. It wasn't hard. All it took was one well-chosen comment about his mother's unmarried state at his conception and birth.

That afternoon, Mrs. Gridley, as usual, spent

her time correcting papers. With her thus occupied, Sid had plenty of time to work on Liz. She sat across the room from him, but no matter. Sid knew what he was doing. He spent many minutes just staring at her ample bosom. When Liz finally noticed him staring at her, he made a couple of insinuating gestures with his tongue. She looked at him like she couldn't believe what she was seeing. Sid maintained the same maneuvers through the whole half hour.

Mrs. Gridley dismissed Sid first. He waited outside the door for Liz. She came out five minutes later.

"Come here, Liz," said Sid, taking her arm and pulling her around a corner. "I've got to talk to you."

"No way, faggot. I don't want to be seen with you."

"In the first place, I'm not a faggot. In the second place, there isn't anybody here to see us. This place is deserted. I ought to know. I get on detention more than anybody."

"Alright. What do you want?"

Sid backed her up against a wall and leaned over her.

"You."

She gaped. "You were coming on to me in there."

"You bet I was. I'm so horny even old Gridley's looking good."

"What are you? Bi?"

"No. I'm hetero. Very horny and very hetero. Give me fifteen minutes to an hour of your time and I'll prove it to you like you've never had it before."

Liz glared at him.

"Quit trying to act so cool," she growled. "I know what you are. You're just another horny freshman trying to lose his virginity on me. Well, I'm getting sick of it."

"I bet you are. But who says I'm a virgin?"

Sid moved in and French kissed her.

"Does a virgin kiss like that?" His hands wandered confidently. "Does a virgin move like this, huh?" He slipped a hand underneath her blouse.

"Not here, you idiot," she hissed pulling his hand out. "You want to get us suspended?"

"Come on, I know a place." He grabbed her hand and pulled her. She followed willingly.

"Fifteen minutes to an hour, huh?" she asked.

"That's up to you. How long you want it is how long I take."

"You sure know how to talk."

"I perform even better."

Liz was impressed, very impressed, and she talked, too. Two days later, when Sid came into the locker room for P.E., the guys were waiting for him.

"Liz Warner says you're no fag," said Tom Freeman, the spokesman for the group.

"Uh-huh."

"She also says you laid her."

"Uh-huh."

"She said you're no virgin, either. In fact, she says you're pretty good."

"Uh-huh."

"So what gives, Hackbirn?"

"I laid Liz Warner, several times. I've laid lots of girls."

"You're kidding."

"No, I'm not. You guys are all talk and I know it. I've messed around with more girls in one month than all you guys together have in all your lives. And you guys are calling me a fag?" Sid twirled the combination to his locker.

"How come you never talked about it?"

"In the first place, you wouldn't have believed me. In the second place, when you're doing it, you don't need to talk about it."

[This is also a corrected version, and it wasn't that creative. That's the way it happened - SEH]

"Gin," I said, laying my cards down.

"Again?" It was the fourth hand I'd won since he'd started talking. He picked up the cards, shuffled and dealt them. "Anyway. I got invited to a party that weekend and needless to say, further developed my reputation. After a while when I'd disappear, someone would see which girl was missing and look for which bushes were shaking. I still got into trouble with the teachers a lot. But as long as my love life was secure, I didn't care."

"You sure got into a lot of trouble."

"I only got suspended twice, once when Quickly had a surprise inspection of the P.E. lockers and found my, uh, birth control hidden there. That was spring, my sophomore year. Mr. Frye was happy I was being responsible but had to suspend me because Quickly was making such a fuss. Then I got suspended when I was caught with Liz Warner. We weren't really caught in the act, just the preliminaries. But it was Mrs. Gridley who caught us and she nearly had a heart attack."

"Did you ever get out of the remedial classes?"

"Are you kidding? I was there less than two months and I was promoted to the gifted program. I got out of wood shop then, too. Didn't get to take French, though. Not that I minded. I TA'd for Mr. McCready and ended up playing keyboard for a student jazz combo he put together. I also accompanied the choirs and the school plays. Outside of class time, if I wasn't chasing girls, I was playing piano. The girls still didn't want to be seen with me. I had a reputation and they didn't want one. I found out, though, that most of those nice girls, including Sheila White, were perfectly willing to submit to me as long as no-one knew about it. Except for Stephanie. She really was a nice girl and would have stayed one if I hadn't caught her off guard. I felt kind of bad about that. She said she only slipped with me, but that I was worth it."

"That's nice. Gin."

"Okay. Your deal. And now you can spill your guts."

"What?" I shuffled the cards.

"You've distracted me long enough. It's your turn

to lose a few hands."

I smiled. I should have known he was on to me all along.

"So what do you want to know?" I asked, dealing.

"About your life, I guess."

"It was pretty boring compared to yours."

"I doubt it. There were a lot of things that I consider boring about my life."

"Maybe. But my life, except for the resort, was very conventional."

"Conventional is a little outside my experience."

"I don't know. It was pretty much like your high school days. Only I was a genuine nice girl. I didn't even go to a parochial high school, cause it was too far away. We had a Catholic elementary and I went there, but I went to South Lake Tahoe High. Actually, a resort town is kind of an interesting place, especially Tahoe, which doesn't really have an off-season. There's always a lot of people around there, but very few of them live there. Everything revolves around tourists. My life centered on Daddy's business. Not that I was working all the time. I did a lot of things, and I had several friends. I liked to read a lot. Mama, Daddy, and Mae used to take turns reading to me when I was little, especially when I was sick. Then I started reading to them. Mama also taught me how to knit then. I was probably pretty young to learn, but she couldn't think of anything else to keep me occupied and quiet at the same time while I was getting well."

"Gin."

"Oh. Your deal. Anyway, I was half a tomboy. I liked hiking and water sports and skiing and horseback riding. But I liked my dolls, too. Mama also saw to it that I learned to cook and clean and housewife stuff, in general. I guess that's why I come off so domesticated."

"You do indeed."

"It's kind of a problem for me. Everyone thinks I want to get married. But I don't. There was a time when I did. When I was in seventh and eighth grade, I wanted to be a housewife and mother. That was when Women's Lib started getting big. I looked at what they were saying and I realized I didn't want to be a traditional housewife. I still planned on getting married, but I also planned on running Daddy's business for him when he retired."

"Was he going to let you?"

"I never told him my plans. I just started helping out more. From the time I was twelve and a half, I did a little bit of everything on that resort. The summer between my sophomore and junior year, I worked in my daddy's gift shop on the main drag, and every summer after that, until I got my teaching job. Then I was a ski instructor in the winter. I enjoyed it."

"What changed your mind?"

"My literature course in college and I guess my high school days did, too. I liked school and planned on going to college, preferably one away from Tahoe. Mae and Neil got married when I was fourteen and I used to go down and visit sometimes. I think that had a lot to do with it. I began to realize that all these people who came to our resort came from real places. I got curious and wanted to see the world."

"That's funny. You never struck me as the world traveler type."

"What type do I strike you as?"

"I don't know." He gazed at me thoughtfully. "A nice girl, I guess. But you're not the popular cheerleader type. I know their kind a little too well."

"Hey, watch it. My best girlfriend was a cheerleader and she was just as well behaved as I was. I had friends in high school. But I still felt lonely a lot of times. I used to blame it on the fact that my daddy's place had horses and all the girls only liked me for that. Looking back I can see now that was true only in a very small number of cases. I was different than most of the girls at school. They tended to run to extremes. About half the girls were fast with the boys, and they looked down on me because I didn't believe in going all the way. The other half were even worse prudes than I was. I mean these girls were ridiculous. There was a group of them, and I promise you, this is true, that were so hung up that they spent their time trying to think up different ways they could avoid sleeping in the same bed with their husbands on their honeymoons. Sex wasn't even a possibility."

"They didn't."

"They did. I listened to them once at a slumber party and asked if that was all they talked about. They were flabbergasted. They couldn't even think of anything else. I was considered a wanton woman because I let guys kiss me."

"Oh my, such a loose woman. I wouldn't have thought that you even dated."

"I've been known to neck a little. Of course, I made it very clear from the start what the limits were. That still didn't stop a lot of guys. Sure, I had boyfriends. I remember my first one, Les Rickert. He was a dog. But I was just a freshman and totally thrilled that a boy actually liked me. It lasted two weeks. I realized I was more in love with having a boyfriend than him so I told him to get lost. He was the first guy that ever kissed me. It was pretty bad. He was also the only guy I ever broke up with. After Les, they broke up with me."

"Why?"

"Come on, Sid. How long would you have gone steady with a girl that showed no sign of going all the way?"

"I never went steady. But I get the point. No performance, no boyfriend."

"Precisely. It was very depressing. I began to wonder if anybody liked me for me. It didn't take long before they gave up trying. The only reason I don't hate men now is that I always had a fresh supply of guys readily available during vacations."

"Who?"

"The guests at the resort. Actually, it was an ideal situation. I could fall in love knowing darned well he'd be gone before any of the more difficult complications set in and I never had to worry about the rejection when we broke up because I wasn't being rejected. His cruel parents insisted on taking him back with them. It was great. I had more summer romances. By the time I got to college, I had a very good idea of what kind of guys I liked. I dated a lot in college, somehow managing to avoid getting serious. High school was fun. But my college years were the prime of my life. I had finally found my niche. Academia. I loved it. I loved the research, the BS sessions, I didn't even mind all the all-nighters. You know, not only was I supposed to have my Ph.D. by now, but I was supposed to be well on my way to becoming the head of an English department somewhere."

"What happened? Got tired of it after your Master's?"

"Oh no. I had to support my education habit and myself. My parents footed the bill through my B.A., but after that, I was supposed to get married, or the convent, or something, and if I wanted to go on, fine, but I had to do it on my own. Fortunately, I was able to live with Mae through my M.A. but that house was getting full and I wanted to be on my own anyway. That's why I took that teaching job. I was also hoping I could get the college I was teaching at to fund my Ph.D. They might have, too. But the cutbacks came. I had no seniority and ended up on the unemployment line and you know the rest of the story."

"What made you change your mind about marriage?"

"The guys and my goals. Being a graduate student doesn't leave you much time for a husband. And the same problem that I'd had with the guys in high school popped up again in college, only in a different way. I stopped dating guys who weren't Christian because all they wanted was my body. But after a while, the Christian guys got to be a drag too, cause they wanted to get married and I wanted to head up an English department. It's even worse now. Men my age are looking to settle down and if they aren't, you know what they're after. Very, very few guys are just looking for companionship." I looked at him. "I guess that's what I value about our relationship. We're just friends. I can be completely honest with you."

"Would you mind being honest with me now?"

"What do you mean?"

"Do you still want to head up that English department?"

I thought about it. "Not really. I'd still like to go for my Ph.D. eventually. But not right now. I really like what I'm doing. In fact, the more I think about it, the more I'm convinced it was no accident that things fell out the way they did."

"Who knows?" Sid absently discarded.

I looked down at my hand. "Oh. I've got gin."

Sid looked at me, a little stunned, then started laughing. "It's not my day for cards."

"So let's give it up, then."

"Alright. What do you want to do now?"

"How about telling me some more stories of your wild and wanton youth?"

"They'd only embarrass you."

"I haven't been so far."

"That's right, you haven't. I wonder why?"

I shrugged. "I don't know. Maybe it's because you're not purposely trying to embarrass me. You might want to edit a little anyway."

"I suppose I could." Sid adjusted the pillow on his bed, then leaned back against the headboard. "Let's see. How about the time I single-handedly started the biggest riot my high school ever knew."

"How did you do that?"

"By doing what came naturally, of course. It was at a football came with our crosstown rivals, South High. Let's see, I was sixteen so that makes it junior year. Anyway, the South High guys were just plain mean, knives, chains, the works. But their cheerleaders, well, they were all stacked and wore the tightest sweaters, the shortest skirts, and you know those little leotard panties they always wore?"

"Yeah."

"Pulled up very high. Before the first quarter was over, I was visiting the other side. I returned during the middle of the third quarter to find fights breaking out all over the field and the bunch of guys I hung around with panicking. They had noticed how one of South's cheerleaders had turned up missing and when they couldn't find me, figured out where she had gone. Of course, the South football players on the sidelines knew their girl was getting it from a San Fran guy. They'd heard the girls talking. The subs told the players on the field, who started fights with our players. They did get through the fourth quarter. I think we won. But as soon as the gun blew, there was the biggest fight on that field you ever saw."

"What did you do?"

"I made it with another South cheerleader. The South guys never found out I was the one who did it either. I think it took ten squad cars to break up the fight. When they finally did, it was after midnight. South got sat on for starting it all, even though the cops knew why they'd started fighting. The cops just didn't know who and nobody on our side was going to say, even though they knew there was only one person with that kind of nerve. I got called into Mr. Frye's office the following Monday and he told me that the only reason I wasn't being suspended was because they couldn't prove I was the one who'd been playing with the South Cheerleaders. I, of course, admitted nothing. Stella taught me that."

"What? To admit nothing."

"Mh-hm."

"Was she mad when she first found out you fooled around?"

"Yeah, but not because I was fooling around."

"Then what was she mad about?"

"Well, I'd never told her, even though I think she suspected. Then one day about a month before school let out my freshman year, she got a phone call from an irate father. The inevitable had happened."

"What? You got caught in the act?"

"No."

"V.D.?"

"No."

"Then what..? You got a girl pregnant."

"Bingo. Stella denied any responsibility for my actions and said he couldn't prove it, and even if he could, the most we were going to do was give him the name of a safe doctor. When he hung up in disgust, she turned on me, wanting to know why I hadn't been using any birth control. I had to make the stupid comment that it was the girl's business. Stella promptly retorted that it was stupidity like that that had resulted in my being in existence. If I was going to fool around, I was an idiot begging for paternity suits if I insisted on assuming someone else was going to be responsible. Then she told me I was a bigger idiot if I ever admitted that I had slept with someone. That lecture stuck very well. I think the timing had something to do with it. Diedre had told me she was pregnant before her father called and I was pretty scared. I don't think I ever believed it could happen to me. Anyway, Diedre got her abortion and after that, I kept myself covered. It was a nuisance, but I wasn't going to let it happen again. After I got to Stanford and got my money, I had my minor surgery. I still had to stay covered for a couple months, but I was so relieved afterwards." He looked at me. "I guess all this sounds pretty bad to you, abortion and self-mutilation."

I shrugged. "Not really. I don't agree with it. But what's done is done, nor am I here to pass judgment."

"Thanks. What else do you want me to tell you about?"

"I don't know. You sound like you were pretty popular."

"I was, especially my last two years. Radicals were in vogue then and I was a genuine, real live radical. I was the only kid who got excused from school to attend peace rallies and sit-ins and civil rights marches. I didn't go all that often. It depended on whether or not Stella was on welfare. If she was on welfare, I was left to keep the social workers happy. If Stella was working, she brought me with her. She had to be careful either way not to get arrested, cause then I'd end up in a foster home and Stella didn't want that. I guess she was making one last ditch effort to keep me from becoming a capitalist. She could see I was leaning that way."

"What made you change your mind?"

"Three things. In the first place, there were the peace rallies themselves. As you know, they weren't always peaceful and it was a little too easy to get yourself hurt or even killed. Hell, look at Kent State. The tear gas was the worst part for me, though. That stuff is miserable." Sid shuddered at the memory. "In the second place, my civics teacher held me after class one day and pointed out that while I questioned everything else, I had never questioned my aunt's philosophies. So I did and I found out that I didn't really agree with them. Of course, the thing that really did the communism in was good old-fashioned adolescent rebellion. Most kids then were rebelling by speaking out and taking action. I rebelled by becoming indifferent."

"You're not indifferent, Sid."

"What do you mean?"

"I've noticed that the things you're indifferent about are often the things you care about most."

He thought about that.

"Maybe," he said. "Probably. I guess I've gotten very good at fooling myself."

"We all have. Look at all the years I spent thinking I wanted to get married. You wouldn't believe what a shock it was to me when Rory Scheidler proposed to me and I turned him down."

"Who was Rory?"

"A guy I met while I was working on my B.A. We went together for about eight months. Oh, he was sweet. I really loved him. He was an art major, a very sensitive guy, but crazy. He wore an earring in one ear. You think Daddy doesn't like you, you should have seen the fits he had when I brought Rory home. Daddy almost made me quit school. I still went with Rory for another four months after that and then he proposed. When I turned him down, he really thought I was too scared to tell Daddy I was marrying him."

"Were you?"

"No, I don't think so. I spent a good long week deliberating before I gave Rory my answer and during that time, Daddy never once entered my mind. A lot of other things did, but not Daddy. I thought it was Rory I didn't want, at first. But I really loved the guy and I knew we could have had a good marriage. It was the idea of being stuck, not just with Rory, but with anybody that bothered me."

"You don't seem to mind being stuck with me."

"I know I can be reassigned."

"You didn't always know that and you still didn't mind."

"But we're not married. You still have your life and interests and I have mine. I know there are a lot of similarities. Sometimes they scare me, but I guess there isn't that sacramental element. We share and are close to survive, not because it's demanded of us. That doesn't sound quite right, either."

"I don't have any answers. I vote we change the subject to something on safer ground. I don't mean to pull away, but I'm not ready to deal with where this conversation is headed."

"Me neither." I looked at the cards still laying spread out on the night table. I put them into a deck. "How 'bout some fifty-two card pick up?"

"If you want to pick them up."

We ate lunch after that, ordering from room service. Then Sid decided he had an idea he wanted to develop. He took a nice leather covered clipboard/folder out of his suitcase and got out his fountain pen. He kicked off his shoes and lined them up neatly next to the bed. Then, after propping up the pillows against the headboard again, he sat down and stretched his legs out.

I just sat, thinking. It looked like my plans were going to be ruined. I was going to talk Sid into having dinner at a nice restaurant and present him with his watch then. But Sid showed no sign of leaving the room. I figured I could make do with room service. The reason I didn't want to do that was that I was afraid of what could happen if Sid's birthday present really touched him. It wasn't that I didn't trust him. I didn't trust myself. The very real threat of the thugs somehow diminished next to Sid's hold on me.

I knew going out that night would be taking a stupid, silly chance, but it seemed worth it.

I picked up the cards and shuffled them. Then, sitting cross-legged on my bed, I dealt myself a hand of solitaire. I thought if I could get Sid antsy enough I could get him to take me out that night. Fortunately, I knew all the right buttons to push. I also knew I was asking for trouble at the same time. Sid knew exactly what buttons to push on me.

I played absently, whistling an old forties tune in sharp piercing tones. After a few bars, I knew Sid was glaring at me, even though I hadn't looked up to see. He let me continue for another minute.

"Lisa," he said finally, in a controlled, but irritated tone. "In the first place, you are not In the Mood. In the second place, your whistling, in general, is bad enough without you trying to imitate the entire Glen Miller orchestra."

"Huh? Oh. Sorry." I returned to my game.

A few minutes later, I hummed a Dan Fogelberg melody, then I added what words I knew.

"Lisa," Sid said after about five minutes of my singing only half the lyrics. "I'm trying to concentrate."

"Oh, was I singing again? I'm sorry."

"Why can't you control that mindless humming of yours..."

I decided I was losing my card game, so I shuffled the cards and dealt another hand.

"Sid," I asked, plaintively. "Is there anything you need me to do?"

"No."

"What are you writing about?"

"Hookers."

"You're just saying that to tease me."

"No, I'm not."

"You're not really going to write an article about prostitution, are you?"

"Why not?"

"Who are you going to sell it to?"

"Depending on how I handle it, several places. In fact, I may develop two articles."

"Why?"

"Because you write differently for Playboy and Cosmopolitan than you do for Ladies' Home Journal. You ought to know that."

"Sorry. There won't be anything to embarrass me in the one you send to Playboy will there?"

"Have I ever sent anything to Playboy that's embarrassed you?"

"No, but..."

"Will you get it through your head that there's some very fine writing in that magazine and that they're very nice to freelancers?"

"I know. But that's not why people buy it."

"Well, it's why I buy it."

"That's what you say."

"If I want to look at women, I don't have to waste time looking at pictures. I know where I can find plenty of the real thing."

I didn't have an answer for that. I hadn't been

all that fair to him in the first place. I knew darned well that ninety percent of the many magazines he subscribed to and read, he wrote for. Besides, I couldn't see him leering over the pictures in Playboy. It just wasn't his style.

"So what are you going to say about prostitution?" I asked.

"I haven't made up my mind."

"Then what are you working on?"

"Making up my mind."

"Getting very far?"

His "no" was rather pointed. I returned to solitaire. I lost two more hands, then gave up.

"I'm bored," I announced.

"Why don't you read? I packed a book for you."

"I noticed. You had to bring Victorian poets, didn't you?"

"I thought you liked poetry."

"I do. But I've only got a minimal tolerance for Shelly, Coleridge and Wordsworth et al. 'In Xanadu, did Kubla Kahn/A stately pleasure dome decree...' Do you know why that poem was never finished?"

"I never knew it wasn't."

"You've read it, haven't you?'

"I believe so."

"You know why it wasn't finished?"

"No, and I don't care to, either."

I flopped onto the bed on my tummy and continued reciting "Kubla Kahn".

"I'm trying to work." Sid was getting angry. "Will you put a cork in it?"

I got up and paced back and forth across the length of the room. I really was bored silly by that point. Sid let me go for about ten minutes, then it began to get to him. Sighing, he put down his pen and closed the folder.

"Alright, I give up," he said.

"I'm sorry, Sid. I'll sit down and let you go on working."

"And five minutes from now, you'll find something else to bug me with."

"I'm sorry. This room is getting on my nerves."

"Mine, too. But hang in there. Hopefully tomorrow they'll let us go to Chicago."

"Maybe. In the meantime, I get to go stir crazy. You think maybe we could go out tonight? Just to dinner?"

"You want to get yourself killed?"

"It'll be dark out and if we stay together, I won't be spotted so easily. We don't have to go anywhere where there are bright lights."

Sid shook his head and looked at me bewildered.

"I don't understand you. You were almost raped and killed last night and the guys responsible are still out there looking for you. Why on earth do you want to go out? You're safe here."

"Am I?"

"I am not-"

"I know," I interrupted. "I'm not worried about you. Really. I'm not. I just feel like a sitting duck is all. Do you realize how easy it'd be to poison our dinner when room service brings it?"

"It's not all that easy. Besides, they don't know we're here."

"How do you know they don't? I'm not talking about Mutt and Jeff, either. I'm thinking of whoever hired them."

"I'll admit it's possible, but we can only afford so much paranoia. We have to assume no one knows we're here."

"Why?"

"We'll go nuts otherwise. If someone really wants to do us in, there's only so much we can do to prevent it. More than likely, that's enough."

"I suppose. But I still feel terribly exposed. I'd feel better if we were moving around, a moving target and all."

He sighed. "Unfortunately, this room is getting to

me, too. Alright, we'll go out to dinner."

"Hooray. Thank you."

"On the condition we go armed, wired and you stay right by me except to go to the ladies room. You'll be harder to spot as part of a couple."

"I'll drape myself all over you. I'll be a regular clinging vine."

"I never did like clinging vines."

I grinned at him, bubbling over with excitement.

"I know exactly where I want to go," I said, bouncing onto the bed. "We can get really dressed up for it. Oh please let me make the reservations."

"Alright. But make them for eight or later. We're waiting for the dark to cover us."

"I will."

I made the reservations for eight fifteen. Then Sid went back to work on his idea and I took up the Victorian poets. Actually, they weren't really that bad. While reading some of Lord Byron, I got an idea for an essay. I dug out paper and pen myself and became so absorbed I didn't notice the afternoon slipping away. Sid left to check in and came back and went back to work. I was surprised when he announced he was taking a shower.

"So soon?" I asked.

"It's six o'clock and I assume you're going to want time to get ready."

"Yeah, I will. I think I'll shower, too. Will you do me a favor and dry your hair out here? I want to get in as soon as you get out. You know it takes longer to dry my hair than it does yours."

"I suppose."

It was a quarter to seven when I came out of the bathroom, wearing my robe and with my hair wrapped in a towel. Sid was standing in front of the mirror. He had his suit pants on but was shirtless.

"It's all yours," I said to him, indicating the bathroom.

"Thanks." He gently patted the hair over his right

ear, making sure it covered the tiny receiver hiding there, so small, you had to look for it to see it. He tapped the dresser next to the matching transmitter set lying there. "Don't forget."

I unwrapped the towel from my head and picked up the blow dryer, looking for the diffuser attachment.

"Lisa, could you bring the blow dryer in here?" Sid called from the bathroom.

"Why?"

"Mirror's fogged up and not clearing fast enough."

The lower half of his face was already covered with foam when I handed him the blow dryer. He plugged it in, flipped the switch and began drying the mirror over the sink. I stepped behind him and went rummaging through my carry on for the diffuser so I could dry my hair without trashing my perm. I pulled it out just as Sid finished clearing a good sized space on the mirror.

"Here you are," he said, pointing the dryer at me.

I grimaced as I got a blast of hot air in my face.

"Very funny." I grabbed the dryer from him, put the diffuser on the nozzle and started using it properly.

"I thought so." Sid chuckled as he picked up his razor.

Even in the steamy bathroom, my hair dried fairly quickly. I turned off the dryer as Sid washed off the remnants of the lather on his face. When he turned away to dry off, I looked into the mirror and sighed.

"What's the matter?" Sid asked.

"I wish I had my hot rollers with me. Then I could do my hair really nicely."

You've got your curling iron, don't you?" He stepped around me and started poking through my carry-on.

"Yeah, but I can only do my ends."

"Don't you know how to do it in layers?" He pulled out the iron.

"No."

"It's really easy. Come on, I'll do it for you."

I followed Sid out of the bathroom. He plugged the curling iron into the socket over the dresser.

"I don't know, Sid. You sure you know what you're doing?"

"Of course, I do. I wouldn't have offered if I didn't." He picked up the transmitter and handed it to me. "You go get dressed and made up while the iron heats, and bring me your bobby pins."

I looked at him, rather puzzled, but did as he asked, although it took a little longer than usual since I had to cover up my black eye. When I was ready, he had put on his shirt, tie and vest, but left the vest open and had turned up the cuffs on his shirt.

"You look like a hairdresser," I said, smiling hesitantly.

"That's the idea." He grinned and pointed to the chair he'd set in front of the dresser. "Come on, sit down."

"I don't know. I think I'll stick with just curling the ends."

"Sit down." I sat. "Trust me. I know what I'm doing." He picked up my brush and started in, brushing with firm, professional strokes.

"Where'd you learn to do this anyway?" I asked, still doubtful.

He clipped a section of my hair to one side with a bobby pin.

"Very first time? At a party. It was a particularly good one, too. I think there were roughly three girls to every guy." I snorted. "I was, uh, taking a break, when I got to talking with this gal who was a hairdresser. She was just slightly tipsy and had found a curling iron and was curling all the other girls' hair. So she showed me how and supervised while I did a couple girls. They turned out really nice. Then one of the guys passed out and Shawna and I got hold of a pair of scissors. Between the scissors and the curling iron that poor boy got a shock the morning after that beat his hangover." Sid chuckled.

"Did you do any other girls after that?"

"No, just Shawna." He sighed happily. "Nice lady."

"I was talking about hair."

"Oops. Sorry. I should have known better. There was this one case. I took the whole training course for that. And at other parties I have. Just to keep in practice. Really impresses the ladies. Of course, it doesn't usually last."

"What do you mean?" I was getting nervous again.

"Let's put it this way. Your hair will stay."

"I understand."

I have to admit, I was impressed when he was done. It looked gorgeous. I covered my eyes as Sid lightly went over it with hair spray.

"Not bad," he said, smiling and stepping back to admire his handiwork. "You look very nice."

"Thanks. It does look good. I'm impressed."

"I told you."

"Haven't you ever heard of modesty?" I got up and walked over to my purse.

"Me?" Sid grinned as he buttoned up his vest. "Of course, I've heard of it."

"Your ego is so over inflated." I watched as Sid flipped down his cuffs and slipped the cuff links in place. "I mean look at you. I'll bet you're the only person in the country left who still wears cufflinks."

"What has that got to do with my ego?" He slid his shoulder holster on and adjusted it.

"I don't know. I'll think of something."

He chuckled. But his smile faded as he picked up his gun, quickly checked the clip and put it in its holster. He put on his jacket.

"Ready?" he asked, smiling again.

"Yeah." I picked up my oversized purse. Sid frowned.

"That bag can be spotted a mile away as it is," he said. "It really stands out with that dress."

"I have a smaller clutch," I said, going to my suitcase. I pulled it out.

"That's much better."

"I think I left my lipstick in the bathroom. Would

you get it for me, please?"

"Sure."

While he was gone, I quickly slipped his present and card into the clutch. On top of that, I stuffed in my gun, my wallet, my pen and pad, and my brush. It made things a little crowded, especially when I added the lipstick and the compact Sid brought to me.

Sid took one quick check in the mirror. Satisfied that all was perfect he offered me his arm.

"Shall we, my dear?" he asked in his most pompous tone.

"Certainly, darling." I affected my best highbrow voice, taking my place by his side.

Dinner was delicious. Sid had broiled swordfish while I had prawns in a Cajun white wine sauce. About midway through, I excused myself to go to the restroom and conveniently "forgot" to turn on my transmitter. I didn't go to the restroom right away. Around the corner, where Sid couldn't see me, I stopped our waiter and ordered a fresh fruit plate and split of champagne for dessert.

They did it up beautifully. The busboy had cleared our plates and Sid was shifting liked he usually does when he wants the check. Our waiter appeared with the fruit and cheese.

"What is this?" he asked as our waiter poured the champagne into two flutes.

"Your birthday," I replied, pulling his present out of my clutch.

"I was hoping you'd forget," he said, looking at the gift. "Lord knows I've been trying to."

"How could I when you remembered mine?"

He looked up and smiled gently. "I noticed you were wearing your pearls."

My hand reached up and twirled one of the pearl stud earrings he had given me.

"Yeah, I planned it that way. Aren't you going to open your present?"

"Alright. It's too small to be a sweater."

"You forgot to bring my knitting."

He opened the card and laughed appreciatively at it. I was on needles and pins as he carefully slipped off the ribbon and undid the paper. I held my breath as he opened the box. He just looked at it.

"You're an awful hard person to buy for," I burst out, fearing the worst.

"It's an antique, isn't it?" he asked finally.

"Yes. It has a music box too." I lifted the watch out of the box and wound it.

Sid took it back and opened it. The gentle tinkling music poured out. He smiled.

"Bach's Minuet in G," he said softly. "I've always liked Bach."

I took the watch back and slipped it into his vest pocket, carefully leaving the fob to dangle.

"I thought it would be just the right touch. You're always wearing suits like this." I swagged the chain and looped it through the vest buttonhole. "There, it looks so dignified."

"But will it keep time?" Sid was smiling.

"I think so. It was running okay in the shop."

"Where did you get it?"

"In a little shop off the square."

Sid pulled the watch out and examined it. Then he set it and wound it.

"You must have sunk quite a bit into this."

"It wasn't that much. But I felt it. It was probably more than I should have spent."

"In more ways than one." He was still examining the watch. "Places like that usually have quite a markup. Do you mind telling me how much it was?"

"A hundred and fifty dollars."

Sid was surprised. "Is that all?"

"It was a lot to me." I was hurt.

Sid started laughing.

"Come here, child." He pulled me close to him. "I've got to do something." I tightened. "No, I'm not horny. It's just..." He released me and looked at me fondly.

"You did it again. Yes, a hundred and fifty is a lot of money for you to shell out, especially on me. But you're not out of the bargain basement."

"What do you mean?"

"There's a possibility I'm wrong, but I think this watch could be worth five hundred, up to a thousand dollars."

"You're kidding."

"Of course, it could be worth as little as twenty-five. But I don't think so. It's in excellent shape."

"Oh dear, maybe you shouldn't carry it."

"Oh no. It does look distinguished." He slid the watch back into the vest pocket, making sure the fob was dangling. "It's just what I needed. Just the right amount of panache to set off my style."

"Then you like it?"

"I love it. I'd like to get it appraised if you don't mind, just out of curiosity. But worth twenty-five or a thousand, I still love it. It's exquisite. Thank you." He gently kissed my forehead and then hugged me again. "You are a dear friend. Thank you."

"You're welcome," I whispered.

We held each other for a couple of moments more. There was an awkward pause as we released each other. Then Sid reached over and picked up his glass of champagne.

"A toast," he said, raising his glass. I picked up mine and raised it. "To friendship and to understanding."

"Amen," I said as we clinked glasses.

As we left the restaurant, Sid proposed a walk along the river.

"Well," I replied. "I was planning on going back to the motel and letting you do what you like. I mean I want you to have fun. It's your birthday."

Sid gently squeezed me. "I appreciate that, but in the first place, believe it or not, I'd really rather spend the evening quietly enjoying the pleasure of your company."

"Want to try a different version of gin rummy?"

"And in the second, a second drop got scheduled for you tonight. I found out when I checked in."

"Oh."

"I should have told you sooner, but you were working, and then you were so happy about dinner, I didn't want to put a cloud over it all."

"That's okay."

He smiled softly. "Actually, it's probably just as well in terms of our relationship. The way I'm feeling right now, the way we're both feeling, we're better off on our feet and walking around."

"If you're feeling that way, I don't mind going back to the motel later so you can work it out. Really, I don't."

"If it was just an urge, I'd say sure." Sid stopped walking and faced me, laying his hands on my shoulders. "But it's more than that, it's a feeling."

"I don't understand."

"I don't, either." Sid shook his head and we continued our walk in silence.

It was near midnight when Sid and I investigated the alley where I was to make my second drop. We hid in the shadows, guns drawn and ready. Down the way, I could see Winters' form sitting in a doorway.

"It looks clear," whispered Sid.

Winters flopped over. My stomach tied itself in knots. Sid got a good grip on my hand and all but dragged me along the shadows to the still form. I turned away to face the building. Unperturbed, Sid knelt by the man and began probing.

"Is he..?" I asked, weakly.

"Dead? Yes. I can't quite tell in this light, but it looks like he was strangled. Rigor's just passing off."

"Oh no." I covered my eyes.

Sid sighed. "I remember last month when you insisted on unplugging my toilet when we could have just as easily called a plumber, you not only looked, but reached in and pulled out a far ghastlier mess than this corpse could ever be in its present state."

"That was different. It's the principle of the thing."

Sid didn't get a chance to reply. A bullet ricocheted off the building I was facing. Startled, I looked down the other end of the alley. Silhouetted against a street lamp was a short stout figure and a tall one in a raincoat.

"Let's get out of here," grumbled Sid, grabbing my arm.

Not that he needed to. I ran very quickly and right behind him. The bullets came fast and kept coming. I still say it was a miracle from God that we didn't get hit. [It was because they were running after us - SEH] Sid and I came out of the alley at about the same time. I started up the street, but Sid grabbed my hand.

"Into the square." He pointed across the street to the dark park in Andrew Jackson Square. "There's cover."

I looked back as we ducked through the gate. Mutt and Jeff had come to the head of the alleyway still firing. Mutt had one arm in a sling, but it didn't seem to be stopping him. We ducked behind a park bench. Sid reached inside his coat and pulled out his gun. He turned and took aim. But something I heard made me pull his arm away before he could fire.

"What..?" He looked at me angrily as I placed my hand over his mouth to shush him.

"Listen," I hissed.

"...completely covered," a voice was shouting. "Drop your guns or we'll fire."

"The police," I whispered and pointed.

Through the trees, we could see the officers at the head of the street, behind one of the buildings. Mutt and Jeff turned on them and shot. The police opened up and I gasped as they went down.

In the silence that followed, a crowd gathered as policemen filled the street. Sid smiled at me and holstered his gun.

"Good job, my dear," he said, brushing his forefinger across my nose.

We left the square on the other side, doubled

back around and joined the crowd around the two fallen men. From the various comments we heard, we gathered that the cops had no idea who Mutt and Jeff had been shooting at. Mutt wasn't going to tell them, either. He was dead. Jeff was unconscious and in pretty bad shape.

We left the square very subdued and headed back to the motel.

"That's one less thing to worry about," Sid said quietly, as he shut the door to the room.

I sat down on my bed.

"I'd almost rather be worrying," I replied.

"I know." Sid came around and sat on his bed facing me. "At least we didn't do it. In fact, they brought it on themselves. I'm very glad you stopped me from shooting. If you hadn't, we'd have the cops looking for us now."

I shrugged. "What a rotten way to end your birthday."

"Fortunately, I've still got a chance at another and so do you." He briefly smiled that hot little smile of his. "Naw, I won't."

"What?"

"I was going to tease you. But I decided that wouldn't be nice."

"What were you going to say?"

"Never mind."

"What were you going to say?"

"You asked for it."

"Alright, I'm asking for it."

"Well, I was just going to suggest that we could still end my birthday on a nice high note, that is, if you're, ahem, willing." He smiled again.

I caught my breath and then summoned together what little anger I could find, anything to break the spell.

"Oh!" I threw one of my pillows at him. He laughed.

"You had to ask."

I took advantage of the momentum from throwing

the pillow to get myself up and busy with getting ready for bed. I fled with my nightgown and robe into the bathroom.

While I was washing my face, it occurred to me that that was the first time Sid had out and out propositioned me. True, it was strictly in jest. If Sid had been serious about it, he would have been far more subtle. I wouldn't have known what was going on until it was too late. The fact that he was joking told me that he felt very secure in our relationship. That made me feel good, and strangely enough, safer with him.

I climbed into bed as Sid went into the bathroom.

"Goodnight, Sid," I called.

"Goodnight, Lisa and thanks again."

"You're welcome."

As I settled in, I thought I heard Sid singing. I listened carefully. Softly from the bathroom came the song "You and Me Against the World."

June 2 - 7, 1983

"Hog butcher for the world, Toll maker, Stacker of wheat, Player with Railroads and the Nation's Freight Handler," or as it's better known, Chicago, Illinois. The sun was setting Thursday night as our plane landed at O'Hare airport and it was dark by the time our taxi let us off in front of the hotel on Lake Shore Drive. I stood on the sidewalk with the luggage, while Sid paid the cab driver.

"Show me another city with lifted head singing so proud to be alive and coarse and strong and cunning..," I said to myself.

"What?" asked Sid, picking up the suitcases.

"'Chicago', by Carl Sandburg," I explained. "I can't remember all of it. Just snatches."

Sid just chuckled.

Our room was nice but had only one bed.

"Who had the bed the last night in Florida?" I asked when the bellhop had gone.

"I don't remember," Sid replied digging into his pockets. "Let's flip for it."

I looked at him suspiciously. Flipping a coin to decide something was not unusual for us. Sid almost invariably suggested it, flipped the coin and won. I almost always called heads, and as I thought about it that night, I realized I had never seen that quarter come up anything but tails.

"Call it in the air." Sid sent the quarter flipping into the air.

Instead of calling it, I snatched it as it fell. I looked at it, then at Sid. He smiled sheepishly.

"Double-tailed," I replied, not really angry or even disgusted. "Tacky, Sid."

"A young lady gave that to me, just before I left for Nam. Made me promise to always carry it with me. She said it was a good luck piece."

"Especially when you have to flip for something."

"Well, I was wondering when you'd catch on."

"Just for that, you can sleep on the floor tonight, and as an added punishment for all those months of deception, you can also watch Johnny Carson with me."

"Cruel and unusual punishment."

It wasn't the Tonight Show, or even Johnny Carson, that Sid minded so much. He hates commercials. That's one of the reasons why he almost never watches television. On the rare occasions there's something on commercial television he really wants to see, during the commercials he'll take the remote control and switch channels every three seconds until his program is back on. That drives me nuts. We had a rather nasty fight last spring when I got fed up with his channel switching and hid the remote control during the third episode of a mini-series we both wanted to see. We never did resolve the remote control issue, but we did decide it wasn't worth fighting over. Of course, we've been known to have occasional friendly wrestling matches over it.

Fortunately, the television in the hotel room didn't have a remote control and I made Sid promise not to touch the channel switch. I turned it on just before ten.

"Aren't you turning that on a little early?" Sid called from the bathroom, where he was getting ready for bed.

"I want to watch the news," I answered. "I'm tired of not knowing what's going on in the world."

"But it's not even eleven yet."

"This is the Midwest, Sid. Everything's an hour earlier."

"That's right. Turn it up so I can hear." He opened the bathroom door a crack.

I was already in my nightgown and robe. I took a pillow and lay on my belly with my head at the foot of the bed and chest propped up by the pillow. The anchorman was introduced and the camera zoomed in on him.

"Good evening. In tonight's top story, a shootout with police in New Orleans has solved the murders of two women, one in Orlando and the other in San Francisco. Paul DeNaio, with our New Orleans affiliate, has that story. Paul?"

Sid came out of the bathroom wearing his robe and bottoms, but still brushing his teeth.

"Uh, oh," he mumbled, through the foam.

Pictures of coroner's men taking bagged bodies away in the night filled the screen as the voice spoke.

"Andrew Jackson Square is not known for gun battles, but that is exactly what erupted here last night when New Orleans police officers interrupted and shot two gunmen."

There was a shot of a mustached police spokesman labeled Captain James Wilkes.

"The suspects exited the alley over there, firing their guns," said Wilkes in that wooden tone all police spokespeople seem to use. "We, uh, don't know at this time who they were shooting at. The officers were on patrol, heard the gunshots, and came around the corner, there, identified themselves, and then returned fire."

DeNaio picked it up. "The body of a third man, whose name has not been released was also found in the alley. Police believe the gun battle may be connected. The gunmen were identified as Lyle Kisko and Arnold Shipner. Kisko died at the scene. Shipner died later this morning at New Orleans General Hospital."

"How comforting," I grumbled, crossing myself.

"At least we didn't do it," Sid said, still brushing his teeth.

"Today, a routine check matched Kisko's fingerprints with those found in connection with the strangling death of Laura Fredrickson, a tour director who worked at Disney World. Fredrickson's body was found at the Orlando, Florida resort last Friday, May 27th. Orlando police were already comparing notes on a similar murder in San Francisco on May 12th, that of Gina Delacando, an independent insurance sales rep from Washington D.C. Semen samples from both Kisko and Shipman have been shipped to Orlando and San Francisco police departments and early results look promising. The question now remains why and how did Kisko and Shipman attack two women on two separate coasts and what relation those crimes might have, if any, to the death of the third man here in New Orleans. This is Paul DeNaio, ABC News."

I reached over and turned off the television. Sid returned to the bathroom and rinsed out his mouth.

"Why do I get the feeling that Laura Fredrickson did not show up for her drop?" I asked. "And that you took advantage of the fact that the transmitters were not working to avoid telling me?"

Sid stayed in the bathroom. "I don't know that that's an issue."

"I think it is." I was angry and hurt.

"That was what? Last Friday? I wasn't exactly in any shape for extended conversation then, you know."

"That's no excuse. Will you come out of there? Why didn't you tell me?"

Sid stood in the doorway. "I guess I didn't want you to worry. I don't know."

"That really hurts." I started to cry.

"That's not necessarily why." Trying to keep a grip on his temper, he paced. "Damn it, I was already all tensed up with being horny and all, and then she didn't show, and I had a bad feeling I knew why, and I just didn't want you to have look at another corpse. I was trying to spare you, and that, I swear, is the truth."

I nearly shrieked. "What do I have to do to prove myself to you? Okay, I used to panic because I was new to this, but are you going to hold that against me forever?"

"Of course not."

"Then will you get it through your thick skull that I don't want to be protected? Yeah, I've got a problem, but it's not going to get any better if you keep shielding me from it. I thought we were a team. How can we be if you hold stuff back from me?"

"I didn't mean to." He looked at me helplessly. "Look, I'm sorry. I don't know what happened. I wasn't exactly thinking straight. Anyway, it scared the hell out of me. I was having enough trouble holding myself together. I didn't think I could hold you too."

"Didn't you consider the possibility that I could have held you?" The tears ran down my face.

"I should have." He sat down in a chair next to the dresser. "I don't want to hurt you and I'm sorry if I have. I know it's been a while since we've been working together, but I'm still not used to having another person around. I've been alone all my life and I've preferred it that way." He sighed. "I intensely dislike being vulnerable, and I don't like saying how I feel. It's extremely hard for me to tell you I feel afraid, or that I feel anything at all. Even when I'm angry at you, I have to be in control. That's the worst of what you've done to me, and probably the best. You make me own up to my feelings, at least to myself. Handling all that, I..." He shook his head, unable to finish. He got up, restlessly.

"Sid," I took his hand as he passed close to me and patted the bed next to me. He looked at me puzzled but sat down. I turned his back to me and gently rubbed it in a circular pattern.

"I just want you to understand that I can be strong, too," I said. "And I don't care if you're weak. For heaven's sake, if you keep trying to be strong for both of us, all you'll do is hurt yourself. I don't want to see that."

He turned to me and gently laid his hand on my cheek. It was soft and his thumb tenderly caressed me. He began to move towards me, his lips barely parted.

I let out a strangled little cry, afraid that I could not resist him. Apparently, he thought I could, for he stopped and shook his head, withdrawing his hand.

"No." He closed his eyes and turned his head. "No, I won't."

"I'm sorry."

"Don't be. Don't ever be. You can't be sorry for your need to say no to me any more than I can be sorry for my need to make love to you."

"You don't know how much I wish we could." I wiped the tears from my eyes.

"Someday, Lisa, we will, when I can make you see the beauty and not the guilt."

"No. I couldn't ask you to make that kind of sacrifice."

"I won't. Nor will you. It would hurt both of us too much. When we come together, it will be on terms we both agree on, happily."

"If that could ever happen."

"It will, that much I do know."

"I can't change that way."

"You already are, just like I'm changing your way. We'll change and come together somewhere in the middle."

I smiled at him knowing there wasn't any somewhere in the middle and half-fearing that there was. Sid pulled me up off the bed and took the bedspread, extra blanket, and my pillow. Quickly, silently, he made up the bed on the floor. He turned to me.

"Goodnight, my sweet Lisa," he said softly and kissed my forehead.

"Goodnight, Sid." I reached and my lips brushed his cheek next to his ear.

We looked at each other fondly for a minute. Then Sid sighed.

"Go, now, to bed." He turned me around and gave me a gentle shove. "I have only so much control."

"Maybe I'll make myself scarce tomorrow."

Sid laughed.

"We'll see," I heard him say from the floor.

The next morning, at breakfast, I went over Sid's drop.

"He's Damon Savallo, a top man, adopted in 1979. He's black, about six three, and big. His cover is as a talent scout for the Chicago White Sox. He transferred in from division 57J when our group needed some extra bodies. His references were excellent, and he has exceeded expectations."

"Hm." Sid mulled it over. "Is there anything you want to see or do while we're here?"

"I've heard good things about the Museum of Science and Industry, but that's kind of an all day thing."

Sid's drop was around two, at a coffee shop about a block from our hotel. Sid didn't like the idea but didn't want to drop any clues by changing it.

"Maybe I will make myself scarce this morning. It'll probably be my best chance. Do you mind putting off the museum until tomorrow?"

"Nah. I think I'll just hang around here and relax. What time do you want me at the drop?"

"Given that you picked up a tail on that last one, why don't I just turn up the transmitter and you hang out in the lobby here. If there's trouble, you can catch it, and if I'm tailed, you won't be seen."

"Sounds good."

Sid took off a few minutes later, and I ordered a second breakfast with extra bacon. I had seen a bookshop in the lobby and figured I could augment the Victorian Poets with a good murder mystery but didn't find any to my liking, or anything else I felt like reading. So I explored the hotel.

I was delighted to find a laundromat on the bottom floor. I didn't know what Sid was planning on doing about the dirty clothes situation. But I knew what I was going to do that day. I hurried back to the room.

While gathering together the laundry, I decided

to take a chance on having the dry cleaning done. Not that I was worried about the hotel. I was sure they, or whoever did their dry cleaning, were competent and I was able to get it in in time for one-day service. I was worried about a possible quick departure. Doing the laundry myself, I had a little more control on what would be left behind if we had to leave Chicago suddenly.

The drop went fine, without hint of a tail or trouble. Sid checked in and came back to the hotel around three thirty, humming "Marianne." I was on the bed, surrounded by a pile of underwear and socks.

"Repacking?" Sid asked, not quite sure what to make of it.

"In a minute. I've got to get all this stuff sorted first, then folded and the socks matched."

"What did you do today?"

"The laundry. I don't know if you noticed, but both of us were out of clean clothes."

"Well, I had, but I was going to call the hotel laundry service tomorrow."

"Now you don't have to."

"I would have preferred it." Sid looked around. "Where are my shirts? I assume you washed them."

"And dried them. They're hanging in the closet. They're not a bit wrinkled. I hung them and your washable pants up straight from the dryer. That's one advantage to cheap clothes."

Sid inspected his shirts.

"Oh no," he groaned. He pulled out one of the shirts on its hanger and fussed with the collar. "Look at that. Limp." He turned and gestured with the shirt. "I like my collars, cuffs, and fronts lightly starched. That's why I use a laundry service."

I shook my head.

"He can face gunmen and corpses without blinking an eye," I addressed the air. "But let his collars go limp and the man goes to pieces."

"A- I am not going to pieces, and B- It is the small

creature comforts that make the unpleasant things in life bearable."

"What's comfortable about a starched shirt?" I held up a pair of athletic tube socks. "Are these yours or mine?"

"What did you do with my warm up suit?"

"Are you kidding? I washed the warm-ups first. Those things were beginning to walk around by themselves. They're drying in the bathroom."

"I see."

"I washed everything. Well, not everything. I took your suit, your two sportcoats, my shetland sweater, my black dress, and your tweed pants to the hotel's dry cleaners. They'll be ready at four."

"And you washed everything else?"

"If it didn't say dry clean only on the tag, I did."

"Including my jeans."

"Sure."

"You washed my jeans." Sid sank into the chair, devastated.

"They were dirty." I couldn't help being a little amused by Sid's distress.

"You do not wash jeans. You dry clean them, otherwise, they shrink and fade."

"Not if you don't put them in the dryer, which I didn't. They are also drying in the bathroom." I shook my head as Sid bolted in there.

He sighed as he came out and leaned in the doorway.

"At least you didn't crease them down the center. I really hate those lines."

"Of course I didn't. Give me credit for some know how. When I said I did everything on Daddy's resort, I meant it. Part of that included guest laundry. I also had a girlfriend in college who worked in a dry cleaners. We used to compare notes every now and then."

"And you still washed my jeans." Sid returned to the chair.

I had to laugh.

"What's so funny?" he grumbled.

"You. For heaven's sake, it's not that big a deal."

"Oh, it isn't? I happen to value my personal appearance."

"So do I. But I don't let it bother me if I can't look perfect all the time. Besides, who's going to see you? Just me and I couldn't care less if your shirts aren't starched. And I seriously doubt you're going to have any problems attracting women even with a limp collar and jeans that just might be a touch faded."

"That is the least of my worries." He folded his arms and gazed at the bathroom. "This may sound crazy to you, but I don't really care who sees me. It's like a picture hanging crooked on a wall. Some people wouldn't even care. I'm the type that has to have it straight."

"I understand. My mother is like that sometimes. I remember once when she had a dinner party, she found a spot on her best table cloth at the last minute. For a lot of reasons I don't remember, she couldn't change it. But I do remember that nobody knew the spot existed because the centerpiece covered it. Mama still went nuts. Never mind that nobody else knew. She knew it was there and it spoiled her entire evening. Look, I'm sorry I went ahead and washed everything. I should have asked you first."

"That's alright." He still sounded miserable.

"Listen, if it'll make you feel any better, I'll see about digging up some spray starch and an ironing board."

"Thanks, but don't bother. It's not fair for me to burden you with my personal fetishes."

"I thought that's what you were paying me for."

"For taking care of the mundane trivialities, yes. But while ironing is definitely mundane, it is anything but trivial. Remember, my innocent one, there was a time when if I wanted a shirt without wrinkles in it, I had to iron it myself, and I grew up in the days before permanent press. That is why I'm so glad I can pay to have it done for me. I'm sorry I got upset at you. I shouldn't have. You've obviously been working hard today. I should be thankful."

"Don't worry about it. It was worth it to see you having fits."

"I don't have fits." Sid glared at me.

"Of course not," I replied soothingly. "I was speaking figuratively. Now, will you help me figure out whose socks are whose?"

"Socks?"

"Our athletic socks, dear boss. We both wear tube socks to run in."

Sid came over and helped sort out the athletic socks. Then he refolded all his other socks the way he liked them folded, while I finished folding his underwear. He finished with the socks first and looked at me, puzzled.

"Why doesn't that bother you?" he asked.

"What?" I set his underwear to one side and started untangling a pile of bras.

"My underwear. You always get so embarrassed about things like that, but not that. I don't understand."

"At the resort, I handled all sorts of underwear. It never bothered me. Why should yours?"

"I don't know. I just know people get weird about underwear. I remember once, I was living with this girl and one day I was helping her with her laundry and she went into fits because I was handling her bras. I couldn't figure it out. I'd been removing them from her for three nights and sometimes during the day, too. And, yet, here you are, the most modest person I've met in my life, and not only do you fold my stuff without batting an eye, you let me sit here and watch you fold yours."

"I'll even let you help if you like."

"You don't mind me putting my hands all over your most intimate apparel?"

"As long as I'm not in it."

"You are hopelessly inconsistent."

I just shrugged. Sid shook his head and helped me fold.

That night, after dinner in a fairly respectable restaurant, we went to a movie. The next day, Saturday, was spent at the Museum of Science and Industry. Sid went out that night by himself and didn't come back 'til one thirty a.m., humming "Marianne".

Sunday was another second drop. Sid went with me to church, in his blue sport shirt and navy sportcoat, under which was his model thirteen.

"Why not do what..?" I asked hesitantly as we walked to the church. "Well, you know. What you did the last couple of Sundays?"

"Because of check in yesterday."

We'd been ordered to make the second drop together and try to capture the persons we figured would be there to nail us.

"It'll be faster if we don't have to meet up with each other."

"We can probably ditch after communion, too."

Sid hesitated. "Won't that be a little conspicuous?"

"Hardly," I snorted. "It's almost more conspicuous to stay 'til the end. Are you going to be okay without your fix?"

"That's why I went out last night."

For some reason, I felt very restless all through mass. I couldn't concentrate on the readings or the sermon and during the consecration, I could have been at the drop for all the attention I was paying.

It had been arranged at a park, I still can't remember the name, but there were plenty of nice, leafy trees to discourage sniper fire and give us plenty of cover. Unfortunately, that also gave any bad guys plenty of cover. Sid and I went there in separate taxis. Although I remained more or less within sight of him at all times, I kept a good hundred feet or so between us. It was what Sid called a flanking maneuver.

It worked, sort of. Sid met Savallo at a park bench, and within seconds, gunfire erupted. Sid and Savallo dove behind the bench. I traced the gunfire to a tree across the path and down some, and I mean literally within the branches. The advantage was that the gunman was pinned. The disadvantage was that I couldn't see him for the leaves. He, however, could see me approach.

I dashed for the closest tree. Savallo stood and fired. The gunman put a couple slugs in him and he fell over the bench. I aimed for the branches and fired, hoping for the best. That drew more fire at me. Sid tried shooting from the bench but didn't get much of a chance. It seemed the least movement brought on bullets.

We remained in a standoff for a while. It seemed like an hour or three, but it couldn't have been. Sirens approached. I fired at the tree again and ducked as bullets tore into the tree that hid me. I tried again, but as I ducked, out of the corner of my eye, Savallo raised his head and gun. The revolver snapped back and tumbled, but it had done its work. The branches rustled, and the gunman tumbled to the ground.

Sid scrambled for me, his hand on his left arm.

"The bathrooms," he gasped.

"You okay?" I asked.

"Fine."

We made it to the public restrooms before the police got to the park, and managed to stay hidden long enough for them to get too occupied with Savallo and the guy he'd killed to notice us casually look them over and saunter away. Sid had ditched his sport coat in the restroom and kept his arms folded. His shoulder holster went in my purse.

We didn't say anything in the cab back to the hotel. Sid continued holding his arm.

"Get packed," he said, gruffly when we got back to the room and headed for the bathroom. "We're getting out of here."

As he passed me, I noticed the dark stains between the fingers of his right hand. I stopped him and pulled his hand away. On his left upper arm, there was a bright red horizontal bloody stripe. I looked at him in horror.

"Lord Jesus, have mercy," I whispered.

"I'm alright," Sid replied. "I just got winged. That's why I couldn't shoot back. But it's not serious. Now hurry up and get packed."

"No." There was a silence as he glared at me. I stood my ground. "We've got to take care of your arm first."

"I'm not going to a hospital. That's too obviously a bullet wound and someone will ask questions."

I looked at it more closely. "I don't think we'll have to."

"Alright, I'll clean it up and you start packing."

"I'll clean it up. It's at too awkward an angle for you. The packing can wait."

"We've got to leave Chicago as fast as possible."

"I know. But you need taking care of." I pulled out the first aid kit. "That comes first."

"Alright," Sid grumbled.

"Sit on the bed. I've got to get a washcloth and a towel."

I don't think my touch was as gentle as Sid's, but I tried. He gritted his teeth as I carefully cleaned the wound.

"It burns like hell," he grumbled.

"I'll bet. There isn't any puncture wound. It looks like it just grazed you."

Sid winced as he tried to flex his left hand. "It did enough. I couldn't shoot, damn it. Savallo killed himself plugging the bastard."

"Dear Jesus, have mercy on his soul." I crossed myself and sniffed, then went back to work. "Do you get the feeling we're leaving a trail of bodies?"

Sid winced again as I applied antiseptic ointment to the stripe.

"Unfortunately, yes. I just can't figure out why, or even if I should figure it out."

"Why not?" I carefully cut a piece of gauze padding to fit over the wound.

"We don't necessarily have the need to know."

"Given that we're also the targets, I think we need to know plenty."

"Well, we haven't been nailed yet."

"I suppose."

I wasn't feeling terribly reassured. After I finished bandaging his arm, I washed off his hand. While Sid started packing, I rinsed the blood out of the washcloth and towel.

Less than an hour later, we were at an airline ticketing desk at O'Hare airport.

"We want to go to Yellowstone," Sid told the girl behind the computer terminal.

"The National Park?" she asked.

"Yes."

"Well, sir, the closest we fly to it is Boise, Idaho. Then you can change planes there and fly to either West Yellowstone, Idaho Falls, Jackson Hole, Bozeman or Billings. Oops. Wait a minute, skip Bozeman."

"We want to get there today."

"Well, I'm afraid, sir, that's impossible. The next flight out of Boise to any of those airports is Tuesday morning to Jackson Hole."

"Can we go to Boise today?"

"Yes. We've got a flight in about an hour."

"Fine, put us on it."

"Certainly. I can check your baggage here and assign you seats if you'd like."

"Great. Two in non-smoking, with a window seat."

"Would you like me to ticket you through to Jackson Hole?"

"No thanks. We'll see what happens when we get to Boise."

Sid handed the girl his credit card with some difficulty, given his arm.

"Why didn't you take the flight to Jackson?" I asked as we headed for the gate.

"There's got to be a faster way to get there. We'll find it in Boise."

"You want me to take your carry on? It'll be easier on your arm."

"I can manage."

He couldn't, really, but needed to keep his precious control, pretty gutsy, in a way, when you consider we didn't have any pain pills except some Tylenol.

There wasn't a faster way to Yellowstone. We spent a good two hours at the Boise airport looking for one. The only thing that left sooner than the flight to Jackson Hole was a bus and it left Monday evening. Sid was about to resign himself to spending two nights in Boise when I got a hold of a road map and ascertained that if we drove ourselves and left early Monday morning we could get to Yellowstone by dinner. Sid wasn't overwhelmingly thrilled with the idea but agreed when I pointed out that we would have to rent a car, anyway, in Jackson Hole, as it was still a two and a half hour drive from Yellowstone. I also suggested the possibility of camping, but Sid flatly refused to. He said it wasn't practical for our situation. I had to agree, although I knew darned well the reason Sid said no had little to do with practicality.

Once we saw Boise, Idaho itself, Sid was perfectly happy to be driving out of there the next morning in the four-door sedan we'd rented. Not that Boise is all that bad, in fact, it's rather nice as cities go. But I do have to be honest. Boise, Idaho is not one of the nation's hot spots, especially on a Sunday night. It also had more one-way streets than L.A. Sid and I got turned around three times looking for a place to eat dinner. To make matters worse, Sid was sulking because I had to drive because his arm hurt.

It wasn't bothering him that much, either that or something else was bothering him more. At six thirty, he left me at the motel and drove off to find some nightlife in the deserted city. I had no idea how, but he did. He came back close to eleven, singing "Marianne".

We left the motel at six a.m. Sid drove, saying that his arm felt a lot better. It probably did, but I knew darned well that wasn't why he was driving. [So I hate being driven - SEH] Sid can be a real control freak at times.

We didn't leave Boise until after six thirty. While trying to get to the interstate, we stumbled across a supermarket just opening. I told Sid to stop.

"Why?" he asked.

"We'd better get some more bandages for your arm."

"Alright." He pulled into the parking lot.

Once in the store, I got another idea.

"Hey, why don't we get one of these?" I said, pointing out some styrofoam ice chests. "We can get some ice and some cold drinks and stuff for lunch and have a picnic. Better yet, we'll get some munchies for on the way."

"We won't be getting much exercise all day in the car. Eating on top of that..." Sid shook his head. "Besides, I've got a feeling you're going to want to stuff that thing with soda pop."

"Alright," I groaned. "I'll compromise. Fresh fruit and healthy stuff. You know, if we nibble on the way, we won't have to stop for lunch and that'll save time."

"True. Okay, you're on. But no junk."

"If you insist." I pulled a shopping cart away from the others.

We bought bananas, strawberries, a couple oranges and some peaches. Sid insisted on a quart of non-fat milk, which I drink though I'm not overly fond of it. I tried to get him to compromise with low fat, but he remained firm. We also got several different canned fruit juices (no sugar added). Sid was delighted to find the store carried Perrier and added a six-pack of bottles to the cart. I was able to talk him into a couple packages of Alouette, that French cheese spread, and some unsalted Akmak crackers. When we went past the candy aisle, I tried to sneak a couple of candy bars and a package of raspberry whips into the cart. Sid caught me and made me put them back. He also tried to make me put back the package of fig bars.

"We agreed," he said, getting irritated. "No junk."

"These are not junk," I replied. "See, they're even whole wheat. They're the best thing to keep you, uh, well, moving."

He looked at the package and then at me.

"They do, huh?"

"Grandma Caulfield swears by them."

"She does. Well, what the heck." He dropped the package into the cart. Sid may not agree with Grandma Caulfield's views on sex, but he doesn't argue with her home remedies. I'd had to dose him before and he knows they work.

We got some plastic knives and napkins and the extra bandages. As we headed for the checkout, I added, without thinking, a box of female type personal items. Sid looked at me, rather puzzled.

"I'm due in a few days," I explained, blushing a little.

"I thought you bought those in New Orleans," he said, quietly.

I was caught. "I didn't get a chance to. They got me before I could."

"Come to think of it, you should already be using them."

I bit my lip. "I'm late."

"This late and most women would be worried, and we both know you've got nothing to worry about." Sid's voice had that angry edge to it.

"Well..."

"Why did you lie to me?"

I looked at him. I could see he was hurt.

"Look, I know you're mad and you have every right to be. But can we wait to argue about this until we get back to the car?"

Sid's lips pressed into a tight, straight line. He nodded.

When we got back to the car, I started packing the ice chest immediately. Sid watched for a couple minutes before speaking.

"That really hurts, Lisa." His voice was just barely shaking. "And after you yelled at me in Chicago for keeping things from you."

The tears were already rolling down my face.

"Well, I went to get your birthday card and I knew you'd be really mad if I told you that."

"There was no way you could help being found out. Didn't it occur to you that I'd be even madder when I did?"

"Well, yes, but that wasn't all of it."

"What else is there?"

"It was your birthday and I wanted to surprise you." I broke down into sobs, waiting for the inevitable fury.

"You mean Wednesday night?" he asked quietly.

"Uh-huh." I looked at him, still crying. "Didn't it mean a lot to you?"

"Well, yes." He sighed, helpless, the anger draining from him. "Oh, Lisa. Come here." He reached over and pulled me to him. Gently, he held me. I sobbed onto his shoulder. He sighed again. "Woman, what have you done to me?"

"What do you mean?" I asked.

He released me enough to look into my face, his hands still holding my shoulders.

"I ought to be giving you the chewing out of your life. Instead, I feel like a heel for getting mad at you in the first place. What you did was stupid, even without Mutt and Jeff around, risking your neck just to buy a birthday card for me. Then to lie about it just for the sake of a silly celebration..."

"Sid, that's the only thing I ever lie about, honest. Just birthday surprises, and Christmas, and things like that. You've got to believe me."

"I believe you, and your little celebration meant a lot. I was very touched. But in the final analysis, it wasn't that important."

"It was to me. You were so nice to me on my birthday."

"I didn't expect..."

"I know." I sniffled. "It's just that, Sid, you're my best friend. I'm closer to you than I am to Mae. I had to do something."

"Oh, Lisa." Sid opened the front door to the car and reached in and pulled out a tissue from the box that had been left on the dash. He put it to my nose. "Come on, blow."

I pulled my head away.

"Thanks, but I can blow it myself." I gently took the tissue from his hand and blew my nose. With one arm still around me, I felt Sid kiss the side of my head. He walked over and finished packing the ice chest.

"You know, Lisa," he said fitting the lid on. "You're one of the best things that ever happened to me." He opened the door to the back seat and put the folded shopping bags on the floor. "You're right up there with losing my virginity."

"Thanks a lot," I grumbled.

Sid looked at me for a moment.

"That wasn't meant to be as tacky as it sounded. Give me a hand with this, will you?" He grunted as we picked up the ice chest and swung it onto the back seat. "Maybe I'd better put that into perspective." He shut the car door, looked away for a moment to think and then back at me. "I've got a good life. Sure, it's had its low spots. But a lot of very good things have happened to me." As he spoke, he walked around to the driver's side of the car and opened the front door. He paused, not getting in. "The women I've known, getting published, getting my money." He looked at me intently. "There is a reason I'm exceptionally horny. I get a tremendous amount of pleasure from sex. Until I met you, losing my virginity was the very best thing that had ever happened to me."

I was speechless. What was there for me to say? I

knew how hard it was for him to go without sex. I cared for him so much but was powerless to express it.

"We'd better get going," he said, getting into the car.

I got in on my side, slowly putting on my seat belt. Sid waited until it was buckled before starting the engine. He looked at me.

"You mean a lot to me, Lisa," he said quietly.

"Oh, Sid, you mean a lot to me, too."

He put the car in gear and pressed the accelerator.

"Let's go find that interstate," he said, jovially, purposely shattering the mood that could go nowhere.

As we came into Twin Falls, Idaho, we saw several signs for the local McDonald's.

"Oh, Sid, please stop," I begged, teasing. "I really need a junk food fix."

"Come on," said Sid, laughing. He accepted a cracker that I'd just spread with cheese. "Are you seriously telling me this isn't better than McDonald's?"

I finished licking the cheese off my fingers. "Well..."

"You're hopeless, woman."

"My tastes just aren't limited, that's all. I'm open-minded."

"I prefer to be discriminating."

"You'd never know from the women you date."

"I'm open-minded. There are times when that's appropriate, too."

I chuckled. "It seems so weird, you know? We're so different sometimes, and yet we do work well together, and we're such good friends. It's not supposed to work this way."

"I'm glad it did."

"And the really funny thing is, if it hadn't been for one chance meeting, it would never have happened."

"But fortunately I came along and rescued you from a fate worse than death."

"Just so I could risk my neck with you, and Larry wasn't that bad."

"A- He was, and B- You'd already ditched him. I

merely provided a more graceful escape."

"Then what, pray tell, was the fate worse than death you were talking about?"

"Working for your parents."

"That's not fair."

"That's the way you described it."

"Well, maybe I should have gone back to Tahoe. I would have been safer. Working for you, if I'm not trying to save my life, I'm defending my honor."

"Now wait just one minute. I have never made any serious attempt to deflower you."

"But the thought has crossed your mind."

"Of course it does, frequently. That doesn't mean I'm going to do anything about it."

"I know. That's why I'm still around."

"Still, I won't turn down any invitations."

"Well, don't expect any."

"I'm not."

We lapsed into a silence.

"Do you really regret coming to work for me?" Sid asked suddenly.

"No. Not in the least. I like the excitement. I can't imagine living a dull normal routine life anymore."

"Good."

There was another silence.

"Sid?"

"What?"

"Do you regret hiring me?"

"Oh, no."

"You keep saying that I'm doing things to you."

"You are. You've managed to turn my life upside-down."

"I'm sorry."

"For what? Making me think about things? For reaching out and touching me? For making me share myself with you? Lisa, you haven't got a thing to be sorry for."

Shortly after one, we stopped at a rest area to stretch and use the facilities. I always take longer than

Sid, so he was waiting for me when I came out. Smiling, he put his arm around my shoulders and suggested a short walk around the rest area before we got back to into the car. I agreed.

About halfway around, we both saw at the same time what looked like a New York model getting out of a little Fiat with the top down. I heard Sid catch his breath.

"What?" I asked.

"That is one gorgeous woman," he said softly.

He was gazing at her with more admiration than lust. Maybe that's why I reacted the way I did. I still don't know. I do know it was a very unreasonable reaction. I shrugged his arm off my shoulder.

"What's your problem?" Sid asked, genuinely surprised.

"I suppose we don't have to be in Yellowstone by dinner," I replied.

"What do you mean?"

"If you want to go pick up on her. I suppose I could find something to occupy myself."

"I was just looking at her"

"It was the way you looked at her."

Sid looked at me, uncomprehending. Then the light dawned and he chuckled.

"You're jealous."

"I am not."

"Yes, you are. It's written all over you."

"So what if I am?" I glared at him as he laughed harder. "And stop laughing. It's not that funny."

"It's hilarious."

"It is not!" Then I mumbled, "You never look at me that way."

"Why should I?"

"You think I'm ugly don't you?"

"No, I don't. I think you're pretty."

"You never said so."

"I'm saying it now. You're a pretty woman."

"Not like her."

"I'm not going to lie to you. No, you're not. But you're still good looking."

"I'll bet you've never even looked at me." Which really, was pretty ridiculous, and I knew it even as I said it. But I was in no mood to be rational.

"Alright." Sid threw his hands up in disgust. He stepped back a couple of paces and really looked at me, in a very detached manner. "Strictly physically speaking, you've got a good figure, nice hair, a nice face, a good smile, when you're smiling, and beautiful eyes. Your eyes are definitely your strong point."

"That's all?"

"What more do you want?" Sid was very frustrated. He came over to me and put his hands on my shoulders. "I'm sorry, Lisa, but you are not unutterably gorgeous. You are, however, a very very beautiful woman."

"But..."

"Lisa, what makes you beautiful has very little to do with your physical features, which are, nonetheless, very nice." He put his arm around my shoulders and walked me back to the car. "What makes you beautiful is your character, your personality."

"That sounds kind of funny coming from you," I replied, somewhat mollified.

"Why?"

"You don't seem to be terribly worried about whether or not a woman has a personality."

"I'm not. But then, the women who have no personalities that I know usually make up for it in bed."

"That's sad."

"Why?"

"To have being good in bed as your only positive quality. I don't know. It just seems like so little."

"It can be a great deal."

We fell silent and remained so until we were back on the highway.

"Sid?"

"What?"

"Does it ever occur to you that you use women for

your own personal gratification?"

Sid was unfazed. "Yes. But I don't quote unquote use anyone who doesn't want to be."

"I don't know. It just seems very selfish."

"It probably is. But then, they're using me in the same way."

"Doesn't that bother you?"

"No." It didn't.

"Why not?"

"Why should it? I'm happy, they're happy. They know that sex is all I want from them and that's all they want from me."

I frowned. "There's got to be more to it than that."

"Why?"

"Well, what about relating to them as human beings? Like we do."

"Lisa, what you and I have is an exception. You are a very unusual person in that you work on your relationships. I work with you on ours because we have to."

"Is that hard?"

"Yes, it is. I'll admit it is very rewarding, and I don't mind the work anymore. But most people don't want to work that hard on a relationship, myself, for the most part, included. I know that sounds terribly cold-hearted to you, but it is a fact of life."

"Facts of life have a nasty habit of being very brutal, don't they?" I sighed.

"Not always." He could see how depressed I was getting. "Flowers are a fact of life and they're not brutal."

"No." My spirits lifted a little.

"So is fresh fruit. Speaking of which, why don't you hand over a strawberry?"

"They're all gone."

"You don't mean to tell me you ate that entire basket full?"

"No, you ate half."

"No, I didn't."

"You did too."

"I did not. I only got, what, three?"

"Four, but whose counting?"

"That's not half the basket."

"Alright, so I got three-fourths. You've got to learn to eat faster, Sid."

"Well, you could try not inhaling everything edible within reach. Would you mind peeling an orange for me?"

"May I have some?"

"You'll probably get most of it, but alright."

I made a point of giving him most of the orange. As I peeled it, the juice ran all over.

"Orange juice is a fact of life," I moaned, trying to keep it all on the napkin.

"But it's not brutal."

"Just sticky. I'd better pop these sections straight into your mouth. You don't want to get everything all sticky."

"That would be highly distasteful."

The first section didn't quite make it all the way in. I still had the piece that didn't make it. But the juice dribbled down his chin. Laughing, Sid grabbed a tissue and wiped it off. The next piece almost went down his windpipe.

"No more throwing," he gasped, as soon as he could speak.

"I'm sorry." I was, too, though I was laughing with him. "You ready for the next section?" He nodded. "Okay, open up."

As I gently pushed the section in, his lips caught my fingers and he licked the juice off of them.

"Yuck!" I snatched my hand away.

"There are a lot of women who like that." Sid grinned mischievously.

"I know." I licked my fingers myself. "Licking is supposed to be really sexy. Well, it's just gross to me. Like French kissing. I never could figure that one out."

"You seriously don't like French kissing?" Sid

asked. "I thought you were just joking that time you told me no tongues."

"Not entirely," I said. Sid had only kissed me that one time in the entire ten months we'd known each other. It was under the mistletoe, and he'd set me up. "And believe me, I was glad you didn't."

Sid shook his head. "I'll never get you figured out. You say you like necking."

"That doesn't mean I want someone else's tongue in my mouth." I shuddered. "There was this one guy, it was just so sick. We'd barely held hands and all of a sudden he kissed me with his mouth wide open and his tongue going for my tonsils, and he was drooling and slobbering. Yick."

"How old were you?"

"Fifteen. You think I was too young or something?"

"Or something. You just weren't ready for him to intrude past your personal barriers like he did." Sid shook his head. "There are a lot of men out there who forget that sexual activity is a physical invasion of a woman's body. You have to respect that, and there are too many jerks out there who don't." [Jerk was not the term I used - SEH]

I flushed. "I'll say. Is it my imagination, or is it really true that all men think about are sex and sports?"

Sid laughed. "You're asking me that?"

"Yeah." I was serious.

Sid glanced over at me, then studied the road. "In all honesty, I have to admit I do not spend most of my time thinking about sex, and I almost never think about sports. But a lot of the men I know are obsessed with getting their rocks off one way or another. A good many of them suppress it, which is where I think the sports thing comes in. At least that's physical. Steve and Eric and Dave, you know, the guys from the gym? They are not into messing around like I am. Eric and Dave are as faithful to their wives as they come. Steve's too much of a romantic. But they're all hung up on sex, and I really think it's because of the prudish nature of our culture. They repress their sexuality and as a result, they see sex in everything."

"I repress and I don't see sex in everything."

"You're also not a man, and a large part of how manhood is defined is by the ability to perform. A woman's femininity is defined by fertility, which may be why women nurture." Sid smiled at me. "And you may say no, but you don't repress your sexuality that much. If you did, you wouldn't admit to ever having been horny or enjoying necking, and yet you do. You may deny yourself the pleasure, but you don't pretend you're not interested."

"What good would that do? It's going to come out one way or another. It's like being angry, in a way. And I am curious. It's like the French kissing thing. I mean I never understood it as an intrusion issue until you said so. I just thought it was over-rated, and I couldn't figure that out. There are a lot of things that are supposed to be sexy that I can't figure out."

"Like what else?"

"Like bucket seats. How could they be sexy with that gear shift between you?"

Sid's eyes twinkled. "Who says it has to be between you?"

"You mean two people in one seat?"

"Mm-hm." Sid's grin was knowledgeably smug and a little reminiscent.

"Well, I suppose if it reclines."

"Even if it doesn't."

"You mean you can still...you know..?"

"Mm-hm."

"That's physically impossible. Oh, geez. this is embarrassing." My face was almost purple.

Sid laughed. "Will it embarrass you too much if I tell you how it's done?"

"Probably. But I'm dying to know."

"Your problem, Lisa, is that you're limiting yourself to one position. There's no law that says you have to be lying down, face to face."

"I guess not, but..." My voice trailed off in confusion. Sid laughed, again.

"The girl sits on the guy's lap," he said, gently.

"Oh. But where do her legs go?"

"It depends on whether or not they're facing. Generally, the legs go where there's room."

"I take it you know from experience."

"Oh, yes. I remember this one girl I knew, her dad had one of those little two-seater T-birds. He'd drive to work during the day and she'd have it at night. We used to drive up to Mount Diablo. It put a lot of miles on the car, but her dad figured if we were driving so much, we couldn't be doing much else. Boy, was he wrong. On warm nights, I'd bring a blanket and we'd make love under the stars." He sighed and then looked at me. "Maybe we'd better change the subject. You look like you're about to crawl under the seat."

I shrugged. "You want some more orange?"

We got to the entrance of Yellowstone National Park around two p.m. After paying the entrance fee, we pulled over to look at tourist brochures we'd been given and figure out where we were going to stay and what we were going to do. Sid chose Old Faithful Inn simply because that was the closest to where we were. It took us almost another hour to get there because the roads were so twisted and narrow we couldn't drive all that fast. I further delayed us when I saw a small herd of elk and made Sid stop so I could take pictures. He just smiled and said I played the tourist role very well.

While we were checking in to the hotel, I noticed on the sign board that Old Faithful was about to blow.

"Come on," I said, pulling on Sid's elbow. "Let's go see it."

"I'd rather get settled first." Sid put his charge card back in his wallet.

"But you know how one thing leads to another. I don't want to take a chance on missing it."

"I seriously doubt we will. There is a reason they call it Old Faithful."

"Please?" I blinked twice.

He weakened. "But what about our luggage?"

"I can have the bellhop take it up for you while you're watching Old Faithful," said the desk clerk. "You can call for the key here when you're ready."

"Great," I said excitedly and grabbed Sid's hand. "We will."

Sid refused to be dragged, insisting instead on holding me back. His pace was maddeningly slow. Still, we joined the crowd surrounding the geyser in plenty of time.

By the time Old Faithful finished blowing, it was getting close to three fifteen. Sid made the check in call, then we got settled into our room. I suggested an early dinner. Sid wasn't all that hungry after nibbling all day in the car but agreed amiably. He didn't eat much. I did. We ate in the hotel dining room, relaxing and taking our time. It was five fifteen when we walked back into the lobby. I noticed that Old Faithful was due to blow and tried to talk Sid into watching.

"Why do you want to see it again?" he asked, chuckling.

"Why not? It'll be fun."

But as I looked outside the windows, I noticed the crowds walking away from the geyser.

"She blew early," I heard someone remark.

"Too bad," replied Sid.

I continued gazing at the people heading our way when suddenly my heart froze.

"Oh no," I gasped.

"What's the matter?" Sid asked in a low voice, sensing my urgency.

"My parents."

"What?"

"They're here."

I pointed to where Mama and Daddy were in the crowd. They were with another couple that was vaguely familiar to me. It had to be the Shakespeares.

"What the hell are they doing here?" Sid growled

in shock.

"Mama said they were coming. It's part of some timeshare thing Daddy's thinking about getting into. But Mama said they were coming next month."

"Have you talked to them since Washington?"

"No."

"Then you talked them in May," Sid snarled. "This is June. It's next month."

"Oh, help. What are we going to do?"

"Good question."

"Maybe we ought to just brazen it out."

"Do you want to try to explain to your father why we are sharing a room and wearing wedding bands and using phony names?"

I paled. "Are you kidding? He'd tear you apart in no time. Oh my god, they're coming in here."

Sid noticed an open stairway on one end of the huge room. It led to two lofts, one above the other, overlooking the lobby. We scrambled up to the uppermost loft. Just as we reached it, I looked down and saw my parents and their friends entering the lobby.

"Stay away from the edge," Sid hissed.

He pulled me back into the shadows of the dimly lit loft. I looked around. Scattered about were well-cushioned love seats and chairs.

"Damn," Sid growled. "They're coming up here."

"We're trapped." Then a ray of hope dawned. "Maybe they won't come all the way up. Mama can't stand heights."

"But what are we going to do if they come up here?"

"What are you asking me for? You're the boss."

"Real cute. We'd better ditch these rings just in case. Damn, I've never had a cover blown before."

"Wait a minute. It may not be blown." An idea congealed as I gazed about the loft.

"How?"

"Now this is going to sound like a B-rate movie, but..."

"We don't have time for lengthy explanations."

"Would you be able to recognize that couple over there if you saw them again?" I pointed to a dark corner, where two young people were necking.

"You know, I think you've got something."

"And most people wouldn't look that closely. It'd be too embarrassing."

"Hell, I don't even look." He stopped and looked at me, concerned. "You don't mind, do you?"

I swallowed. "As long as it's perfectly clear that it's strictly in the line of duty."

"Of course. Uh oh, they're coming up."

Sid and I made for the nearest dark corner.

"Let's see, my back isn't as familiar as yours, so you sit here." He sat me down facing the stairway and sat down, next to me and turned.

"You can put your hands on my face to help hide it," I said nervously. "And I'll put my arms around your neck to help hide your face."

"Good idea." And we positioned ourselves accordingly.

I looked at him.

"You won't get any ideas, now?" I asked.

"Never."

"And you won't get carried away?"

"Strictly business, I promise." He glanced over his shoulder quickly. "Here they come."

He moved in. It was strictly business, too. Thinking about it later, I got very disgusted with myself. I had always wanted to do a little necking with Sid, although I never told him. I was too afraid of what it would lead to. But there I was, necking with Sid, with a virtual guarantee that nothing would come of it and do you think I took advantage of it? No. I was too busy trying to follow my parent's movements. I strained to catch every sound I could. I peeked through half-closed eyelids.

"Now, Bill, you stay away from that edge," I heard Mama drawl.

"Althea, there's a good strong railing here," Daddy

replied. "I ain't gonna fall."

"Then don't lean over it and don't tell me not to worry. You know how I am about edges. And heights, too. I don't see why we had to come up here."

"It's a nice view." I assumed that was Bill Shakespeare.

"These men are so thoughtless," said Dottie, Mr. Shakespeare's wife. "Come on, Althea, we'll wait for them downstairs."

"Well, we'll come down with you," Daddy drawled. "This place is worse than a drive-in movie."

"Now, Bill," Dottie laughed. "Don't Althea and you want to join them?"

"This here's a public place." Daddy didn't sound in the least perturbed. "Althea and I don't need to do that kind of stuff in public."

"I wonder if he does it at all," Sid muttered.

I took a chance and kicked him in the shin.

The voices trailed away. Sid carefully looked over his shoulder.

"Okay, they're gone." He pulled away.

"Low blow, boss," I growled, still steaming.

"Alright, it was a tacky cut." He stood up. "I apologize."

"Apology accepted." I let him help me up.

We cautiously went to the head of the stairs and watched them descend. It took forever. As they got to the main floor of the lobby, they headed for the door. We took a chance and went down the stairs, just far enough to keep them in view. We came all the way down when they got into a car and drove off.

"Whew," I sighed in relief. "Oh, be calm my beating heart."

"That was too close."

"Well, we're safe."

"For how long?" Sid headed for the desk and I followed.

"It's a big park."

"Well, I'm not taking any chances. We're going to

our room now and staying there unless it's absolutely necessary to go out."

"Terrific." I sulked.

The room was small. The bathroom had only a sink, toilet, and cramped shower stall. About the only thing the room had going for it was the pair of twin beds. Sid wasn't very thrilled about sleeping in a twin-size, but he had to admit it was better than the floor.

"Shades of New Orleans," I grumbled. "We're gonna go nuts."

"They're your parents."

"It's not my fault." I sat sulking on one of the beds.

Sid gazed at me with a strange look on his face.

"What are you looking at?" I asked, grumpily.

"You. I'm trying to analyze what happened while we were necking."

"Nothing."

"Are you sure?" His tone was not challenging, more like he wanted to know.

I thought for a moment. "Yes. Nothing happened. I was too busy trying to keep track of my folks."

"Same here. In fact, I'm afraid I shortchanged you. I could have made a better effort."

"Well, it's alright by me that you didn't."

"We'd better file that little trick for future reference. It might come in handy again."

I shrugged. Gloomily, I found myself gazing at the phone. Then I got an idea.

"I'll call Mae," I said, reaching for the phone. "She'll know when they're going to leave."

"Not from that phone," interrupted Sid. "It's too easy to trace."

"Well, we've got to do something. We can't just stay here. The hotel staff'll notice and I know they'll talk."

"They'll just have to."

"Sid, Yellowstone is not the sort of place where people stay in their rooms, and it was blatantly obvious, we aren't honeymooners."

"I know. But the whole park isn't even open yet.

That increases the odds of our running into them again."

"But I have to make that drop, and there's check in."

"Alright, I'll go. They won't recognize me as easily."

"Try again. Mama'd spot you just as easily as she would me."

"What do you mean?"

"Those lovely distinctive features of yours. On top of that, Mama says you're a dead ringer for some old boyfriend of hers."

"She's never said anything to me about that."

"And she never will. In fact, I wasn't even supposed to tell you." I mimicked my mother. "'Tisn't nice."

"What?"

"Any relation to you would be probably on the wrong side of the blankets."

"Big deal."

"To Mama it is. She didn't want to cause trouble. I didn't have the nerve to tell her you were born on the wrong side of the blankets and never really cared. She did tell me the name of the gentleman in question. A John something. Caponetti."

"Hoping to track down my erstwhile father, I presume?" Sid smiled gently and shook his head. "It won't do any good. I got all my distinctive features from my mother."

"How do you know?"

"Because Stella and I look almost exactly alike, and I do have a photograph of my mother somewhere. When we get home, I'll dig it up for you."

"Oh, and your baby pictures too." I smiled happily, somehow forgetting our current dilemma.

Sid shook his head. "I have no baby pictures. We were too broke for a camera and Stella didn't care, anyway. I may have one of my senior pictures around and I've got my high school yearbooks. But that's about it. Something about being in the spy business made me rather camera shy after that."

"Wow. That's weird. You should see all the pictures of us that Mama has."

"Which is very nice, I'm sure. But speaking of your mother..."

"What are we going to do about that?" I looked at Sid hopefully.

He shrugged.

"Play a lot of cards," he said.

Later, as I was getting my nightgown and robe from my suitcase, I noticed a tuft of blonde hair sticking out of a pocket. I checked to see if Sid was looking. He was absorbed in a hand of solitaire. Smiling, I pulled the wig out and slipped it between the folds of my robe.

Before I left the bathroom, I put the wig on.

"It's all yours," I said, coming out.

"Thanks." Sid glanced up at me, then dropped the cards he was holding and stared, squinting.

"You're not going to laugh, are you?" I asked feeling very foolish.

"No." He stood, and looked at me more closely. "I think you've found the solution to our problem." He paused. "I am a little worried, though. Is that really going to get you past your parents? Keep in mind, your face is particularly familiar to them."

"Well, I also have a pair of those indoor/outdoor sunglasses and I have some tricks I can do with my makeup. I have to cover up my eye, anyway."

"That might just do the trick."

"Now, if there was just something for you." I pulled off the wig and laid it on top of my suitcase. "How long would it take you to grow a beard?"

"We'll be out of here by the time it was grown enough."

"How about glasses?"

"Well, I do have a pair, but A- I seriously doubt they'd be that effective as a disguise and B- I can't see out of them anyway."

"Why not?"

"I think it's because I've been wearing contact lenses

exclusively for so long. You have to focus differently with glasses and my eyes just won't anymore."

"It sounds to me like a bad prescription."

Sid shrugged. "Who cares? I never wear the things anyway. I hate how I look in them."

"I'll bet they're not that bad."

"That is irrelevant. I don't like how I look and that is enough."

"Could you put them on for me?"

"Why?"

"I want to see how you look in them."

"Why?"

"Because I'm curious."

"That's ridiculous."

"Come on, Sid, please."

Sid shook his head and rolled his eyes skyward, but he walked over to his suitcase.

"For crying out loud." He pulled out a simple brown eyeglass case. He slipped out the glasses and put them on. The frames were dark but very stylish. "Are you satisfied?"

"I like them. They make you look very intellectual. You really look good."

Disgusted, Sid pulled them off his face, jammed them back into the case and put the case back where it belonged.

"Sorry, it won't work. I still won't wear them, unless absolutely necessary."

"Doesn't it feel funny when you put them on with your contacts?"

"I took my lenses out while you were in the bathroom. My eyes were getting sore."

I got into bed as Sid came over to his bed and picked up the cards he'd dropped. I watched him fondly. He neatly put the deck in its box and then, looking up, somehow caught me gazing at him. We looked at each other for a long moment, then he smiled warmly and headed for the bathroom.

I had the weirdest dream that night. I was

walking down an aisle that split in the middle. One aisle led to an altar with a priest waiting and another man, my groom. The other aisle led to a platform with a group of people in caps and gowns sitting on it, my PH.D. Then out of nowhere Rory Sheidler and George Hernandez came up and took me to a park. There they each took turns kissing me. But then Sid came up and they stepped aside. Sid held me and began kissing me also, albeit more passionately. Then all three men ran away and Daddy was chasing them. I tried to hide, but I couldn't. Daddy started after me. I ran as fast as I could, but it was in slow motion. I looked back and it wasn't Daddy chasing me but an army of strange, shadowy men, all with guns. I ran even harder, but couldn't go any faster. I ran and ran.

I woke up. My legs twitched. I sat up in bed and looked around the dark room. Sid was babbling away in his sleep. He'd been doing that the whole trip, talking in sleep, that is. I'd never said anything to him about it. But I was beginning to wonder if it had something to do with why only a few of his girlfriends stayed the night. I was having enough trouble sleeping through it and I wasn't even in the same bed.

I took a deep breath, trying to calm myself. Sid rolled over and began chuckling.

"Come on, come on, come on," I heard him mutter. He sighed happily. "Oh, Lisa."

I looked at him shocked. Then I realized I'd been dreaming about him. I felt my face growing hot. He snorted and rolled over again, remaining silent. I laid back down again. Surprisingly, I fell asleep almost immediately.

If Sid had been somewhat skeptical about the wig Monday night, Tuesday afternoon he was even more so.

"Having them catch us would be bad enough," he said, about mid-morning. "If they catch you in some crazy disguise, it'll really be awkward."

"It fooled you at first."

"But A- I didn't have my contacts in and B- I wasn't expecting it."

"Well, neither are my folks. They don't know I'm here. Why should they look twice at a blonde with glasses and heavy makeup? Besides, I know some contouring tricks that'll make my face look different."

"Where did you learn that?"

"High school drama classes. I was the main make-up person."

"Well, I suppose. I still don't trust disguises. It's too hard to get out of trouble if you're caught."

"I won't get caught, then." I pulled out my makeup case.

Sid picked up his pen and folder from the nightstand.

"Well, the drop's not till tonight," he said, watching me start to apply my make-up with a disapproving eye.

"We've got check in coming up, and I'm going to call Mae."

"I don't know if you should call her at all."

"Sid, I've been gone almost three weeks. She'll be worried if I don't call soon, and she'll probably start asking questions, too."

"Alright. Do what you want." Sid sounded perturbed.

"Sid, are you alright?" I asked. "You're not getting horny already are you?"

"Oh, no." He looked at me. "I'm just feeling a little like a caged animal, I guess."

"My sympathies. I know how it feels."

Sid just shook his head and returned to his work.

The check in call was pretty standard. I hung up and called my sister.

"Hello?" Mae did sound rather distant.

"Hi, Big Sis, it's me."

"Lisa. It's about time. How are you?"

"Oh, fine. How's it going with you?"

"Really good. Of course, Darby and Janey are a little wired 'cause school's almost out and the others are picking up on it. But they haven't torn down the house yet. I figure if I can just hang on for the next three months, I'll have Ellen in kindergarten and just the twins to deal with."

"Ellen's in kindergarten already? It just doesn't seem like it's been that long since you first brought her home from the hospital."

"I was thinking the same thing last week when I registered her. Still, she doesn't start 'till September. I'm beginning to think it's going to be a long summer."

"Why?"

Mae laughed. "Just my active, healthy children. Yesterday morning I left the twins playing in the backyard while I was cleaning up after breakfast. There's nothing back there for them to get into trouble with. So, naturally, they couldn't stay there."

"Naturally. But I thought you kept the gate latched."

"I do. I don't know how, but they unlatched it. Anyway, I got this phone call from Carol Lester, they're down at the end of the block and she's having fits because Mitch is down there teasing Roddy's whippets. I went running down there to get him, wondering where Marty had gotten off to. The little rascal, he was digging up the Lesters' flower bed looking for buried treasure."

"Oh, no." I was laughing.

"For once there wasn't too much damage, thank heavens. Carol was having kittens over the whippets as it was. They baby them too much, if you ask me. It's no wonder they're so high strung, and they're so skinny, too. Ugly dogs."

"They're built for racing."

"Whatever. Anyway, when I got the boys back to the house, there was Ellen in the middle of a mess, as usual. This time she'd decided she wanted a drink of grape juice and had spilled the whole pitcherful all over the kitchen floor. When I got back, she was dropping slices of bread into the juice because she said they soaked it up just like paper towels."

"You're kidding."

"I wish. She ruined over half a loaf. And before I could clean everything up, the twins got into it and the three of them tracked grape juice onto the family room carpet. I'm thanking God they didn't go into the dining room. We're having Jack Laird's birthday party here Friday night. Granted, they're all people from the church, but you know how it is."

"Yeah, I do."

"So, where have you been? I haven't heard from you since before you went on that retreat."

"I've just been really busy. But listen, the reason I called is that I'm wondering where Mama and Daddy are. They're not in Florida or Tahoe. That's not like them to leave Tahoe at this time of year."

"Oh no, they're in Yellowstone Park. I talked to them the other day. Remember Bill and Dottie Shakespeare? They had those three boys, one of them was kind of stuck on you?"

"Oh, them." I groaned in disgust at the memory of those really awful boys. "What about them?"

"Well, Bill Shakespeare's got some big timeshare investment. I don't remember all of it, anyway, they brought Mama and Daddy out there to check it out."

"Oh. So when are they going to be home?"

"They leave Yellowstone tomorrow morning. They've got to get back to Tahoe. Mama wants me to call her again on Wednesday when they're more or less settled in."

"I might call then too. But don't tell them that. I don't know if I'll get a chance to. Look, I've gotta run. Give my love to the kids. Bye."

I hung up fast before Mae could ask any questions. I turned and looked around the big, echoing foyer I was in. A second later, my father appeared from one of the hallways. He seemed to be looking for something. When he saw me, he looked at me for a moment puzzled. He looked down the other hall, then back at me. Shaking his head, he withdrew.

I found out later, he'd heard the last couple of sentences of my phone call, had recognized my voice and come looking for me. He was surprised to find nobody but a "blonde tart". Mama insists it was his imagination, especially after what happened that night, when I went to make the drop.

My contact was Daniel Pusnell, six three, blonde hair, green eyes, football player figure. He'd been with Quickline since its inception in the 1960's and was considered the cleanest of everybody in the suspect tree. His cover was as director of concession sales, and he lived in a small cabin just outside of the National Park.

I didn't see him, or anyone else worth noting when I first walked into the bar at the Mammoth Hot Springs Hotel. I sat down at the bar and ordered a ginger ale. About twenty minutes later, Pusnell stepped up to me and asked me what I was drinking.

"Swamp water," I replied, smiling coolly.

"I've been looking for someone drinking that." He smiled.

I furtively slipped my hand into my purse and handed him the envelope.

"Now do me a favor and make tracks," I said.

"Sure thing. You might consider doing the same thing. That tall guy over at the table near the moose head has been staring at you since you walked in."

"Thanks. I'll watch out for him."

Pusnell returned to his friends, smiling and shaking his head. They laughed rather crudely. Slowly I turned to see who was staring at me. It was my father.

He was sitting with Mr. Shakespeare. They'd been friends in Tahoe, which is kind of surprising because Bill is loud and rowdy and a little radical and Daddy doesn't usually like that type. What drew them together is that they're both named after old English playwrights. Bill Shakespeare has the worst time of it, though. Very few people have heard of the Restoration playwright, William Wycherly.

I wasn't sure if Daddy recognized me. I didn't think so. But he was trying to. I knew I had to throw him off. I tried to think of the last thing I, as myself, would ever do. Hanging around Sid had certainly rubbed off on me. I put on what I thought was a sexy smile and blew a kiss at my father.

His brow wrinkled and he glared at me. I smiled again and ran my tongue along my teeth. That did it. He stopped staring. With a very affected sigh, I left the bar. When I got back to the car, I sat behind the wheel for five minutes before I could stop shaking enough to drive.

Sid laughed when I told him what happened.

"You came on to your father?" he gasped. "I don't believe it."

"That was the point," I snapped. "It was the last thing I'd ever do."

"That is priceless." Sid sank onto his bed chuckling helplessly. "I wish I could have seen it, oh, I wish."

"Well, it was pretty scary when it was happening."

"I can imagine. But to see you come on to anybody, and on top of that, your father. I wish I could have seen his face. It must have been something else."

As I thought about it, it had been. In spite of my irritation, I found myself giggling. Sid looked at me and we both burst out laughing. I hurried into the bathroom to take off my makeup and get ready for bed.

As I came out, I saw Sid sitting on the edge of his bed, dealing out a hand of solitaire onto mine. He was smiling to himself in a way that made him look particularly handsome. My camera was close at hand. I picked it up, grabbed the flash unit and retreated into the bathroom, so he wouldn't hear the faint whine of the strobe warming up. After slipping the flash unit in place, I set the shutter speed.

"I thought you were finished," I heard Sid call.

"I forgot something." I hoped he hadn't moved.

Fortunately, he hadn't. I focused quickly.

"Sid."

"What?"

In a brief second, he looked up and I released the shutter. A second later he was recoiling and blinking from the flash.

"What did you do that for?" he groaned.

"I just realized I didn't have any pictures of you."

"It's just as well."

"No, it isn't. I'd like to have a picture of you."

"There aren't any of you."

"I'm taking them all."

"Then hand over that camera."

"No."

Sid came over to me. "Why not?"

"I don't like having my picture taken."

"Neither do I. Give me the camera."

"Not now." Switching off the strobe, I walked away from him over to my suitcase. "I just washed my face and it's all blotchy, and my hair's dirty, and I'm in my nightclothes."

"Will you let me tomorrow?"

"No."

"Why not?"

"I don't photograph well. Really, I don't. I guess I just don't have that much to work with."

"Are you still bugged about that stupid woman yesterday?"

"No. I hadn't even thought about that." But suddenly, remembering the incident brought tears to my eyes. "But maybe I am. No. It's not that so much as... Well, Sid, I guess what hurt so badly was that, well, all my life I've been good looking, but not really pretty. I've been smart, but no genius. I tell you, being in the bottom half of the top ten percent is really the pits. I hate second place. I'm sick of it. At the end of my junior year in high school, I ran for senior class president. We had a run-off between me and this other guy. It was close, but he won. I just barely missed getting on the pep squad. I almost got into Chamber

Singers. The only reason I got to play Annie Oakley in Annie Get Your Gun my senior year was because the other girl who'd been cast broke her leg skiing two weeks before dress rehearsals. I didn't even get my name in the program 'cause they'd already been sent to the printer. In college, I almost got the department scholarship. My thesis was almost published. Darn it, Sid, I know I'm pretty. I'm just not pretty enough. I know I'm smart, just not smart enough. I'm good. I'm just not good enough." I sank down onto the bed sobbing.

Sid sat down next to me and put his hand on my back.

"Lisa," he said, softly. "You're good enough for me."

"Am I?"

"Yes." He reached over to my suitcase, pulled out a small travel packet of tissues and handed it to me. "We all have our moments of self-doubt. But don't give in to it. You are beautiful. You are intelligent. You're extremely competent. Based solely on the work you do with the business and with my writing, you are invaluable to me. As a friend, well, you're the only person who's ever broken through."

I sniffed and wiped away my tears. "Thanks, Sid. I just wish I had more of your self-confidence."

"You do?" He smiled gently, then looked away. "That's funny. You know, there's a reason I don't like having my picture taken, and it has nothing to do with the spy business."

"Oh, you don't think you're..."

"Not always." He looked at me. "Heaven knows I hear otherwise often enough. But I'm not convinced. I guess I have my moments too." He paused and looked away again. "There are days when I wonder if I really am that good looking, that good of a writer or spy, if I'm really that good in bed."

I couldn't reply. I knew how much it had cost him to say what he had. Wordlessly, I put my arms around him and laid my head on his shoulder. He slipped his arm closest to me around my waist and with his other hand, stroked my cheek. Gently, he rubbed his cheek across my hair. I felt his gentle kiss on the top of my head. His hand slid to my chin. He lifted it and my head to face him.

"I'd better get ready for bed," he said, quietly.

I released him. Sorrowfully, he got up. He paused for a moment, then shook his head and went to get ready for bed. Frustrated, for some reason, I grabbed my book of Victorian poets and turned to Tintern Abbey. I flopped face down on my bed, yawned, and began to read. I heard the shower going in the bathroom.

I was barely a third of the way through the poem when I began to nod off. Soon, it was impossible for me to keep my eyes open, or to make sense of what I was reading. Strange images filled my head; of the abbey, the grassy fields, cliffs, and Sid in Dickensonian dress.

I was only dimly aware of the book being removed from my hands, of being lifted by strong, gentle arms and set down again. I curled up comfortably. The hands returned again, this time deftly removing my robe. I was lifted again. I snuggled in. My forehead and my cheek rested against flesh. It was warm and smooth. I was laid back down again and the blankets were pulled gently over me. A hand tenderly removed the hair from my face and brushed against my cheek. Then his lips caressed mine, tenderly, gently, warmly. They were soft and I reached for more.

I opened my eyes and found myself looking into his beautiful blue eyes as he pulled away.

"I'm sorry," he said, very softly. "I didn't mean to wake you. But you looked so lovely."

I reached out and touched his cheek. My fingers brushed over the beard that was just barely starting to come in, to the softness just above it.

"You are beautiful," I replied. His hand covered mine and pulled it down to his lips. Gently, he kissed the backs of my fingers. "Maybe a little too beautiful," I continued. "For my own good. Goodnight, Sid."

He kissed my fingers one more time before releasing them.

"Don't worry." He smiled gently. "Not without your permission. Goodnight, Lisa."

I rolled over, perilously close to saying yes. Later that night I dreamed I had. I don't remember much of the dream, just his warm, gentle kisses.

[And all I could think of that night was how wonderful it felt just to hold you next to me. It's funny, for all you said you were on the brink of giving in, I knew you were nowhere near ready, and I couldn't understand why, but it didn't bother me. Many other times that trip, I felt frustrated and fearful that we would not have our consumation, but not then - SEH]

June 8 - 11, 1983

One of the things that really amazed me about Sid that trip was his ability to act as if nothing had happened the morning after one of those wonderful, frustrating moments of closeness that kept popping up. I would be very subdued, but Sid would tease me out of it by the end of breakfast. Well, not that Wednesday. I remained somewhat lackluster until mid-morning. We got on a tour bus right after breakfast, having decided that the odds were against running into my folks since they were leaving.

We were at the Fountain Paint Pots when Sid insisted on having his turn with the camera.

"You sure you know how to work it?" I asked, reluctantly handing it over. "This isn't surveillance photography, you know. I've only got one hundred A.S.A. film in there."

"I've been playing around with all kinds of photography for years," said Sid, checking the light. "I always figured if I was going to be freelancing, it would be worthwhile to be able to take my own pictures. Why don't you sit... here on this rail."

I did as he asked. "So why aren't you into it now?"

He shrugged. "I mostly write business articles, and most magazines would rather use their own art for that. Now put your hands here and lift your chin." His finger softly did the lifting. He stepped back and fussed with the light meter and focus ring. "Alright, now, smile. Think of something fun, like sex."

"Oh!" Caught off guard, I ducked my head, covering my face with my hand. But I was laughing.

"Come on," he coaxed. "Let me see your face."

"I'm blushing. Why do you do that to me?"

"What did I do?" He was so innocent.

"You know darned well you told me to think about sex just to make me blush."

"You're so cute when you do." Then more gently, he said, "You're also smiling now."

"What?" I looked up involuntarily.

Sid removed the camera from in front of his face and smiled.

"Beautiful," he said, quietly.

I found myself almost mesmerized by his piercing blue eyes. I had to look the other way. His hand touched mine as I slid off the rail.

"Why don't we check out what's down this path?" he said, jovially.

I stopped him.

"How do you do it?" I asked.

"What?"

"We have moments. They're incredible. They've been happening ever since New Orleans, at least. But the moment passes and the next thing I know you're acting like it never happened."

"Oh, they've happened, alright." Sid leaned on the rail and gazed at the gurgling geyser pots. "But I have to bury my feelings. What I feel for you, I cannot deal with right now, any more than you can deal with your feelings for me." He paused. "I'm sorry. I had no right to speak for you."

"Maybe not. But you're right. I don't know what's happening to us, but whatever it is, it's happening way too fast. I'm having a terrible time coping with it. I don't understand my feelings right now."

"Me, neither. But it's not just lust anymore."

"Please. Don't try to put a name on it. You think we can't cope now..." I bit my lip as a new thought occurred to me. "Maybe, when we get home, I'd better ask Henry to have me reassigned."

"No. Please don't." Sid walked over to me with a

strange urgency. "At least not right away. Seriously, I think a lot of this is our current situation. We've been living very closely together. But when we get back home, we'll have all our old distractions and friends. I'll have more accessible women. You'll have your boyfriends."

"Okay. I see what you mean. But maybe our next trip, we'd better find another cover."

"That might not be a bad idea." Sid put his arm around me and guided me up the path. "We'd better get back to the bus before we get left."

One nice thing about the weirdness that was going on was that Sid started being extra nice to me. The tour bus driver told us about this Old West barbecue at the park. The only way to get to it was to ride a horse or in wagons. Although, Sid adamantly refused to ride a horse, he consented to going to the event, and he let me sign up for a horse.

That was before he made his check in call. He came back to the room with a scowl so threatening and dark it could only mean misfortune of the gravest kind.

"What's wrong?" I asked.

"We have to leave tomorrow morning," he said.

"Isn't there going to be a second drop?"

"No. They believe they have something, so they're stepping up the schedule."

"That can't be all."

"That's just it. The Dragon didn't say anything else. But there was a lot more to be said. She sounded nervous. It was nothing I could put my finger on, but she wanted off the phone."

That really put a damper on the evening. At least, I got a couple good gallops in.

We left early the next morning, actually getting a flight out of Jackson Hole to Denver and from there we just barely made the connecting flight to Flagstaff, Arizona, and from there got a shuttle to park. We were settled into our hotel room at the Grand Canyon by five o'clock.

We got lucky again and got "stuck" with a double: two full sized beds. There was a sink in the room, but the baths, showers, and toilets were down the hall. While Sid was making his second shave, I thumbed through the schedule of events.

"You want to take the all-day mule ride?" I asked. "It goes all the way to the bottom of the canyon."

"No."

"How about the half-day trip?"

"It's not the time involved, but the mules that I object to."

"But don't you want to go down into the canyon?"

"I could live without it. But if I have to, I'd prefer to walk."

"Great. They've got an early hike on the Kaibab Trail, or we could take Bright Angel all the way down even earlier and come up Kaibab. That's an all day hike, but we're in good shape."

"Remember that the next time I wake you up to go running."

"Boy, if you weren't shaving."

"Don't know yet."

"Hm. Why don't I just brief you now?"

"Okay. Who do we have?"

"Amanda Whitefoot. Black hair, brown eyes, five seven. She has a P.O. box and lives on the local reservation. She handles the public relations for Bright Angel Lodge. She has a small problem with mobility, but has an otherwise good record."

"Sounds good." He wiped off his face, then turned and smiled at me. He was wearing jeans, but his lightly tanned chest was bare.

"What are we going to do tomorrow?" I asked.

"I'd rather know what we're going to do about dinner."

"How about the coffee shop?" I suggested. "The only other restaurant in this hotel is a steak house, which I admit sounds rather attractive to me."

Sid shook his head. "It would. I bet you also like

your steaks rare."

"And still mooing." I grinned mischievously.

"Disgusting." Sid picked up his shirt, the blue one that I'd made. "Let's try the coffee shop. I should at least be able to get a salad."

"Okay," I sighed exaggeratedly.

"Alright. I'll compromise. The steak house some other night. Hopefully, they have seafood."

Just before check in, we decided to go ahead and hike the next day, depending on when the drop would be set up. Sid figured that the less we hung around the hotel, the safer we were. The Dragon agreed, especially since we would not be making any drops for the time being. I took that as a sign that they had pretty much caught their leak, although both of us knew better than to ask. If we had a need to know, we'd be told.

I was quite happy and talked Sid into an extended all-day hike, which meant we had to buy the things we needed for the hike. We were okay on clothes and shoes, but we needed water bottles, knapsacks, hats, and snacks. The last two items, Sid questioned. Well, he didn't question the need for a hat, just the one I chose for him, a cowboy hat.

"I despise western wear," he growled.

"It's not all that bad," I replied. "It's more dignified than those baseball caps."

"Why not this?" Sid pulled a tweed alpine hat off the shelf.

"An alpine hat in the Grand Canyon? Come on."

"It's more my style." He tried it on and examined the effect in the mirror.

"That wool is going to be miserably hot and the brim is so narrow it defeats the whole purpose of having one." I pulled it off his head and replaced it with a natural colored straw western hat. "There, that's light weight and it'll give you plenty of shade."

Sid sighed as he adjusted it. "Whatever. I guess if I don't have to look at myself in it."

"Don't worry, you look great." I pushed him away

from the mirror and tried a similar hat on for myself. "If you start smiling, I might just throw myself at you."

"No such luck." He did smile, but he took the hat off.

The snacks proved to be another obstacle.

"I gave in on the granola bars," said Sid, firmly. "I gave in on the cheese, but all natural or not, these crackers are out. They're loaded with salt."

"And it's a darned good thing they are, too," I retorted, equally firm. "Do you want to get dehydrated? They aren't kidding when they say it's hot down in the canyon. I've hiked it before. It's no pleasure walk."

"Then why are we doing this?"

"Because it's a lot of fun when you're adequately prepared. But not having enough water or even the right stuff and it's a killer."

"Hm."

"Don't worry, it's not that bad, and we're in good shape."

Sid chuckled. "I'm not worried. I'm just fascinated by the risks you choose to take."

"What?"

"Never mind. It's just another one of your inconsistencies."

I just shrugged and slipped a can of beef jerkies into our growing load then went to eat dinner at the coffee shop.

We were up at the head of the trail just before dawn. As the sun rose, I got a beautiful picture of Sid and the rim silhouetted against the bright colors of the sky. As soon as there was light to see, we were on our way.

We climbed out again shortly after four.

"That's the rotten part about hiking in this canyon," I said, slowly stretching out. "The hard part gets saved for last."

Sid finished off a long drink of water.

"I presume you mean the climb back up," he said, breathing heavily. "They're right. The air is thinner up here."

"But it's fresh." I headed for the road. "Come on, we've got a long walk back."

Sid sighed, took off his hat, wiped off his forehead with the back of his hand and replaced the hat. He smiled at me.

"That was quite a hike," he said.

We heard a car approach. Sid stopped walking and faced it, holding his thumb out.

"Will you stop clowning around?" I giggled.

"Who's clowning around?" Sid flashed a smile at me. "I'm tired."

"Sid. Hitchhiking is dangerous."

"It's not that bad." The car passed without slowing. We continued walking. "Besides, the likelihood of the enemy knowing that we're on this road at this moment in time is pretty slim."

"I don't want to chance it."

"Relax. I've never had anything happen to me, and until I got my money that's mostly how I got around."

Sid tried to thumb down yet another car. It didn't stop. A third car did.

"Come on," Sid said, as we trotted down the road to where the car had stopped.

It was a station wagon with Wisconsin license plates loaded with camping gear and three college students: two guys and one girl. The girl was behind the wheel, one guy was in the front passenger seat and another was sitting in the back seat with his back to the door and his legs along the width of the seat. The guy in the front rolled down his window, as we approached. We could hear the rock music while we were still fifty feet away. Unperturbed, Sid walked up to the open window.

"Hi," he said. The girl turned down the radio.

"You guys look like you could use a lift," said the guy.

"Sure could," replied Sid. "We've been hiking all day. You headed for the village?"

"We sure are, hop in." The young man turned around and swatted his companion's legs. "Hey, Brett, move over."

Yawning, Brett sat up straight. Sid opened the door.

"After you, my dear," he said to me gallantly.

Still, hesitant, I got in. Sid climbed in after me and shut the door. The car pulled back onto the road.

"Hi, I'm Stan," said the guy in the front seat, twisting to face us. "That's Margie driving and Brett back there with you. You'll have to excuse Brett. He's been smoking too many of those funny cigarettes."

"Stan," groaned Margie, slapping his leg. "Will you quit saying that? You know Brett doesn't do drugs."

Stan chuckled.

"I just haven't slept since we left Madison," grumbled Brett, yawning. Clearly, the trip wasn't agreeing with him.

"I'm Ed and this is Janet," Sid said. "Where you guys headed eventually?"

"We're making the grand tour of the western half of the U.S," answered Stan. "This is our second real stop. We stayed in Denver a couple nights. After here it's Vegas, then California. We're going to Disneyland, Hollywood, the Sequoias, San Francisco, Tahoe, Crater Lake..."

"That's in Oregon," interrupted Margie. "And we're stopping in Ashland first. Besides, they don't want to hear every little place we're going."

"Camping all the way?" asked Sid.

"Half and half," replied Stan. "and half. We've got relatives in some spots, we're staying in motels in others and camping. We're staying at a motel in Vegas."

"I hope so," said Brett.

"You guys camping?" Stan asked us.

"Fortunately, no," replied Sid. "We're staying at Bright Angel Lodge."

"Bright Angel?" asked Margie. "Isn't that the where they had all that trouble this morning? We heard it on the radio."

"Trouble?" I asked, getting worried.

"One of the employees got the you-know-what kicked out of her," said Stan. "A couple of hoods worked her over in her office. It was just luck that a couple guests heard the racket and barged in on them. They had to airlift her to Flagstaff."

"That's too bad," replied Sid, casually. But I could see he was afraid of the same thing I was. "Did they catch the hoods?"

"Nope. It had to be drugs," said Stan. "That whole business is so stupid. I know a couple of guys at the dorms in Madison who are pharmacy students. They're strung out half the time on Tylenol and codeine. They're just barely passing. How, I don't know."

"You ought to see the idiots on my floor," said Margie. "They're smoking grass in the hallway, right under the smoke alarm and it's not like it's that easy to miss."

"That's what smoking that stuff will do to you," agreed Sid.

We arrived at the village shortly after that. Our ride was nice enough to drop us off in front of the Lodge. We discreetly asked a few questions about that morning's accident and found out that Amanda Whitefoot had indeed been the victim, and that she was still kicking. They hadn't found the two men responsible. Sid and I didn't think they would.

Sid insisted on checking in himself and told the Dragon everything. He was not happy as he hung up.

"Well?" I asked when we got back to the room.

"We stay until Sunday," he said, scowling again. "At least, that's the plan. Not making that second drop in Yellowstone triggered something, but the Dragon didn't say what."

"That's nice. Does this mean we have to stay cooped up again?"

"We were specifically requested not to, unfortunately. But I think we will stay wired, and you can carry your gun in your purse. I don't think I can get away with a blazer." Sid sat down glumly on his bed. "I was thinking of skipping out tonight by myself, but I don't think that would be a good idea."

"There's always Sunday morning," I said.

"I don't think you want to listen in on me. Besides, how am I going to hide the transmitter?"

"So don't use it. I'm sure a couple of hours isn't going to hurt, especially during the day."

"Well, we'll see."

Saturday, I got depressed. Very depressed. That trip I'd been at times a little blue, lackluster, crying and even out of it. But Saturday, I was hit by a depression as deep as the Grand Canyon and as dark as a night in the desert. I was feeling fine when I woke up, not even tense really, but as I was getting dressed, after a shower down the hall, it enveloped me like a huge black sheet and took over.

The worst of it was, I couldn't figure out for the life of me what was causing it. It wasn't the tension of the situation. I was worried about it, but not in a depressed sort of way. It wasn't Sid. He'd been very sweet the night before, offering to eat at the steak house. Unfortunately, we weren't able to get in at a reasonable hour, so we went elsewhere. Sid made reservations for Saturday night at seven thirty just to be sure. I knew he didn't want to eat there that much, so I was pleased by the effort he made to make sure we got in. We weren't close that night. If anything, Sid was a little distant, but still very pleasant to be around.

Trying to put a finger on what was depressing me only depressed me more. I shoved my feelings aside and went back to the room. I guess I was hoping my mood would just go away.

I should have known better, and to make matters worse, Sid was very distant and touchy to boot. He didn't seem to notice me and my mood at all. In all fairness, I was working very hard at hiding it. But the perverse nature of the mood was such that I began to get a little irritated at Sid for not noticing.

At lunch, I more or less picked a fight with him. It was a little too easy. We were in the cafeteria. Sid held a table for us while I ordered.

"Well, here we are," I said, all but slapping the tray onto the table. I handed him my sandwich. "You get turkey, no mayonnaise, on whole wheat, and milk."

Sid morosely unwrapped the paper.

"This is roast beef, rare roast beef."

"That's mine." I traded sandwiches and plopped a carton of milk in front of him. Sid looked at it, then glared at me.

"This is whole milk. You know I only drink non-fat."

"Well, that's all they had, so tough. I know plenty of people who'd be more than happy to have that."

"I know. I was a deprived child once, too. I still don't want it."

"You are so picky. It's disgusting. Can't you be happy with what you've got?"

"Will you leave me alone?"

"Alright, what's eating you?"

Disgusted, Sid laid his sandwich down looked away, then glared at me.

"No-one," he said, extremely irritated. "That is the problem."

It took me a minute to figure out what he meant.

"That is sick," I replied, blushing and angry and still not completely sure what was involved.

"Tough. I would have thought by now you'd be able to pick up on the signals and have some sensitivity."

"You're a fine one to talk. All you think about is yourself and your needs. Well, what about mine?"

"I'm not the one saying no."

"See what I mean? That's the only need you ever acknowledge. I've got other needs too, you know. I operate on more than one level. I'm not just a physical person."

"I am sorry. But in my current condition, I cannot

deal with this.”

“Then why don’t you just go out tonight?”

“Not tonight.”

“Then tomorrow, while I’m at church.”

“It’s too dangerous.”

“Well, it’s better than this. You’re not livable when you’re this way.”

Sid looked at me, then sighed. “Alright. But while I’m gone, you stay away from the rim.”

We finished eating in silence. Sid’s mood picked up a little, now that there was light at the end of the tunnel. Mine got worse. Later that afternoon, I went shopping while Sid checked in. Our transmitters were on and functioning. I thought I heard him hang up the phone without saying anything. I backed into a corner and put my face into a book.

“What’s going on?” I hissed into the transmitter.

“No answer,” grumbled Sid.

“Oh no.”

“Don’t panic. It doesn’t mean anything yet. I’m going to relax in the lounge.”

The souvenir shop was only across the hall. It was a little confusing dealing with the noise from the lounge at the same time as the noise from the shop. I managed by tuning out the lounge somehow.

It was impossible to tune out the woman’s voice, though. It was a little before five when it sounded in my ear, deep and sensual. She was talking to Sid, however.

“I notice you’re alone,” she said.

“I am.” Sid’s voice was receptive.

“Looking for some company?”

“I could be. What kind...” The sounds of Sid’s voice and the lounge faded out.

I had a feeling I knew why Sid had turned his transmitter off, but the way things were, I didn’t feel it would be a good idea to bank on that. I put the mug I’d been looking at down on its shelf and went over to the lounge. From where I stood in the doorway, I could see Sid sitting sideways at a table. Across from him was a casually dressed woman. She was rather pretty but had a hard look about her. Sid had his wallet in his hands. He held it low, underneath the table top and removed a bill. After casually shoving the wallet back into his jeans, he slipped the bill under the table to the woman. She looked at it and smiled.

I nearly wretched. It had never occurred to me that was how Sid was meeting his needs. Thinking about it, it made sense. Shaking, I left the lounge.

"Sorry about that." Sid's voice in my ear made me jump. "I didn't think you'd want to listen in."

"I figured. Thanks." I spoke softly and headed down the hall. "Um, I'm going back to the room."

"Are you alright?"

"Fine. I'm just tired."

"What about dinner?"

"You go on without me. I'm not hungry."

Inside the room, I sat down on the bed. As ugly as I found the situation, I knew I had no right to condemn Sid for it. The action maybe. But I still had to accept it as a part of his life and continue actively caring for him. It wasn't easy for me to accept. That's why I'd gone back to the room, so I could work it out in my head before I faced him. I didn't get much of a chance. Less than three minutes later, I heard the key in the lock and Sid came in.

"What's the matter?" he asked, concerned.

"Nothing. Please just leave me alone for a bit." I couldn't look at him.

"Sorry. You don't leave me alone. I reserve the same right."

"Please. I'm trying to work something out."

"What?"

"Will you?"

"Something is bothering you."

"It's not that bad."

"You can't tell me you're not hungry and expect me to believe it's not that bad."

"Alright, it is. But it's something I've got to work

out myself."

"No way. You wouldn't let me get away with a stunt like that. I'm not going to let you. Now spill it."

Miserable, I took a deep breath. "When you turned off the transmitter, I got concerned and went to the door of the lounge. I saw you hand her some money."

"So?"

"You're paying her to... you know."

"You knew that's how I've been getting it, didn't you?"

I shook my head.

Sid shrugged. "Oh. I thought you knew, or at least figured it out. I keep forgetting how naive you are. Sorry about the rude awakening."

"Sid, please."

"What are you so upset about? I'll admit it's a little on the sordid side."

"A little? It's repulsive!" I blurted out. "It's bad enough you use women the way you do. But that. It's the most degrading, selfish-"

"Now, you just hold on one minute, little lady," Sid snapped. "Get off your high horse right now and start facing some facts. One, I am horny and I am very limited at the moment as to how I can relieve it. Two, hookers are people too, and they don't particularly get any big kick out of the way they make their living. But for a lot of them, it's the only way they can. It's either hustle or starve. Three, hookers are also very efficient. At the moment, I don't have time to seduce someone. I've got to get it where I can find it and get it fast. Four, as for being selfish, I don't suppose it occurred to you that I might have something to offer them. Women like me for a reason."

"Oh, come on. You don't honestly expect me to believe your primary motivation is to make some hooker feel good. You said it yourself - get it where you can find it and get it fast. You're just out there to satisfy yourself."

"I care about my partners."

"Yeah, but when you're doing it, you're not thinking about them. You're thinking about how good you're feeling, and nothing else."

"You don't know the first thing about it."

"I know enough."

"No, you don't. You have no idea." He glared at me, his eyes blazing, and his voice got soft and even. "You don't know what it is to want and I mean want so badly it hurts."

I stood my ground. "You're wrong, Sid. If there's one thing I do know, it's want. I'm very good at that."

Suddenly, his manner changed. His eyes were still intense, but not with anger.

"Yes, I believe you are," he said softly. He shook his head, then fixed his eyes on me. "This is ridiculous. We are responsible adults. We desire, we crave each other. Why are we saying no to ourselves?"

"You know very well why." But I was beginning to wonder myself.

"It's not like there isn't anything between us." He took a step towards me, his eyes pleading. "Lisa, please, will you let me make love to you?"

I couldn't answer. I couldn't even look away. Sid slowly moved closer.

"Please?" he asked.

His arms slid around me, across my back, with his hands up into my hair. I held him, enjoying the feel of his solidness. His mouth kissed mine with a fire unlike anything else I had ever known.

Somewhere in the back of my mind, a little voice reminded me that this was not right. Big help that was. I had always figured the moment would come when Sid's desire would overwhelm my better judgment and it had arrived with a vengeance. The poor man was desperate, so why not get it over with?

"It's time," he whispered, his voice thick and husky. "I promise I'll take very good care of you. It's going to be beautiful."

Again, he kissed me, and nervously, I held him.

One of his arms dropped and he picked me up and carried me to my bed, his mouth still on mine. Gently, gazing into my eyes he laid me down and smoothly laid down next to me, then halfway on top of me. One of his arms remained underneath my shoulders, the other hand gently caressed my face.

He kissed my mouth again, and I tasted his tongue as it lightly slipped between my teeth. I still didn't like it much, but it was part of it all, so I went along with it. He pulled away and looked tenderly into my eyes, his hand brushing the hair away from my face.

"Please relax, Lisa," he said, very softly. "It'll be so much easier for you."

Taking what deep breaths I could, I tried to relax and calm my trembling limbs.

Sid's gentle kisses followed my jaw back to behind my ear.

"I won't hurt you," he whispered. "Just relax."

He kissed my mouth again.

"Relax," he whispered again, but this time there was a touch of urgency in his voice.

I concentrated solely on that one word, trying to forget anything else. I could feel myself loosening.

"That's good," he whispered. "Hold me. Keep relaxing."

I put my arms around him, as he continued kissing and caressing me. Effortlessly, he rolled us onto our sides. His hands gently rubbed my back. It felt good, soothing. I let myself enjoy it and tried to kiss him back as he kissed me. I didn't realize he was pulling my t-shirt out of my pants. He rolled me back onto my back. His kisses worked their way down my neck and along my collar bone.

"Nice and relaxed," he whispered. "You're doing good.

His hand slipped under my t-shirt just below my ribs. The shock of his soft warm hand on my skin made me stiffen.

"Dammit, will you relax!" He fiercely pulled away.

"I'm trying." I started to cry. "I'm trying."

He looked at me tenderly, but all the passion was gone.

"Yes, you are," he said very softly. He bent and gently kissed my lips. It was gentle and inviting and I tried to respond, but his tongue hit my teeth. He sighed as he pulled away. "It's no use." He sat up. "You're worse than a cold shower."

As I rolled over, sobbing uncontrollably, I felt Sid's hand on my shoulder.

"Lisa, I'm sorry," he said, urgently. "I didn't mean it that way."

"I don't care how you meant it." I was even more miserable than I had been. "How'd you like to be frigid?"

"But you're not." His strong gentle arms picked me up and held me close to him. "The passion is there. I touched it. It's just locked away for the time being. I was a fool to push you."

"And I was a fool for falling," I sniffed.

He lifted my chin and smiled warmly.

"Looks like we both blew it," he said softly.

I sniffled. Sid reached over to the bedside table and grabbed a tissue.

"Here you go," he said quietly.

I took the tissue and blew my nose, while he held me and kissed the side of my head.

"You want to try again?" I asked.

"Oh, no. One failure is all I can handle." He looked at his watch. "It's time to get going anyway. You've got just enough time to wash off your face."

"For what?"

"Dinner."

"Oh. I almost forgot." I scrambled off the bed and tucked in my shirt. I looked back at Sid. His face was unreadable, but he did look rather forlorn. I realized that as bad as I felt about what had happened [or not happened - SEH], he must have felt worse. His ego had probably taken quite a beating from my inability to respond. [Actually, I was berating myself for pushing you - SEH] But there wasn't anything I could say.

He couldn't find anything to say, either. In silence, we walked to the dining room. In silence, we ate most of our dinner.

A woman played a harp at one end of the room, accompanied by a young man on guitar. They did instrumentals of mostly contemporary music. It underscored our silence nicely.

We were almost through our meal when I recognized the melody she was playing. I looked at Sid.

"I know that song," he said, thoughtfully. "Now, what is it?"

"Send In the Clowns," I replied.

We looked at each other. At the same time, we both started breaking up. I think we just sat and laughed for about five minutes solid.

"Was that a farce?" Sid asked, as the laughter finally began to subside.

"Oh, it was awful," I giggled. "I hope you're not too mad at me."

"Why?"

"Because you couldn't... I don't know... Melt me down, I guess."

"That's not your fault. It's good that you're that committed to your values. I know better than to try making it with a woman like you. That's why I don't usually fail. Don't worry, I'm not in the least bit mad." He paused as a new thought occurred to him. "Actually, I'm relieved."

"Relieved?"

"Yeah. I think we proved to ourselves that a sexual relationship between us is just not going to work, at least not for the time being. And neither of us is at fault, really."

"I guess so. It does kind of let the pressure off, doesn't it? Now we're free to be just friends."

The waitress came and took our order for dessert. I was surprised when Sid requested a cup of de-caf. He wasn't surprised when I asked for a slice of fresh peach pie a la mode.

"Um, this is going to sound a little strange," I said when the waitress had gone. "But do you still... You know, want me?"

"Oh, yes." Sid reached out and touched my cheek. "Very much. In some ways, more than ever. But it's different now. I know the damage it can cause. I may never make love to you. Before this, the thought was unbearable. Now, it doesn't bother me. I'd still like to. But if I never find the key to your mental chastity belt, then what we've got right now will be enough."

"Thanks. I needed to hear that." I paused. "I think it's only fair to tell you I know what that key you're looking for is."

"What?"

"Marriage and that includes fidelity."

He sighed, then looked at me. "That's asking a lot. I don't think I could."

"To be honest, I'm glad. I really don't want to be married, at least not now. My independence is very important to me. And there's also the fact that you're not Catholic. It's no big deal now, but when you're married, man, those values, they're everything."

"Hm. I suppose they would be."

The waitress arrived with my pie and Sid's decaf. Sid pulled her aside and whispered in her ear. She smiled and nodded. He slipped something into her hand.

"You're going to be busy tonight," I said, my voice far snider than I'd intended.

"What? Oh. No. My appointment is for tomorrow morning, and I think I will be keeping it. What I slipped to the waitress was for something entirely different."

"I'm sorry. I guess I'm still uncomfortable with the idea of you buying it. I've just got to get used to it. It's a part of you, and I've got to accept it as such."

"If it'll make you feel any better, it's not my favorite way to go. I rarely do it. They're hard women and not terribly willing to let go. It's not a lot of fun always, but it's adequate."

"I'm sorry."

"For what? For being yourself?"

"No. For you, for having to deal with it. I'm trying to understand."

"So am I, my dear little ice-maiden."

"I'm sorry I'm so cold."

"I only called you that because you're not." He leaned over and gently kissed my lips. I softly returned it. He smiled. "Yes, it's there. It's just not mine. Yet."

I chuckled. The harp began to play "You and Me Against the World". I looked over at Sid. He nodded. I smiled at him. Then, impulsively, I leaned over and kissed his gentle mouth.

June 12 - 13, 1983

Sundays, Sid lets me skip running and sleep in. That Sunday I woke up early with a familiar dull ache in my lower abdomen. I tried sleeping through it, but it had to get messy, and wouldn't you know, Sid had to come back in after his run.

"Awake already?" he asked, with an amused grin. He was wearing a tank top and running shorts instead of a warm up suit, even though it seemed fairly cool out. Then again, that was probably why he wasn't sweating like a horse.

"Uh, yeah." I pulled the covers to my chin. "You going to be here long?"

"My appointment's not 'til eight, and I wasn't going to shower until after."

"I guess if you're paying, she can't complain." I was more interested in my robe, which was at the foot of the bed because I knew I'd stained, and that was more embarrassing than I was ready to handle.

Sid sniffed his armpit. "I'm okay." He still grabbed a towel and rubbed down.

I wasn't doing too well. Keeping my covers over me, I sat up and got my robe. It was a bit of a struggle getting it on without sitting on it and making things worse and still not letting Sid see anything, and by that point, he'd figured something was up and was watching. I got my clothes and my carry on.

"Wearing your jeans today?" Sid asked. He rinsed a washcloth out in the sink.

"I can still stay fully armed," I replied. "I'll strap my twenty-two to my shin like you do."

"True." Sid wrung out the washcloth and turned off the water.

"Don't!" I yelped as he lifted the covers to my bed.

"I thought that's what I saw." He pulled the covers back to reveal the stain. "Well, it's about time. I was getting ready to put a candle in the window." He went to work.

"You don't have to make it any more embarrassing than it is," I grumbled.

"What's embarrassing about it?" he asked. "It's just a natural process."

"So is going to the bathroom, and I seem to remember you getting pretty grossed out when I unplugged that toilet of yours."

"That's..." Sid looked up at me and smiled. "You've got a point. However, the one is merely waste." He pointed at the stain. "This can be considered a celebration of fertility."

"Since when are you so interested in fertility?"

"Yours I have no problem with." He chuckled. "You know, you could look at this as evidence that your virginity has been lost. It's the traditional sign, you know."

"Hm." I squeezed my legs together, thinking that I really needed to be going.

Sid looked at me. "Are you still feeling upset about something?"

"I'm not depressed anymore, but my cramps are pretty bad, and don't lay any psychosomatic BS on me, okay?"

"I wasn't planning on it. I am sensitive to the needs of women."

"Then why don't you have a trash can in your bathroom? That's why your toilet got plugged, you know." I started feeling really messy. "Listen, I've got to get going. Figures this month would be a gusher."

"I'll meet you back here at nine thirty. And stay away from the rim."

We spent most of the day reading. Around a

quarter til three, we found a pay phone and I made the check in call. I swallowed when it wasn't answered after the first two rings. I let it go a little longer.

"What's up?" Sid asked, a little nervous himself.

"No answer." I held on, hoping. "It's gone at least ten rings." I hung up. "It's the second time."

Sid checked his watch. "It's early yet. Maybe she's just not there."

We called again right at three, then at five after, and ten after. At a quarter after, Sid hung up the phone, his face as pale as a ghost.

"Nothing," he said softly. He took a deep breath. "We've got to get out of here."

I touched his arm. "Sid-"

Glaring, he laid his finger on my lips. "From this moment on, Sid Hackbirn and Lisa Wycherly are dead. You and I are now Janet and Ed Donaldson."

"I know."

He nodded sadly. I managed to hold my tears until we got inside the room. As soon as Sid closed the door, I sank onto my bed and sobbed.

"We've got to get packed and out of here now," said Sid urgently.

"I'm never going to see my family again," I cried.

"That's not for certain." Sighing, Sid sat down next to me and held me. "We'll find a way to go back to being ourselves. We just can't count on it is all. I know it's going to be hard. But you'll have to cry later. We've got to go now."

"I know." I tried pulling myself together. "Just give me a couple minutes, will you?"

"Sure." His lips softly pressed against my hair.

I got a tissue. "I suppose it could be worse. It's not like we don't have feelings for each other, but I just don't want to be married."

"It's the last damn thing I want," Sid grumbled.

"Well, you don't have to make it out to be something really awful," I snapped.

"It's not. Except..." He turned away. "You can't be

a real wife."

I bit my lip. "Can you be a real husband?'

Sid gave me his only too obvious look. "I don't think there's any question about my interest in that issue."

"I didn't mean conjugally. There's a lot more to marriage than just sex."

Sid picked up his suitcase and set it on his bed.

"I suppose there might be," he grumbled. "What are you thinking of?"

"A relationship for starters."

"Didn't you just imply that we have one?" Frustrated, he jammed some socks into the case. "I mean, I'd like to think the past few weeks would count for something."

"Of course they do." I fidgeted with my tissue. "It's mostly just..."

"Just what?"

"Will I be the only one?" My voice grew small and uncertain.

Sid stepped back. "Oh. That."

"Well?"

"Believe me, after what we've been through and as close as we've become, anyone else wouldn't mean a damn thing."

"Then why not just be faithful?"

"If you weren't around for some reason." Frustrated, Sid went back to packing. "Why is it so important that I be faithful anyway? I'm not expecting it from you, although I have to admit, I find it a little hard to imagine you sleeping around."

I grimaced. "I couldn't. Our sex life should be something very special and unique."

"What makes you think it won't be?"

"How will I know it is?"

Sid chuckled lecherously. "You'll know."

"Really? And how will I know that the words you whisper to me are not whispered to some other woman? That you don't touch another woman the way you touch me? And what about whenever something starts itching or dripping and I'm wondering if I've got some social disease?"

"I'm very careful about that, and if you want, I'll be extra careful." Sid came around the bed and held me. "But don't ever think for a second that what passes between us could be anything like what I do with another woman."

"Then why aren't I enough?" My eyes caught his.

He pulled away. "Enough has nothing to do with it. I don't even know why we're discussing the possibility. You're not ready for sex any more than I'm ready to lock myself up if you're not there. And that, my dear, is precisely why we've got to find a way out of this. We've wasted too much time already. Come on."

Sadly, I hoisted my purse onto the bed.

"Wait a minute," I said suddenly, digging through the huge leather sack. "We still have the drops."

"What?" Sid came over to me.

I shoved the envelopes in his face. "The drops for Seattle, San Francisco, and San Diego." I opened one. "I'm going to see what they say. They may give us a clue."

"We don't necessarily have the right."

"Neither of us wants to be married, and I want to see my family again."

Inside was a second envelope. Sid peered over my shoulder.

"It's addressed to the floater team," he said, deciphering the code faster than I could.

I hesitated. "Oh, hell. In for a penny..."

I opened the inner envelope and gave the card inside to Sid. He read it and swore.

"What?" I asked.

"It basically says that upline knows they're leaking. This was Seattle. What do the others say?"

I ripped away to find exactly the same messages.

"Get finished packing," ordered Sid, doing the same.

I grabbed my stuff. "What are you thinking?"

"I don't know yet. It just doesn't make sense. Obviously, they were looking for whoever was opening stuff."

"And then setting us up for an attack with that second drop."

"Which the suspect couldn't have known was coming, but would probably take advantage of to save his or her own skin."

"But it's the suspects that keep getting killed."

"And these are addressed to the floater team, which is going to be the same for this line, and they knew that second drop was coming in Chicago."

"But did they in New Orleans? That's probably why I was followed."

"But I wasn't in Chicago, which must mean they were looking for you."

"And then I had that blonde wig in Yellowstone."

"Nor was there a second drop." Sid stopped. "It must be the floater team that's leaking. That's the only thing that could account for what's going on, and they must have gotten a hold of the Dragon somehow."

"So what do we do?"

"We're going after that team."

"We don't know who they are."

Sid thought that over. "But we have Amanda Whitefoot's address. She's still in the hospital." He looked at me and smiled. "I think a nice little break-in is in order." He checked his watch. "We'd better hustle. I'd like to be in and out of there before dark. We'll need the light to see, and if we make any of our own, it could attract attention out there in the middle of nowhere."

I thought it was going to be tricky getting onto the reservation, but Sid pulled out an F.B.I. ID and said we were there to question some people about some antiquities that had been stolen from them. We found the house without problem, and it was pretty isolated. Someone else had found it first. The place had been trashed, naturally after every trace of Whitefoot's double life had been removed.

"It's not an unusual procedure when one of ours goes down," explained Sid with a frustrated sigh as he looked around the room.

I picked up an address book and flipped through the pages.

"I doubt you'll find anything in there," said Sid.

I stopped flipping. "Care to put some money on that?"

"You got something?" Sid came over.

"Recognize that phone number?"

Sid took the book. "I'll be damned. Harry and Carol Beldon. I wonder who they are."

"How about Whitefoot's floater team?"

"It wouldn't be out where anyone could find it."

"Why not? Don't you have Henry James in your address book? You had him in the Rolodex when I started working for you and had a reasonable excuse for knowing him." Henry is our floater. Sid ostensibly knows him as a contact for his writing. "Why wouldn't Whitefoot have a visible reason for knowing her floater?"

"That makes sense, and it's about all we've got." Sid thought it over. "There's a CIA base in Manhattan. We've got to get our passports through them, anyway. Let's see what they can do with this."

We had to fly to Denver first and spent the night there. Neither of us felt up to saying anything. Sid got us a double at the hotel next to the airport, neatly avoiding any discussion about who would sleep on the floor. [Or whether one of us would - SEH]

We caught an early morning flight out to New York. As usual, Sid boarded the plane, took his contacts out and went to sleep, waking up just long enough to recline his seat after the captain said we could. I read the magazines I'd picked up at the airport in Denver. I didn't want to think about being married, let alone to Sid. As for never seeing my family again, I found that even harder to face.

We hit some nasty turbulence about two hours

into the flight.

"What? Help," Sid muttered, then snapped awake. He swore and blinked.

"You okay?" I asked.

"Yeah," he gasped and blinked again. "Just had a bad dream. Why aren't we landing?"

"We're not there yet."

The plane took a sudden dip.

"What the hell..?" Sid gripped the armrest.

"It's just turbulence."

Sid snorted. "I was dreaming there'd been an explosion and everything was blown all over."

"Good timing." I smiled briefly, then gazed out the window.

Sid leaned back and tried to go to sleep again, but the plane kept bouncing. He squinted and leaned over me towards the window. He always gets an aisle seat, which is fine with me because I prefer a window seat.

"Is that the wing bouncing up and down?" he asked.

"Yes."

"Wonderful." He settled back into his own seat.

"I've been told it's supposed to do that."

There was a pause. I looked at the magazine in my lap. About five minutes before it had seemed incredibly inane. One of the headlines promised me "Fabulous Sex Secrets To Keep Your Man."

"Your cramps feeling any better?" he asked quietly.

"Some."

"Good." There was another pause. "What are you thinking about?"

"Things. Trying to get some perspective."

"On what?"

"On me, you. Our relationship. I don't know. It's like what you said about it counting for something. These past three weeks have been pretty intense. The day you came to get me at the retreat, Father John suggested I try to understand you a little better. It's kind of weird how important that is all of a sudden."

"If I believed in that nonsense, I'd call the man psychic. He had a little chat with me before I left."

"What did he say?"

"Not much. He just expressed some concern for you and said that you needed my support." The plane lurched. I slid my hand into Sid's. His grip tightened as the plane bounced again. "I told him I was doing what I could to give it to you. Then he suggested I try to understand you better. That's why he talked me into sticking around through dinner."

"I wondered about that."

"Well, I owe that man one, assuming I get a shot at payback. If I'd known what trying to understand you was going to do to me..."

"If I'd known the same thing." I looked at him warmly. "It hasn't been easy, and I can't say I've gotten very far, but it's been worth it, at least to me."

"To me, too." Sid smiled. This time his squeeze was gentle.

"I don't want to stop trying, either."

"No, we can't afford to." He looked away for a moment. "You know, yesterday afternoon, what I said about being married, it really wasn't you."

"I know. But I couldn't help thinking so."

"I was a little rough about it. In a way, I'm still in shock. I don't like the idea of leaving my life any more than you do."

"Are you sure we'll have to?"

"We'd better assume so." He looked me over with a warm smile. "I don't mean to balk so much on the fidelity thing. I really don't mind the idea of being faithful to you. I'm just not sure I can. I haven't been faithful to one woman for more than two weeks at a time in my life."

"Two and a half weeks. Remember Kathy Preving?"

Sid chuckled, then squeezed my hand as the plane jolted.

"That was something altogether different, and I wasn't faithful. There was that trip to Washington. I figured she'd never know."

I picked up a second magazine. "Maybe you'd better read this article."

Sid put the page in his face. "Sex addiction? Oh, come on. Sex is not an addiction."

"I don't know. There were some things in there that reminded me an awful lot of you."

"Well, maybe. But it's harmless."

"Not when it starts messing up a relationship. And besides, when you get horny, it distorts your judgment."

"I couldn't have survived this long if it distorted it that much."

"You don't let yourself get that horny that often."

"True. But there were times..." His voice trailed off and his grip on my hand changed. I could see him trying to deal with memories that were very painful. "Maybe it was my fault after all."

"What?" I asked very gently.

"Decisions I made a couple times while I was in Viet Nam. I can't say they were bad decisions. But I knew, even then, they weren't the best. I couldn't think of anything else to do. Three weeks on patrol in those jungles and no women at all. Nothing helped."

"That's in the past. There's nothing you can do about it now."

"Except learn from it. But, damn it, I can't change who I am, and I'm not sure I want to."

"That's why you can't change. And I don't know if you should try, except that..."

"Except that now we're a married couple, and unless I change, we're not going to have much of a sex life."

"We could still catch these Beldon people and everything will go back to normal."

"More likely we'll spend six weeks wandering the continent, then settle in somewhere as that nice couple next door."

"And then I can get myself reassigned."

"Don't do that." His hand didn't squeeze but

tightened in such a way that I knew he wouldn't let go easily. "Look, if I have to be married, I'd rather it was to you than anyone else."

We fell silent for a few minutes.

"It's not like we have an option," said Sid finally. "But if you can put up with me, then I guess I can find a way."

"I can put up with you." I gave his hand a little squeeze.

He reached over and kissed my mouth.

"You think we could get it blessed after we get settled?" I asked.

"What do you mean?"

"Get married again in the Church. Lots of couples do. They get married in a civil ceremony for all sorts of reasons, then years later have a priest bless it. I suppose we could draw up some fake annulment papers for you, just to make it look more legitimate, and I'd have to get another baptismal certificate, but that shouldn't be too hard."

Sid sighed. "It sounds time-consuming. Do we get to share connubial bliss before or after?"

"Well..."

"If you want it official, why can't we just visit a judge?"

"Why? Our business has done it for us. As for the connubial bliss..."

"Is it my imagination, or are you saying that the moral issue is resolved?" Sid chuckled.

"I guess I am. But it's by no means definite that we're forever doomed to new identities."

Sid gazed at our hands. "You're still not ready."

"I'm sorry."

"Don't be. After a lifetime of saying no, you can't just turn around and say yes. We'll take our time getting you used to the idea."

"Oh, great."

"Don't worry, my darling ice maiden. We'll take it very slowly." His free hand reached over and touched my cheek. "I've done a fair amount of work as a surrogate partner for women in sex therapy, and I've dealt with a lot of trauma. I'll take very good care of you."

"Can we wait until we're sure who we are?"

"Sure." Sid sighed. "It's probably just as well. If we don't, we'll for sure have to go back to our own lives and you'll be feeling guilty as hell, and I'll never get you back in my bed."

He leaned back in his seat and was out cold within a minute. He didn't even fully wake up when it came time to straighten his seat for landing. But he didn't let go of my hand until the plane had stopped at the gate and the seatbelt sign was turned off.

Manhattan, which had seemed like such a great place three and a half weeks before, suddenly grated on my nerves. We checked our bags at Grand Central Station and went straight from there on the subway to the C.I.A. offices, which were on the east side near the U.N. Sid flashed his phony F.B.I. ID, which got our thumbprints taken and then into the back office after a twenty-minute wait.

The man behind the desk was not particularly little in size, but seemed little, and had that prissy, bureaucratic attitude one finds a lot of in government clerks.

"Clearance?" he asked us.

"A-1," said Sid. "Division 53-Q, code 6-A."

"Personal code?"

I turned away and hummed so I wouldn't hear Sid give his. A second later, he tapped me on the shoulder, and started humming, while I softly gave mine to the clerk.

"Code names?" he asked.

"I'm Little Red," I said. "He's Big Red."

Sneering, the clerk double checked our info against a printout.

"Well, your thumbprints match," he grumbled, then smirked. "I hear you 53-Q guys are having a little trouble with security."

"We're working on it," said Sid. "We need passports."

"Oh, hell," said the clerk. "Where do you people get the idea that we can just snap our fingers and produce decent documents? We need descriptive info, we need photos. We're not the State Department."

"How long will it take?"

"You can have them by eight thirty. You'd just better hope we can get your pictures done now."

"While we're waiting, we need a priority one background check on some names."

"Why don't you just ask for the moon while you're at it?"

Sid leaned over the desk. "We have a priority one need to know. Our offices are down. Last I heard, we're ultimately working for the same boss. Why not cooperate?"

"What's the name?"

"Harry and Carol Beldon."

"Beldon, Harry and Carol. Fine. But I'm telling you, you domestic people with your attitudes can blow it out your ears as far as I'm concerned. We're out there doing the real work."

Sid hung onto his temper while I bit my tongue. The clerk had to take our passport photos himself and complained every step of the way.

"I'd like to blow it out his ears," said Sid as we left the building. [Correction, I wanted to blow it out his ass. What is it with you and swear words? The religion thing I understand, but the rest of it... - SEH]

He hailed a cab, which didn't stop, all the while complaining about the lousy attitudes of CIA personnel in general, punctuated with an assortment of swear words.

"What do we do now?" I asked as a third cab passed us by.

"Go shopping. We need to look a little more affluent if we're going to be bumming around Europe for a while."

"If we're bumming, why can't we just go the poor student route?"

"Because, as the saying goes, poverty sucks. I know. I've done it."

"What about alterations?"

"This is New York City and we don't have a credit limit on our cards. We can get alterations."

We also found a twenty-four-hour laundry and dry cleaning service and were able to get the clothes we had cleaned. By eight thirty, we each had two suitcases, a carry-on, and I still had my cavernous purse. We also had passports for Ed and Janet Donaldson, some extra equipment, and a file on Harry and Carol Beldon.

"Well?" I asked as we sat down at a coffee shop at Grand Central, our luggage gathered around us.

Sid opened the file. "Let's see. They're floaters, alright. We've got a note here dated the other day that they were cleared to go to Paris and another date yesterday that their line is officially down and that they're under suspicion. Their basic cover is as clothing importers. Apparently, Harry has an office in Paris. And looky here, Carol has contacts among the Red Brigade in Italy."

"Aren't they communists?"

"Definitely, and there are not a few rumors that there's Soviet money behind them. It could be the Beldons are just taking advantage of an opportunity and playing double agent."

"But if they're the source of the leak, then that's less likely."

"Not necessarily. You never really know what side a double agent is on. It looks like that was why they ended up domestic, though. According to this, they were doing some good work in the early sixties, but were suspected of walking the fence and ended up charter members of Quickline."

"I guess the next step is to go to Paris, then." I sighed. "Just how are we going to catch up with them?"

"We've got the address to Harry Beldon's office

here in the file. We'll just wait for them to show. We've got six weeks."

"And if they don't?"

"Mr. and Mrs. Donaldson take up residence in Podunk, Iowa as that nice couple next door."

I crossed myself. "Dear Jesus, please let them be there."

We found a travel agent in the station to get our plane tickets. The only two flights to Paris left that night were booked solid. I suggested going stand by and the agent giggled. Sid booked us on a flight that left the next afternoon at five.

As we waited for a cab outside of the station, I talked Sid into staying at the Algonquin. The room was tiny, but we only stayed there long enough to change into going out to dinner clothes. Sid took us down to the Village to a jazz club there, and then we went dancing. It was a lot of fun because Sid is a good dancer, and how many guys dance at all, let alone well? But it was also a little nerve-wracking because we were drilling each other on our new identities the whole time.

"Is there some reason we haven't gone back to the hotel?" I asked Sid as we held each other through a slow dance.

"We've got a long flight tomorrow with a big time change. Tell me about your parents."

"Curtis and Lynn Mayfield. They live in a condo on Rosewood Court in Diamond Bar. They moved there three years ago. Dad works in computer sales. Mom's an administrative clerk in the Diamond Bar school system. I've got two younger sisters, Jean and Doris, both still in school. Doris goes to Berkeley, Jean is at U.C. Santa Barbara. Tell me about your parents."

"Jim and Rhonda Donaldson. They live in Walnut Creek at 1531 Seeley Drive and have for fifteen years. Dad owns Donaldson Printers, Mom helps out. I've got a brother, Lee, a resident surgeon at County U.S.C. Medical Center in Los Angeles."

"Why is it you get to be two years younger and I

get to be two years older?"

Sid smiled. "It wasn't my idea, but I'm not complaining."

"How did we meet?"

"Larry Everett, a venture capitalist, introduced us five years ago when you were fresh out of college and looking for a business partner with strong sales skills. With your unique approach to service oriented office supplies and my smooth talking, the business clicked, and a year later so did we." Sid gave me a warm look. "You're good at the shy routine."

"That's because I am shy. I don't mind getting up in front of a group if I have something specific to say, but I really hate trying to talk to strangers at parties and things. It's really hard for me to get to know people."

"You got to know me pretty quickly."

"That was one on one, and I don't think I really did know you until these past few weeks. You're not an easy person to get to know."

Sid snuggled in closer. "Neither are you. You talk, but you don't really say much about yourself. It's one of the reasons you're such a good spy."

"I am?"

"Mm-hm. Tell me about our place in Sunny Hills."

I found out why Sid had been stalling about going back to our room when we finally got there. I started to make up the bed on the floor. He stopped me.

"We can't do that anymore," he said sternly. "We're married now, and even if we're not physically doing anything about it, we can't let even the least hint drop that things aren't the way they appear."

"I suppose. I've never shared a bed with a man before."

"What's so immoral about just sleeping in the same bed?"

"Well..." I thought. "Nothing, I guess. But there's the temptation factor."

Sid yawned. "Not tonight. I am beat."

He let me have the bathroom first, and was sitting

in the room's one chair reading a newspaper when I got out.

"Which side do you want?" he asked, getting up.

I shrugged. "I never gave it much thought. Which side do you like?"

"That one." He pointed to the side of the bed closest to the door.

He stopped as I pulled back the covers. "If it will make you feel any better, I sleep by myself."

"What do you mean?" I asked.

"I'm not going to use you as a human teddy bear. Sleeping tangled up in someone else gives me a crick in the neck."

"Oh. Okay. Thanks."

I got in and laid on my back as close to the edge as I dared. Sid took his time in the bathroom. [I was trying to give you a chance to get to sleep before I climbed in - SEH] When he finally came out, he turned out the lights, slid under the covers and true to his word, rolled onto his side away from me. Tired as I was, I still couldn't sleep.

"Um..." I looked over at Sid and debated poking him. "Um..."

"What?" grunted Sid.

"While we're trying to get you know who, are you going to... Well, you know..."

"Have sex with other women?"

"I was more wondering about buying it."

"That's the most efficient, and let's face it, discreet way." Sid rolled onto his back. "I don't know yet. Let's see how long I last."

"Oh."

"Are you really that bugged about it?"

"In some ways. I guess I'm scared, too. We have to be so careful if we want to stay alive, and it just seems to me that when you're... I don't know... Involved with a woman, you're terribly vulnerable."

"For a very short period of time, I assure you, and usually, she's equally vulnerable."

"You know more about it than I do."

"I've been at this business a long time."

"True."

Sid looked over at me and smiled softly. "I'll be alright. Goodnight."

"Goodnight."

I rolled over, telling myself that cricks in the neck are no fun.

June 14 - 18, 1983

We had one tense day, killing time in Manhattan until our plane left for Paris. We slept as late as we could and still be on the streets before we were charged an extra day at the hotel. Sid can be pretty extravagant, but even he's not that crazy. We checked our luggage at Grand Central again, then found a guided bus tour that would finish before we needed to be at the airport.

It's a good thing we slept on the plane. It landed in Paris the next morning at six a.m. Sid slid his hand into mine as we took off and didn't really let go until we landed. Well, I did have to go to the bathroom once, but I took his hand back as soon as I returned to my seat. We waited a long time at the baggage claim, then customs took forever, but only because of the long lines. The guards didn't even ask us to open our luggage.

Then Sid made what we discovered was the ultimate mistake in Paris. He hired a cab to take us into the city from Orly airport. The highway wasn't too bad until we hit the city and joined everyone else trying to get in to work. We crawled, then spent, I swear, thirty minutes stopped waiting for some truck that was unloading merchandise in the middle of the narrow street. The cab driver told us in his broken English that sort of delay was not unusual. Of course, the fare was adding up as we waited.

We'd gotten francs at Kennedy (another mistake, we found out later). When we finally got to our hotel off the Place de la Concorde, Sid found he had to shell out a good chunk of our cash to pay for the cab.

"How much was that American?" I asked nervously.

"Enough to make even me wince," he said. "I've been told France is expensive. At least the dollar's been doing better lately."

The hotel had a nice room available right away, with a private bath.

"Boy, I hear these aren't too easily gotten here," I said, admiring the bathroom.

"This is a three-star hotel, that's why," explained Sid. "They aren't hard to get, you just pay for them."

"What's this?"

It was a funny little toilet bowl without a tank or seat. In fact, where a toilet seat reaches your knees, the top of this thing only came mid-shin on me, and it had two little nozzles that aimed up.

Sid chuckled. "That is a bidet."

"Oh. I've heard of those." I looked at him. "What are they for?"

"You use them instead of toilet paper."

"That sounds kind of messy." I went back into the room and sat on the bed. "Have you ever been to Europe before?"

"Besides 'Nam, this is only time I've ever left the country." Sid prowled.

"Gee, you know so much about it."

He chuckled. "I have a couple friends back home who have bidets, and while you had your nose in that woman's magazine, I read the guidebook."

"I was going to read it on the plane, but I fell asleep." I gazed out the window to the cars rushing around the fountains in the circle below. "What are the odds we'll get some sightseeing in?"

"Pretty good. The last thing we're going to want to do is give our quarry any reason to believe we're not who we say we are."

I picked up a brochure off the bureau. "Hey, this is in English. And German, and Italian, even Japanese. They've got all the bases covered."

"What does it say?"

“It’s bus tours.”

“That might be just the ticket to orient ourselves.”

We had to move quickly, but we caught a general city tour by the skin of our teeth and spent most of the day on it. Our tour guide gave us a lot of pointers on how to get around, too.

“But it doesn’t give us a lot of information on how we’re going to get the Beldons,” said Sid as we relaxed at the sidewalk cafe near our hotel.

“Where did you say that office was, the Rue St. Denis?”

“Mm-hmm.”

“Would they even go there?” I looked up from my map of the Metro. “I mean, if our theory’s right that they’re the ones responsible for the leak, they’d have to know they’re under suspicion and figure that someone is watching them.”

“Possibly. Then again, they were cleared without problem to come here, and the note that they were down came in after they’d left, so it’s also possible they don’t realize that they’ve been tracked this far.”

“When are we going to stake it out?”

Sid checked his pocket watch. We’d changed for dinner already only to find there weren’t any restaurants open.

“Well, we’re not going to get dinner before seven thirty,” he said. “Why don’t we head on over that way? There’s enough tourist stuff in the near vicinity that I think we can get away with ambling through.”

Sid swears it was just luck. I say it was God, Himself. We turned onto the Rue St. Denis several blocks away from where the office was located. Walking toward the office, Sid happened to look up a side street and saw what could only be Harry and Carol Beldon heading away from us. She was average height, with fluffy, streaked hair, and a nice motherly look about her. He looked like your basic, slightly paunchy American businessman.

Sid and I slid around the corner. I grabbed the

transmitters and receivers from my purse. Sid stopped me.

"We may as well stay together," he said. "It's too obvious we're Americans. If we split up, they'll know we're tailing them."

Fortunately, they went straight to a bistro that was around the next corner and down a block.

"Make contact?" I asked, a little nervous.

"Yep."

We took a chance and went around the block, entering the bistro from the other way. The Beldons were still there, conferring over a small table. Sid and I threaded our way through the tables. As we passed theirs, Sid stopped.

"You guys are Americans," he said jovially.

Carol's eyes narrowed for a second, then the mask fell, transforming her into the warm, cozy matron. Harry gave us both the once over and likewise adopted a "glad to meetcha" demeanor.

"Well, howdy," said Harry, standing up. "Why don't you join us?"

"Why not?" said Sid, pulling over a couple chairs. "I can't tell you how good it is to hear some good old American English."

"How long have you been in Paris?" asked Carol.

Sid chuckled. "Not long, but it's a real freaky feeling when people don't sound like you're used to."

"I'm Harry Beldon," he said, offering his hand. "This is my wife, Carol."

"Ed and Janet Donaldson," said Sid. "We're here on vacation. My wife twisted my arm. She's always wanted to come."

"Ed," I said quietly. Sid had slipped into his salesman persona, and it was a little unnerving to see the quiet dignified mann I knew acting like he had several used cars to sell.

"So you folks here on vacation, too?" Sid asked.

"Business," said Harry. "I've got a women's wear company in the States. If it's going to sell, it's got to come from here."

"No kidding," said Sid. "You in the business, too, Carol?"

"Oh, no," she said. "I just come along for the ride. What business are you in, Ed?"

"Office supplies." Sid reached into his back pocket and his wallet. "Golden State Office Supplies. Janet and I own the company. Let me get you a card." Sid thumbed through the wallet. "Damn. I'm out. Honey, you got any cards in your purse?"

"No," I said. "I left them at home. We are on vacation."

Sid laughed. "You are so right, sweetie. So, where are you guys from?"

"Chicago," said Harry. "We also have a home and outlet store in Santa Fe. Where do you folks hail from?"

"Los Angeles area," replied Sid. "Orange County, actually. You know where Disneyland is?"

The conversation went on. Small talk and Sid did most of it. Neither Carol nor Harry were particularly quiet, but I got the awkward feeling that they had more than a casual interest in us. They invited us to dinner, and we accepted. We went to a lovely place on the Champs Elysee, a few blocks down from the L'Arc de Triomphe. I had lamb. Sid had fish. Both of us drank water. The Beldons split a bottle of red wine.

Sid and Harry were really great pals by the end of dinner. As we left the restaurant, Harry had his arm around Sid's shoulders as they laughed and carried on about who was worse: the Cubs or the Angels. They shook hands and we agreed to meet again the next day at the Place St. Germain, a common meeting spot. Sid slid his arm around my shoulders and hailed a cab.

It was just barely getting dark even though it was close to ten at night. The city showed no signs of closing either.

"Speak English?" asked Sid, still the salesman.

"Yes," answered the driver.

"Eiffel Tower. You know?"

"Yes. Eiffel Tower." The accent wasn't French.

"Hey, an Arab," chuckled Sid as we got in. "We might as well be in New York." We got settled in. "Well, Janet, what do you think of the Beldons? Great folks, huh?"

"I suppose. They seem nice." I was puzzled.

The Beldons weren't anywhere around, and we'd been with them the whole time, so they hadn't had a chance to call for a tail, and it didn't look like we had one. Sid rummaged around in my purse.

"Yep, top of the line. I sure can pick them, can't I? This may work out better than I thought. You got any of those antacids in here?"

"I think so. If not, they're back at the hotel."

"How do you find anything in here?" Sid pulled out what looked like a beeper.

It was actually a signal receiving device that, when turned on, would flash if there was a listening device in operation within five hundred feet. We could also use it to track a bug. Sid showed me the glowing red light with a disgusted look on his face. He dropped it back in the purse and left it there until we got to the tower. We walked around, heading toward the river. Sid made loud fun of the French all the way while I tried to isolate the bug unobtrusively.

It didn't seem to be in my purse, which seemed strange. That would have been the first place I would have dropped something. I teased Sid by tickling him. Well, I tried tickling him. He's not ticklish in the least. But I did find the bug in the upper breast pocket of his suit jacket.

At the top of a bridge, Sid stopped.

"Hey, look at all those gawkers on those tour boats," he chortled. He pulled the silk color from his pocket. Sure enough, in the folds was what looked like a button off a suit jacket. I looked at it more closely. Tiny mesh covered the holes. Sid knocked it from my hand. "Honey, get a picture of me waving my hanky at the boats."

"I don't think so," I said.

I doubt the Beldons heard my reply. Sid just happened to walk on the bug at that moment. I surreptitiously showed Sid the bug finder. No light.

"We're safe for the moment," he said with an invisible sigh of relief. "I don't think we have a tail, but let's not go back to the hotel until we're sure."

There was no tail.

"But why?" I asked.

"When did they have a chance to call one?" replied Sid as we got on the Metro train. "They were probably counting on us not noticing the bug and telling a cab driver where to go."

"And on us not having the means to find a bug, and not suspecting we'd have one. That's just too much to swallow. I've got a really bad feeling they recognized us from somewhere."

"If they were watching the drops at all, they could have, which is probably why I was bugged in the first place. There couldn't have been any planning involved."

"Maybe you shouldn't have gotten rid of it."

Sid shrugged. "I hope I accounted for it."

"Yeah, but wouldn't you be a little bit suspicious?"

"I'd be a lot suspicious, especially as paranoid as those two must be by now." Sid thought. "I move we search their office tonight, and let's just hope they decide to move it legitimately to keep their butts covered."

If wishes were horses, we should have had a herd of them. And Sid wonders why I believe. Paris nightlife being what it was, we had to wait until three a.m. to leave the hotel. That wouldn't leave us much time before sunrise at four thirty. Sid had us put on light colored shirts with dark jeans and black zip front sweatshirts.

"I don't get it," I asked as we laid out our equipment. "Don't we want to be all in black so we're not seen?"

"That's what the sweatshirts are for," he answered, more preoccupied with the lockpicks and flashlights.

"But if we have to make a run for it, we can ditch the sweatshirts and bluff our way through because nobody will be looking for burglars wearing white. Damn. We've got to hide the masks and the gloves, and still find someplace to carry a gun or two."

It was tight, but we managed. I vowed to do something about the problem the first chance I had with a sewing machine, preferably my own back in California.

Around the corner from the Rue St. Denis, we faded into the shadows and put on our sweatshirts, gloves and the all-over ski masks. We slid around the buildings to the office. Sid ran a beam from his flashlight all along the door jamb, looking for alarm wires, then picked the lock.

We weren't worried about the police. They were the last people the Beldons would call. But we didn't want the Beldons alerted either.

The office was at the top of a narrow flight of stairs. Sid got us in within seconds and shut the door. I went for the file cabinets while he checked the desk and shelves. Orange light from the street gave the room an odd glow.

I found the file in the bottom drawer of the end cabinet. It contained a host of surveillance photos, but I saw a picture of Amanda Whitefoot and knew I had something. Sid and I heard the footsteps on the stairs at the same time.

I shoved the file drawer shut and followed Sid under the desk. I crossed myself. Sid lifted his pant leg and drew his gun. I got my twenty-two, also.

"Somebody's been in here," grumbled Harry's voice as they entered.

"You'd just better hope they didn't find that file," said Carol, as she pushed past him.

Awkwardly, I jammed the file into my sweatshirt. Sid nodded at me and slid away from the desk on the side where the Beldons weren't. I started after, but in the next second, the office door burst open and bright light circled the Beldons.

There were two figures silhouetted in the doorway, one very short, one rather tall, both lean, and both had .45 (at least) automatics trained on the Beldons.

"Don't you Americans take this overtime business a bit too far?" said the larger figure, a male, in a smooth educated British voice. His face had a rather horsey profile.

Sid nodded at me, and I followed him silently to the wall away from the light.

"Since when does it make any difference to you what time we come here?" said Carol.

"Let's just kill them and be done with it," said the short figure. She was also educated and British.

Harry looked over at Sid and me and laughed and pointed. Before the two Brits could swing the light our way, Sid charged with me on his heels. The Beldons charged also. The Beldons broke first from the ensuing tangle, with Sid and me close behind. On the sidewalk, the Beldons went one way, Sid and I went the other. I glanced back to see the short figure running after us.

We had a good lead on our tail and bettered it, charging around the first corner and down the street to a wide avenue lined with trees. Sid and I ducked into an alcove between two sidewalk cafes. The short Brit came running past.

We stripped masks, gloves, and sweatshirts in seconds.

"Let's neck," Sid whispered, stashing everything behind us.

I ended up with my back to the street and gasped as Sid undid my shirt. I didn't have time to complain. The Brit was on her way back. Sid exposed my shoulder as I covered his face with my hands. He let out soft little moans as we kissed, his tongue everywhere but beyond my teeth. I still wasn't up to that.

Heavy footsteps and breathing announced the return of the large Brit. He met his partner not far from where we stood.

"Lost them, damn it," he complained. "How'd you make out?"

"Not any better. I checked the Metro. The train was just leaving."

He chuckled. "Have you tried asking them?"

She laughed also. "I doubt they saw anything. We're for it, you know. They won't be going back to that office now that they know we're watching it."

"Can't be helped. Let's be off."

Sid peeked around my hair as the two disappeared into the night.

"We should be safe now," he whispered, pulling my shirt back into place and buttoning it. "Sorry about that. I wanted it to look good."

"I'll live."

We gathered our belongings and the file and headed back to the hotel, checking for tails every step of the way.

I barely remember going to bed, I was so tired. It was full daylight when I awoke. Still heavy with sleep, I rolled over. Sid lay on his side, fully awake and watching me. I stared back for a minute.

"What are you looking at?" I asked finally.

"What does it look like?" Sid rolled away, and grabbing his robe, got up. [Let's hear it for denial - SEH] He squinted at his pocket watch. "It's already nine thirty."

I flopped onto my back. "Do we have to run today?"

There was a park, the Jardin de Tuilleries, just off the same circle as the hotel, with a straight, broad unpaved walkway down the middle which was just perfect as a running course.

"Much as I hate giving in to your sloth, we're not," said Sid. "It would make us too conspicuous as Americans. Do you have any compelling desire to shower first?"

"Uh-uh." I yawned and closed my eyes.

Sid was out, fully dressed in designer jeans and sport shirt, within twenty minutes, which isn't bad for someone as fussy about his appearance as he is. I dragged myself in, and eventually put on a full-skirted strapless sundress and petticoat with eyelet trim that peeked out from under the skirt.

It was already a habit. I didn't even feel the straps anymore. But I made sure my twenty-two automatic handgun was in its holster on the top of my thigh, as high up as possible.

As I left the bathroom, Sid had the pictures from the file spread out over the dresser top.

"You were right," he said, holding one up for me. "They recognized us from the drops."

It was pretty grainy, having been shot with a light magnifier and all, but you could see Sid leaning over Blaine Winters' body in that alley in New Orleans, with me facing the wall.

"Terrific," I said.

"They caught me making the first drop in Chicago," said Sid. He picked up the picture to hand it to me, then stopped. "What's this? Get the micro magnifier, will you please?"

I dug the viewer out of my purse. It looked like one of those handheld doohickeys for viewing slides and basically served the same purpose except the magnification power was considerably stronger. Sid scraped something off the photo. I handed him the magnifier and looked at the pictures.

"It looks like they've got shots of their entire line. There's even the guy from Washington, D.C. in here."

"Yep." Sid switched the magnifier on. "Well, I'll be damned. Looks like we've stumbled onto the Beldons' record keeping system."

"What?"

Sid handed me the magnifier. "That's all the information on the Chicago killing, right down to the return of the deposit money found in the killer's apartment. It's the same accounting code we use for our expenses."

"Except theirs are for killing people." I thought. "If

they recognized us, then the Beldons had to figure we would be watching them and their office."

"Yeah, and they probably went back at the same time we did for the same reason."

"What if the file they came back for is this file?"

Sid nodded. "Given the evidence in here, it would be worth the risks to get it."

"And they never got a chance to look for it."

"You're right. They'll have to go back for it one way or another."

"Could they have already?"

"They have no way of knowing that we, or anyone else, have called off the search, and they were caught within seconds of entering." Sid thoughtfully gathered the pictures together. "The trick now will be in capturing them. I don't want to meet at the Place St. Germain. It'll be too easy for them to hit us."

I grinned. "That's it. We draw an attack on us in a public place, then scream for the police."

Sid snorted. "That's the last thing we should do. Local law enforcement just makes things more complicated..." He stopped. "And it's the last damned thing the Beldons will expect. It seems to me that there is a hotel across the street from their office. We'll get a room and monitor them from there, and let them catch us monitoring them. That should do it, especially if we let them know we have their file."

"And with the hotel room, we're not set up for an obvious sniper attack."

"Bingo. We'll leave the file in this hotel's safe, too. It'll be just that much more secure."

We emptied a couple suitcases and only packed our guns and a couple changes of underwear. We wore our transmitters. At the second hotel, Sid got a single room overlooking the street and the Beldons' office. We sat in the window watching, or rather, Sid did most of it. He thought he spotted the Beldons once, but couldn't be sure.

I read for a little while, then Sid and I made up

a list of article ideas I could query on when we got home. After a while, Sid got progressively more antsy and distant. He made his second shave around five and took his time doing it.

At seven thirty, he broke away from the window.

"Why don't you watch?"

"Sure." I took his place.

He paced restlessly. "Listen, I hope you don't mind, but I'd like to go out for an hour or two."

"Let me guess," I said softly. "You're horny."

"Hey, it's been four days. I think I've been doing pretty good."

"Pretty well." I sighed. "I was thinking the same thing, but I didn't want to bring it up."

"I'm glad." He came over to me. "I don't know why, but last night when we were necking, it really turned me on. It wasn't the open shirt. It was probably the fear element. But it was all I could think about this morning. And there you are in that lovely little sundress."

I turned my gaze out of the window. His hands gently cupped my shoulders, and his nose cleared my hair away so his lips could softly grasp my ear. His kisses, sweet and gentle, slipped down my neck. I leaned into it, even as the fear and guilt crept in.

"I can't tell you to get the hell out and get yourself laid," I said. "And I just don't feel right about taking care of you myself."

"No." He pulled back a little. "I can't dump the decisions I have to make on you." He took a deep breath. "I've got to do something. I'm obsessing on this. I can't think straight."

"It's an awful risk."

"We have no reason to believe the Beldons know we're here, and I can't help but think we're better off if I clear my head." His finger turned my chin to face him. He pressed a kiss to my forehead. "It's only for an hour or so. I'll leave my receiver on. You can tap in a message if you see anything."

I didn't say anything as he left. Not ten minutes

later, I saw him leave the hotel with a blonde woman. They went up the street and turned the corner. Tears filled my eyes.

A minute later, the door burst open. Two huge and ugly men swarmed inside with guns drawn. I reached for my model thirteen on the dresser, then quickly drew back.

"The hands in air," growled one with a very strong French accent.

Slowly, I raised mine. The one held me at gunpoint while the other tore the room apart. There was nothing to find. I'd even left my purse back at the other hotel. Angry, the two eventually pulled me from the room, holding me close to hide the gun in the small of my back.

They took me down the street to a warehouse. I stumbled and tried nudging my twenty-two more between my legs. Once inside, I was greeted with a fist to my ear. The receiver went flying. One of my captors held me as his partner pounded my stomach. I tried to relax, but it hurt and I couldn't breathe. The pounding stopped, but before I could get my breath, my scalp flamed as the man grabbed my hair and yanked my head close to his face.

"You have pictures," he demanded, his breath as sour and foul as anything I'd ever pulled out of a toilet, and I've pulled plenty in my time.

I gasped.

"Pictures!"

"I don't know what you're talking about," I sobbed.

He backhanded me three times, or maybe it was more.

"Where are pictures?" he demanded.

"What pictures? I don't have my camera."

I got another cuff in the ear. My head spun and rang, and by that point, I was so disoriented, I really didn't know anything about pictures. The man holding me growled in French.

His partner replied, lighting a cigarette.

"Tell me," he said, pulling my hair again. "Where are the pictures, or this makes the fat marks on your pretty face."

I whimpered. The cigarette came closer.

"Tell me."

I could feel the heat of the glowing end on my cheek. Ignoring the pain in my scalp, I jerked my head away. The cigarette pressed into my neck, just below my ear. The pain was incredible. I screamed and screamed, and even being backhanded however many times couldn't get me to stop.

My hands were jerked behind me and bound very tight. The one who spoke English patted me down fairly thoroughly but missed the gun completely. I'm guessing he couldn't feel the straps through my nice full skirt and petticoat, and the gun was safely tucked between my legs as high as it would go. [There are more concise ways of describing its location, albeit cruder - SEH]

I was dragged up four or more flights of stairs and tossed into a small room. At first, all I could do was reel with the pain. My entire body ached, and my hair tickled the burn, irritating it and making it hurt worse. Slowly, my wits settled. If I was alive, it was only because someone believed I knew where the pictures we'd stolen from the Beldons were.

I didn't know how much time I had. Listening would do no good because nobody was speaking in English. Sid's instructions from my training days slowly filtered in. The first thing would be to get my hands free.

They were bound with bright orange strapping tape. I couldn't reach the little piece of spring steel hidden in my hair, but I could get to my shoes. Groaning, I sat myself up and wiggled my feet around. I slid my thumbnail between the insole and top of the heel on my right shoe. Like magic, it popped open. It hurt like hell, but I twisted so I could see what I was doing.

I wriggled the small serrated blade out of the heel

and went to work on the tape. It only took a minute or so to cut it open, and another minute to get braced so I could tear it off. It took my wrist hairs with it, leaving bright red welts across my wrists. But I was free.

I rescued my gun first. Peashooter or not, I wasn't going to make that mistake again. I put my heel back together, then slowly got up. The room had two windows, one overlooking a tiny alley festooned with clothes drying on lines, and the other facing the street. Through it, I could see the hotel facing the Beldons' office and the open window where Sid's and my room was. So that was how they knew we were there. There was also a skylight, but no way to reach it. Climbing down would be far too slow.

I listened at the door. There was silence on the other side. I tried the handle. It was locked.

Sid swears by spring steel. I have decided it is handy stuff. I pulled the piece from my hair and went to work on the lock. It took me a few minutes, but I popped it open.

The hallway was empty. I silently shut the door behind me and slipped across to the stairs. I could hear the thud, thud of feet climbing, and a second later, my captors spotted me. The pea shooter did a good job on their guns. The men dropped the weapons and grabbed their hands.

They also got mad. I popped the English speaking one in the shoulder. He fell backward onto his partner, and they tumbled down the stairs. I grabbed the two automatics they'd dropped. There wasn't any other way to go, so I ran after them. They landed in the middle of a flight. One reached up for me and I kicked him in the face. I crawled over the banister and jumped to the next flight.

I hit the ground floor running. The door to the warehouse was barred with a huge metal arm. I could hear shouting above me. Summoning whatever little strength I had left, I slid under the arm and shoved. It scraped on the catch but went over. I danced out of the way, then leaned on the door. Feet pounded behind me. I tripped over the threshold but scrambled out.

I ran as fast as I had ever run, cursing and thanking Sid for dragging me out of bed every morning. I found a newspaper in the gutter, swiped it up and wrapped the three guns in it. I dodged cars, then ran the long way back to the hotel on the Place de la Concorde, checking for tails and finding none.

I had been tapping messages to Sid since I broke free. With no receiver, I had no way of knowing if he'd gotten them. When I got to our room, I checked the transmitter. It had died in the rough treatment. I hoped Sid would find the destruction in the other room and come back to the first hotel. He wasn't there. I checked the time: eleven fifteen.

I bandaged myself as best I could, then took a hot bath. Sid didn't come. I slept restlessly, fully dressed. No Sid. Dawn broke and the sun rose slowly into the sky, filling the room with light. Sid didn't come.

There was no doubt in my mind that Sid was in trouble. Just how much, was the question. The best I could figure, he had gone back to the other room and had been caught by the Beldons or whoever else had figured we were there.

Maybe it was a silly chance, but that's where I went. I had dressed carefully in jeans and jacket with my armored running shoes. In my shoulder holster was one of the stolen automatics. I put the other in my jacket pocket. The twenty-two was strapped to my shin, and I had various other pieces of hardware stashed all over. In my other jacket pocket were the bug finder and a small roll of duct tape. I also wore my blonde wig and phony glasses. The wig periodically jabbed my burn, but I wasn't up to taking chances.

Frankly, I was terrified, and felt very lost and alone in a huge city I didn't know and where I couldn't speak the language. I dreaded going back to that second hotel, but there was nothing else to do. I checked out the lobby first, then found the stairs and went up that way. The room was shut. I unlocked it. Everything was as it had been the day before. I even found my model thirteen still on the dresser. I removed the automatic in my holster and replaced it with the revolver. I jammed the automatic in the back of my pants.

I checked out the window. I couldn't see who, but there was definitely movement in the Beldons' office. I dashed downstairs. Slipping out of the hotel, I looked up. Whoever was still in there. I slid in the building's door and into the shadows of the tiny foyer.

A woman left the office and came down the stairs. I couldn't quite see her in the shadows. She wasn't Carol Beldon, but I wasn't going to assume that she was on our side. As she reached the door, I put the muzzle of the model thirteen in her neck.

"Move and you die," I told her as coldly as I could manage.

She froze.

"Hands up and turn slowly."

She did. I almost dropped the gun.

"Dragon," I gasped. She looked at me, cool but unsure. "I'm Little Red, Division 53Q, code 6-A. Come on, you saw me in Washington. I'm wearing a wig."

"You also have a gun in my face," she pointed out.

"I'm sorry." I lowered the gun but hung on just in case.

The Dragon headed out the door with me following.

"What are you doing here?" I gasped. "We thought you'd gotten it."

"No. I had to intercept Yellow Ribbon and Yellow Knife before they left." She went across the street.

"The Beldons you mean?"

She smiled. "Very good. How did you find that?"

"We searched Amanda Whitefoot's place before we left the Canyon. It was in her phone book. We recognized their number."

The Dragon led me into the hotel and went straight to the elevator.

"We got background on them from the Company

when we got our passports," I continued.

"Excellent. I was hoping you'd come here." The elevator opened and we got on. "Where's Big Red?"

I swallowed. "Missing." I tried not to sniff. "He left the room here, and I got captured and got away, but he never returned to the room where we're staying or the room here. Something's wrong, and I can't get through on my transmitter because it died."

"And it seems our friends have slipped through our fingers again. They know we're watching the office. They've got a second hiding place, but we haven't been able to find it."

"It's a warehouse down the street. That's where they took me, and you can see this hotel, and their office just fine from there."

We got off the elevator on the fourth floor.

"That makes sense." The Dragon got her room key out and unlocked the door.

She let me in first. I kept a good grip on the model thirteen, which was a good thing because in the room was a largish man with a horsey profile and a small almost fluffy woman - the Brits from the night before. I braced and aimed.

"What in heaven's name is going on here?" demanded the woman.

"Enough," the Dragon told me. "They're with us."

I lowered the gun, still wary. "They crashed in on the Beldons last night in their office."

"That was you in the mask?" asked the man.

"We were there to capture them," said the woman.

"You were there to kill them," I said.

The Dragon glared at the couple. "We have the assurances. They won't be back." She waited as the couple basically ignored her. She looked at me. "Little Red, this is A12 and A45. They're CID, and have an interest in this case."

A12 was the woman and A45 her partner.

"We've been watching that office since we heard the Yellows were on their way," said A12, looking me over shrewdly. "I can't imagine why they chose last night to return. They had to have been here a few days."

I squirmed. "Big Red and I made contact with them the day before yesterday. We found them in the neighborhood. They bugged us, and when we got rid of it, they must have figured that we were the ones watching them and that they'd better get to the office and get their records."

"That can't be it," said A45. "We searched that office. There weren't any records."

"There was a file of surveillance photos on their line," I said.

"There's nothing unusual about that," said the Dragon.

"We found microdots on the photos with the payoffs to the hired assassins listed." I bit my lip.

"They are clever, aren't they?" said A12 with a lady-like chortle.

"The question is, where are they now?" said the Dragon, going over to a table spread with more photographs. "We can try staking out that warehouse, but I doubt that will do any good."

"I suppose we'll have to continue identifying and interrogating their acquaintances," said A45.

I went over to the table.

"That's rather awkward security-wise," said A12.

I picked up a series of photos of Harry Beldon and a blonde woman that looked vaguely familiar. They were in various attitudes on the streets of Paris, including some rather passionate ones.

"Have you identified her?" I asked the Dragon.

She looked bored. "She's a hooker. Owns a stable not far from here."

"Oh no." My mouth went dry as my heart stopped. I looked at the back of a single shot of the madam. "Is this her address?"

"Yes." The Dragon picked up another photo. "This fellow bothers me."

"That's where he is." I tossed the hooker photos

onto the table and headed for the door.

"Who?" asked the Dragon. "And where are you going?"

"Big Red," I said, leaving. "He's got to be at the brothel. I'm going after him."

The Dragon hurried after me, followed by A12 and A45.

"You don't know that," the Dragon said.

I pounded the elevator button. "The last time I saw him, he was with that woman."

"Sounds like it might be under control then," said A12.

"It's been too long," I groaned. "Come on, you stupid machine." I ran for the stairs, then stopped. "It's... He was horny. He wasn't thinking straight. He's in trouble and I've got to get him out of there."

I flew down the stairs with the others after me. They nearly ran me over as I stopped short on the final landing. Downstairs, Carol Beldon handed a note to the desk clerk.

"My, isn't she the brazen one," said A12.

"It's rather encouraging, actually," said A45. "She must have a hostage, and if it's your Big Red, he must still be alive."

"That's our room number," I said as the clerk filed the note in a pigeon hole. I looked over at the Dragon. "Why don't you follow her?" I pointed to A45, then A12. "You can keep an eye out in the lobby, and you can keep the desk clerk occupied so I can get a look at that note without anyone knowing it's been seen."

"Of all the ruddy-" began A12.

"Marian, do it," said the Dragon as she took off.

A12 and A45 ambled down the stairs together. While A12 addressed the clerk in rapid-fire French, I also ambled down. A12 directed the clerk to a room in the back. As soon as they had disappeared, I scrambled over the desk to the pigeon holes and the note.

"If you want to see your lover again, bring the file to the Place St. Germain at 6:00 tonight."

Disgusted by the assumption, however valid, I replaced the note, hurried over the counter and to the front door. A45 held me back.

"Where do you think you're going?" he demanded.

"That was a ransom note for my partner," I said. "I know where he is and I'm going after him."

I headed for the sidewalk. A12 came back into the lobby. She joined A45 as he followed me out.

"What on earth?" she asked.

"It was a ransom note," explained A45. "For her partner."

"They want us to take the file we have to the Place St. Germain at six o'clock," I said. "It's ten forty-five now, but that doesn't mean they won't hurt him in the meantime."

A12 caught my arm. She had quite a grip for such a small woman.

"Why not just wait until six and get them at the Place St. Germain?" she asked.

"It's a setup," I said. "Wednesday night, they arranged to meet us there yesterday morning. After that, we found we were bugged. They recognized us from some drops we'd made in the States. That's why they went to their office that night, to get their file before we got it."

The Dragon quietly walked up. "Good work, Little Red. She went right to the whorehouse."

I thought quickly. "We've got to find a way in there. If there's an alley near there, I could climb a wall and get in through the roof."

A45 smiled. "Actually, there's a vacant building two doors down. We can get to the roof from there."

"Great." I turned to the Dragon. "Why don't you and A12 go check out the Place St. Germain? If we miss them at the brothel, we can still get them there."

"What is it about Americans?" asked A12, but she tapped the Dragon on the shoulder and turned. "Let's be off, Lillian. Are all your people like this?"

I looked at A45. "Come on."

"Perhaps we should cover ourselves better," he suggested as we headed down the street.

"Perhaps, but I'm wearing a wig, and it wasn't in any of the surveillance photos."

A45 held me back before turning the corner. We slipped into the doorway of an old, old building of gray brick, long gone black with soot. Inside was layered with centuries of dust, it seemed. We got to the roof without a problem, and made our way over it to a building two roofs down. The buildings were literally side by side, so it was no trouble.

A45 stopped at a small dormer window and forced it open. He crawled in first, then helped me into a nice little bedroom, complete with sink and worn towels. We slid out and down a flight of stairs.

Near the next floor, A45 waved me back into the shadow of the stairwell. He went ahead casually and tried to embrace a young woman in drab gray clothes carrying a pile of towels. They went back and forth in French for a couple jovial minutes, then she went on her way and A45 waved me into the hall.

"Well?" I asked. "I don't understand French."

"I didn't get much," he said. "The girls are angry with Madame because she has locked them out of her room, and there's a new favorite in there."

"Which room?" I asked anxiously.

"It's a customer. Quite a man, too. The girl said they haven't heard Madame scream like that in quite some time."

"That's him," I sighed, somewhat chagrined. It figured Sid would find a way to get relief before he got captured.

"Dark haired fellow? Rather handsome?"

"Yes. Which room?"

"This way."

It was down the hall. A45 listened at the door and shook his head. I pulled a piece of spring steel from my hair and went to work on the lock.

It was a fairly small room, and not at all what I

expected for a madam. There was a sink, and a huge wardrobe that I'm certain was an antique, and a brass bed with a flowered spread and Sid, barechested, laying face down on it. His hands were bound behind his back.

Fighting tears, I rushed to the bed and carefully turned Sid over. He groaned. His eyes were huge and black and puffy, and what I could see of the whites were blood red. There was dried blood all over his upper lip, and fresh bruises on his arms and chest. He groaned again and sort of squinted.

"Who..?" he asked.

"It's me," I said quickly. "Are you alright? I mean how bad are you?"

"Li-" He stopped and swallowed and sighed. "You found me."

A45 broke open the wardrobe and began a methodical search.

"It's okay. I'm here now," I told Sid. I looked at his wrists. "Good lord, there's this big heavy cable on you."

Sid nodded. "I heard a church bell ring ten o'clock, and a little after that, they came in and put it on me, as if I was in any shape to do anything."

"It sounds about the right time," I said, picking at the heavy coated wire to untie it. "I cut through some tape, must have been an hour or two before that."

"They got you?"

"Not for long. Here it comes." I pulled the cable away, then popped open the sole on my left running shoe. "You've got duct tape on you, too."

"Goody." He grunted as I helped him sit up.

I slashed it. "Listen, I'm going to have to pull this off now. It's going to hurt."

Sid snorted. "That's like telling the Ancient Mariner he's walking under a ladder."

I yanked and Sid swallowed his yelp. I put the knife back in my shoe and closed it. Groaning, Sid slowly moved his arms around front. I rubbed his shoulders. Sid groaned some more.

I stopped. "Am I hurting you?"

"Yeah, but it's what I need. Got to get the circulation going again."

"I believe I've found your things," said A45 suddenly.

Sid stiffened and tried to make him out.

"He's CID," I explained, still rubbing. "A45. He's helping the Dragon."

"The Dragon?" asked Sid.

"She's here."

A45 brought over Sid's running shoes and shirt. Sid groaned as he lifted and rotated his arms, then leaned into my hands as I massaged his shoulders.

"Think you can walk?" I asked softly.

"Do I have a choice?" he returned. I slid around and looked at him. He gazed softly back. "I'll make it."

Sniffing, I bent forward and carefully kissed his lips. He returned it generously, carefully wrapping his arms around me.

"Hep," hissed A45 suddenly.

He stood with his ear next to the door. On the other side, we could hear Harry Beldon yelling in French and a young woman crying. It came closer.

Sid put his hands behind his back and laid down on them. I grabbed his shirt and shoes and dove under the bed. Harry burst into the room and went straight for Sid, swearing like a Marine. He reached for Sid's arm and got a good solid kick in the chest instead.

Harry recovered quickly, and I rolled out from under the bed right into his legs as he started for Sid again. Harry fell onto the bed. Sid dodged, then jumped on him. Harry threw him. I charged Harry from the side while Sid recovered, and the two of us caught Harry in a squeeze play. I swung my elbow up and into Harry's nose. His head jerked back and the blood flowed freely. Sid shoved his elbow into Harry's stomach, then pulled Harry forward onto the floor. Together, Sid and I got Harry's hands behind his back.

I got the duct tape from my jacket, and ripped off a piece big enough to cover Harry's mouth, then handed the roll to Sid. Sid whipped the roll around Harry's wrists, then held his head still so I could tape his mouth.

Gasping, Sid and I got up. I groaned and doubled over.

"You alright?" Sid asked his hand on my shoulder.

"I got knocked around yesterday, too," I whispered. "I guess I'm not entirely recovered."

Sid nodded. He looked at A45. "Can we count on CID to help us take care of him?"

"There's a simpler way to deal with it," said A45.

Taking a switchblade from his pocket, he walked over to Harry, popped the blade open, lifted Harry's head, and I didn't see the rest.

The room started spinning and I slipped into the hall. Swearing, Sid joined me.

"You might consider that he won't be haunting you now," said A45 calmly, handing Sid the shoes and shirt I'd left behind.

"Let's be thankful for small favors," grumbled Sid. He eased into his shirt. "How do we get out of here?"

"His partner should still be in the building," said A45. "I recommend we find her."

"I'm not big on your tactics, buddy," growled Sid, getting into his shoes.

A45 shrugged. "Nonetheless, unless you are more seriously injured than you appear, it would not be a good idea to forgo the opportunity."

I handed Sid the automatic I had in my jacket pocket.

"Why don't we keep going through the house?" I suggested. "At the rate things are going, she'll find us soon enough."

Sid checked the clip and took off the safety. "Sounds good. Let's just be careful."

"Do you speak French?" A45 asked him as we moved down the hall.

"I only kiss," said Sid.

A45 shook his head. "Why don't you two have any

language skills?"

"It's a fluke we're here," said Sid, getting irritated. "We're strictly domestic."

"Seriously? Well. You'll need to stay with me, then."

"Sh," I hissed. I nodded at a nearby stairwell.

We faded into a doorway, but the steps on the stairs continued up. It was just one of the girls. She paid us no mind and went into one of the rooms.

We found Carol on the bottom floor. The three of us peered out of the stairwell and across a hall at her as she paced alone in a well-appointed living room. A45 raised a small automatic.

I put my hand on it and shook my head. He withdrew. Upstairs, a woman screamed. Carol tensed, listening. The hysteria grew. She marched into the hall, right into three handguns.

"It's over, my dear," said A45. "You couldn't expect to keep it up forever, could you?"

Behind us, more screaming erupted, and the hall filled with young women and a few men in various states of undress. Seeing the guns, one drunk fellow decided we were the source of the trouble and jumped us. In the confusion, I lost my model thirteen. I reached for Carol and got one of the hookers.

The fighting escalated into a full-scale brawl. I elbowed my way through the crowd and suddenly found myself in a headlock. I tried to flip the one who had me and nearly choked myself. She gripped tighter. I stopped struggling.

The fight slowed and stopped as everyone watched Carol drag me to the hall table. Keeping a tight grip on me, she opened the drawer and removed a knife.

She loosened the choke hold, but with the knife against the skin of my neck, I wasn't too inclined to do much beyond what she wanted. She turned me toward A45 and Sid.

"I want cash," she told them coldly. "Fifty million in francs and I want a plane ticket to Argentina."

A45 raised his gun. "My dear, you know the policy. I dislike losing such a good operative, but I will not bargain with a terrorist."

I can't say my life flashed before my eyes. Things went down too quickly. Sid slammed into Carol's side. My forehead stung as I pushed myself away and toward the front door. Carol slammed Sid in the breadbasket, knocking him back, and dashed after me. A45 grabbed her knife hand and forced the blade from her. He tried spinning her back but got kicked where it counts by one of the young women, who wasn't convinced that we were the good guys.

As I opened the door, Carol grabbed me by the hair. I yelped but plunged forward. The wig gave, and Carol stumbled back. I landed on my face. I started up but got tackled.

I screamed for the police as loud as I could. Passersby stopped and stared at the little drama. Blood dripped into my eyes. I wiped it and struggled forward on the sidewalk. Carol desperately tried to pull me back.

"Police! Gendarmes!" I screamed. "Gendarmes!"

I heard a whistle in the distance. It got closer and I blacked out.

I awoke to darkness.

"You are alright," said a woman with a French accent. "Calm now."

"No," I moaned. I felt something brushing my nose, but couldn't feel the rest of my face.

"Lie still. You are fine."

I still struggled.

"She has no head injury. We'll give her something to make her sleep."

"No," I protested. "I don't want it. I don't."

Something pricked my arm. I tried fighting it, but soon I was out.

The light seemed incredibly bright when I awoke. My forehead burned and I felt really nauseous. I didn't feel like getting up, but my stomach left me no choice.

I struggled upright. The Dragon sat down next to me.

"It's alright," she said. "You're safe."

"Barf," I got out through gritted teeth.

"Oh, here."

She pulled a waste can to my face and I tossed it. By the time I was done, Sid was there with a glass of water and a washcloth. He held me as I rinsed out my mouth and wiped up.

"I thought that doctor said she didn't have a head injury," Sid growled at the Dragon.

"Are you better?" the Dragon asked me. I nodded. "How does your head feel?"

"Fine. My forehead burns." I reached up and touched gauze. "My stomach feels better, too. I still feel pretty fuzzy, though."

"It must be the after-effects of the sedative," said the Dragon. "The doctor gave you one when you came to and panicked while she was stitching you up."

"A sedative?" I thought back. "Was it a barbiturate?"

"Why?"

I looked at Sid. "Wasn't that what you gave me when I panicked that time, and I almost threw up when I woke up?"

"I gave you a barbiturate tablet," said Sid.

"Don't ever give me a sedative again," I said.

Sid gave me a gentle squeeze. If I didn't notice his puffy eyes right away, it was because he was wearing his glasses.

"Did something happen to your contacts?" I asked.

"Yeah. I lost them almost immediately," he said. "I went back to our hotel after they patched you together and got our stuff, including that file."

"Where am I?"

"In a safe house," said the Dragon. "We thought it might be a little more comfortable, and it's certainly more discreet."

It was more comfortable. The bed was soft and covered with lavender silk sheets. The room was decorated with purple and lavender flowers.

"What about Carol Beldon?" I asked. "I mean with Harry upstairs, why didn't we get arrested?"

"Our friends from CID," said Sid. "They have some pull, apparently."

"They do indeed," said the Dragon. "Carol's been arrested."

"But Harry. I mean, he just killed him."

"He doesn't like traitors." The Dragon fidgeted with the lavender flowered quilt I was under. "Those two can be very Medieval. It's understandable, given who they are."

I knew better than to ask. The door suddenly swung open and the Medieval pair walked in.

"Well, the extradition papers have been signed," she announced. "They're being delivered Air Express. Should be here first thing tomorrow morning. She'll be shipped out then."

"We can't thank you enough," said the Dragon.

"No thanks needed," said A45. "If it hadn't been for your team here, we wouldn't have gotten them at all."

"It was getting very nasty at our end," explained A12. "But Arthur tells me you two work strictly in the States. What division?"

"53Q," said Sid. "Code 6-A."

"Couriers?" gasped A12. Even A45 seemed taken aback. "Lillian, do you mean to tell me you sent couriers on a job like this?"

"The division frequently handles counter-espionage investigations," said the Dragon. "They haven't been together long, but they're already one of our best teams. In fact, they're the ones that made sure you got that care package we sent you last January."

"Well, if that's the caliber of people you hire for your couriers, it's no wonder." A12 ran an appraising eye over us.

I flushed. A12's gaze lingered on Sid, however. He turned to me, sliding his hand into mine. The Dragon got up.

"I think it's time we let you two alone," she said.

"Quite right," said A12. "Mustn't intrude on two lovers."

"But we're not," I said.

"I should be so lucky," said Sid.

The others laughed and left the room. Sid leaned back on the bed.

"Now where did they get the idea that we're lovers?" he asked, puzzled.

"You didn't say anything..."

"No." He shrugged.

"How are you feeling?" I asked softly.

"Stiff and achy, but much better, thank you." He reached over and kissed the end of my nose. "We sure make a pretty pair, don't we?"

I laughed, then looked at the door, feeling rather puzzled. "I wonder why they decided to kill their operatives. You'd think they'd have just run like heck when it got obvious someone was onto them."

"I don't think we'll ever know," Sid said. "Just like we won't know who they were waiting for here and why they decided they needed that file. I'm guessing they were trying to raise some cash to disappear. And by the way, the Dragon confirmed it. With the way we cleaned things up here, we can go back to being ourselves."

"Oh, wonderful. I can see my family again."

"And we're not married either."

"Yeah." I sighed unexpectedly. "I was kind of getting used to the idea."

"Me, too." He looked at me. "It's probably better that we're not, but however relieved I am, I'm also a little sorry, too."

"So am I." I smiled at him. "We could still get married, I suppose." I shivered. "I don't want to."

"Me, neither."

We laughed, then he reached over and kissed my mouth.

July 28, 1983

My church's youth group holds a week-long retreat at a Christian camp on Catalina Island every summer. Most of the leadership comes from the single adult bible study that did the retreat I was on when Sid came to get me back in May. Father John decided I should be a camp leader too. Sid "just happened" to take off for the Bahamas this week, and doesn't need me around.

It's Thursday evening. The sun is slowly sliding behind the hill. The ocean laps peacefully on the rock where I sit, writing my journal. Maybe I shouldn't have brought it with me. The fact that it's ciphered won't reveal any secrets, but it could make me look a little strange in that planned way that once made me very suspicious of Sid. That was before I knew about Quickline.

But perspective is why I wrote down the first one, and it's why I'm here finishing this bit up. I've been working pretty steadily on it since we got home almost a month ago.

We stayed on a week yet in Paris to recover. Sid's eyes were still a sick shade of green, and the scar on my forehead was a sight. And the cigarette burn got infected. But no one questioned us. Mae just raised cain with me for not calling her and wondered where I'd been. I told her we'd been in and out and all over the place, and never really answered her questions. I didn't even tell her about Catalina. Like Sid says, we can't call attention to our traveling.

The week we got back, Sid picked up a package

from A12 and A45. It was a package of study tapes of French, Italian, and German. We had a good laugh over it. After all, being strictly domestic, the odds of us ever needing to speak those languages is pretty remote.

This morning I gave a talk on sex and the problem of temptation, another one of Father John's ideas. When I told Sid I was giving it, he laughed and said I should use him as a bad example. I did, too. The kids loved it, but I don't think they really believed me about him until lunch.

I sat at the scarfer's table: Father John, Frank, three high school football players, and me. We all have phenomenal appetites and are on fourth and fifth servings before the rest of the camp has finished firsts. [It's not a pretty sight, Lisa dear, and you are the worst of them - SEH] However, today we lingered over dessert. There weren't seconds available.

"Is your boss really that bad?" asked Todd Wilkins, one of the football players.

"Like, you've got to be exaggerating," said Jeff Childs.

"Not a bit," I said. "If anything, I toned it down some."

"She's not kidding," added Frank. "Every time I've taken her home from something, he's got a different woman there. Which reminds me." He got up. "I've got mail duty today."

He picked up the bag of letters and called out names on the dining hall microphone. I didn't get anything, which I expected.

"That's it for today," Frank announced. "Except for one postcard."

"Read it!" someone yelled.

"Oh, I'm going to," Frank snickered. "And this will be uncensored."

Something about the way he said that caught my attention. I looked around. The card was blue, maybe an ocean.

"This hot little number is addressed to our own

Lisa J. Wycherly."

Cat calls erupted from the kids.

"He didn't," I groaned, though why I was surprised, I don't know. "He didn't."

"It goes like this: My dearest ice maiden..." Frank was without mercy.

Some more cat calls.

"He did!" I sank my burning face into my hands.

"No offense, but glad you're not here. Getting a great tan and lots of great dot, dot, dot." The kids roared. "How are the horny juveniles?" Roundabout booing. "Still trying hard to understand. Please, don't eat too much." Cheers, which were accepted by the football players. "And stay away from the junk food."

"Too late!" someone hollered to a big laugh. I'm told my candy bar habit is the stuff legends are made of.

"Your favorite reprobate." More laughter and cheers. Frank held up his hand. "P.S. Don't forget your sunscreen."

The kids laughed really hard and cheered. I did not get slapped on the back because that would have hurt my sunburn.

"Now, Lisa," teased Frank. "You wouldn't happen to know who that was from?"

"He's going to regret this, and so are you, Frank," I called. Silently, I wished sand in Sid's equipment. [So that's how it happened - SEH]

Later, Father John caught me alone, sitting with my journal on my rock.

"Well?" he asked.

"What?"

"You seem to be doing a lot of thinking."

"I guess I am."

"About Sid?"

"Yeah." I looked at Father. "Things got pretty wild on that trip we took."

"Would it be fair to guess that scar on your forehead did not come from a fall on a coffee table?"

"Not quite." I lifted my hair. "That was a cigarette burn. The whites of Sid's eyes had just barely cleared up before he left. He got winged. I got beaten up twice." I looked out over the ocean. "The funny thing is, the violence doesn't seem to bug me. I mean I don't like it, but I'm not scared of it anymore. And I'm not scared of Sid anymore. We tried making love. He asked me, and I couldn't say no or yes. It didn't work. But it really took the pressure off. I mean he still wants to."

"And do you?"

"Yeah," I said softly. "I really want to. And I really don't."

"Why not?"

"Because I'd have to be married to him for it to work, and more than anything, I don't want to be married. It's like I'm finally finding out who I am and what I can do. This trip completely tested all my limits. I don't want to submerge that in a man, and that's what's expected in a marriage. I like being independent and able to make my own decisions without consulting someone else." I chuckled.

"What about Sid?"

"What about him?"

"Someday you might decide that you want to be part of his life in a way that does not submerge who either of you are, but does call for a deep, loving commitment from both of you."

I smiled. "I might, but he can't. I don't think he ever will."

"I guess at the moment, it's much safer for you that way. I'll talk to you later."

I fished Sid's postcard out of my cover up pocket, then pulled out my pen and started writing. Sid says there's a kind of safety in keeping me mad at him.

I keep getting funny looks from the kids as they walk past my rock out here. Lots of people sit out here alone, and quite a few write, so that's not it. I guess I'm the only one who comes out here and whistles "All Day, All Night, Marianne."

About the Author

Anne Louise Bannon is an author and journalist who wrote her first novel at age 15. Her journalistic work has appeared in Ladies' Home Journal, the Los Angeles Times, Wines and Vines, and in newspapers across the country. She was a TV critic for over 10 years, founded the YourFamilyViewer blog, and created the OddBallGrape.com wine education blog with her husband, Michael Holland. She also writes the romantic fiction serial WhiteHouseRhapsody.com, Book One of which is out now. She is the co-author of Howdunit: Book of Poisons, with Serita Stevens, as well as the Freddie and Kathy mystery series, set in the 1920s, and the Operation Quickline series and Tyger, Tyger. She and her husband live in Southern California with an assortment of critters.

Other books by Anne Louise Bannon

I'm so glad you liked Stopleak! Check out my other novels, available in print or ebook at your favorite retailer:

Operation Quickline Series
That Old Cloak and Dagger Routine

Freddie and Kathy Series:
Fascinating Rhythm
Bring Into Bondage
The Last Witnesses

Brenda Finnegan
Tyger, Tyger

Romantic Fiction
White House Rhapsody, Book One

And I would be honored if you left a review for this and any of my books on GoodReads or any other retail site. It really helps.

Connect with Anne Louise Bannon

Thank you for sticking it out this long! Please connect with me on the following social media platforms:

Friend me on Facebook: http://facebook.com/RobinGoodfellowEnt

Follow me on Twitter: http://twitter.com/ALBannon

Favorite my Smashwords author page: https://www.smashwords.com/profile/view/MsBriscow

Subscribe to the Robin Goodfellow Newsletter: http://eepurl.com/zH0Ab

Connect on LinkedIn: http://www.linkedin.com/in/annelouisebannon

Follow me on Pinterest: http://pinterest.com/msbriscow

Visit my website: http://annelouisebannon.com

Follow me on Google+: http://google.com/+Annelouisebannonfiction